# THE AWAKENING

# THE AWAKENING

*a novel*

## Thomas Eno

Covenant Communications, Inc.

Published by Covenant Communications, Inc.
American Fork, Utah

Printed in the United States of America
First Printing: August 1997

04 03 02 01 00 99 98 97    10 9 8 7 6 5 4 3 2 1

ISBN 1-57734-128-7

Library of Congress Catalog-in Publication Data

Eno, Thomas D., 1952-
    The awakening/Thomas Eno.
        p.  cm.
    Sequel to: My Name Is John.
    ISBN 1-57734-128-7
    1. John, the Apostle, Saint--Fiction.  I. Title
PS3555.N65A96  1997
813'.54--dc21

This book is dedicated to my mother, Twila, and to my aunt, Joyce Alderson Ott, both of whom are miracles.

# CHAPTER ONE

It was one of those breathtakingly beautiful mornings in the Pacific Northwest. Bright, fluffy clouds dotted the deep blue of the sky, the sun shone brilliantly across the scattered islands, and the breeze blew light and fresh, filled with the promise of a glorious day.

John shifted on the hard park bench, turning the pages of the newspaper want ads, shaking them out with a snap and squinting to read the tiny print.

"Ah . . . yes, there it is," he said out loud. "That's the one."

Whistling tunelessly, he folded the paper under his arm and stood to stretch luxuriously in the early summer sunshine. Breathing the sweet pungency of the salty ocean air deep into his lungs, he looked across the channel, soaking in the beauty of Puget Sound. *The world is so beautiful,* he thought. *Too bad so few people notice.*

Grinning with the sheer delight he felt in being alive, he headed purposefully to a nearby pay phone. Picking up the receiver and dropping in a quarter, he dialed and waited while the phone rang once, twice, three times.

"Hello," rumbled a deep, gruff voice at the other end of the line. It sounded to John like the voice of someone who ate rocks for breakfast.

John's grin deepened as he spoke. "Mr. Patches? I'm calling about the ad you placed in the paper for a handyman/caretaker. I'm interested in meeting with you this morning. Is the position still open?"

John's eyes flickered as he watched two seagulls fly past and land nearby, hoping for a meal in a discarded McDonald's hamburger wrapper on the ground.

After a momentary hollow silence, the rough voice on the other end of the line grated out, "Are you strong? Got a good back? I don't need any invalids around here. I got one of those already. This here's no pansy job. I need someone who's got some backbone and commitment. If you haven't got that, don't bother!"

"Yes, sir," answered John, "I'm strong as a horse. Haven't been sick in years. I like to work and I like this area, so I can promise you I'm going to stick around."

John waited, but there was no response. Listening, he felt prompted to add, "Look, I think I understand. It's risky to hire anybody these days, sight unseen, and you don't know me. How about if I come out to your place and work a few days for you—no pay, just to let you take a look at me. Then you can decide if I'm working out. That way you won't be out anything, no matter what."

Suspiciously, the voice responded, "What kind of fool do you think I am? Nobody works for free. What's the scam?"

John chuckled quietly, shaking his head. This guy was going to be a real hard sell, but John could feel curiosity and need overcoming fear and distrust. "I just want the job, that's all. It would really suit me and fit my needs. Let me come out to your place and prove myself. You can run me off if you don't like my looks."

"I might just do that," muttered the voice.

"Can you give me the address?" asked John. "I'm on foot, but I can get there in an hour or so, if you're on the island."

Again, the silence. Finally, "I guess there wouldn't be any harm in looking at you. Come on ahead. If you're in town now, take the main road south, and keep going three miles. You'll come to a road on your left, Miller's Lane. Go down it as far as you can, and when there's no more road, you're there. The dogs won't let you get near the house, but they'll let me know when you show up. I'll come out to talk with you. Got a name?"

"John. My name is John. I'll be there before you know it. Thanks for the chance. I appreciate it."

"Humph! We'll see how glad you are when I can take a look at you." There was a click, and the line went dead.

Taking a deep breath, John quietly replaced the receiver. Humming to himself, hands in his pockets, he smiled up into the soft morning sun that warmed his cheeks as he started off across the park to the road that would take him to Miller's Lane. The seagulls watched him, parting calmly to each side to let him pass. John winked at them and strode on his way.

\* \* \*

The white van with rust marks along its left side passed John as he stood at the pay telephone. Inside the van were three men as well as a large box of explosives.

"You sure that stuff isn't going to go off on us?" Hobie, the driver, asked, looking anxiously over his shoulder at the box.

"Yeah," chimed in Skink, the man riding in the front passenger seat next to the driver. "How do we know that junk is safe?"

The third man, Holtz, was calmly sitting on top of the box. "Man, you two are such whiners. How many times do I have to tell you? This kind doesn't go off until you run a charge through it. You can light a match to it, you can hit it with a hammer. Doesn't matter. It won't go off."

A tense silence danced between the men as they drove slowly by the bridge connecting James Island to the smaller island that held the Maxwell Oil refinery. Looking at the bridge, Hobie snorted. "You think you're gonna take down a whole bridge with what you got there?"

Holtz shifted around on the box and smirked, shaking his head. "You ever heard the saying, 'Someone who doesn't know what they're doing needs a bigger hammer to take something apart; a smart guy may not even need a hammer at all'? We don't need to sink the whole island. You only have to blow out the main support areas, then everything comes down by itself. It's all in pressure points and balance." Holtz rolled his eyes and shook his head. "This is for professionals. I don't expect you guys to know anything about it."

"Nutcase!" Skink mumbled from the passenger seat.

Holtz swore to himself. He hated working with idiots. "Look, you guys, I don't have to bring down the *whole* the bridge, just one end of it." Holtz had no love for Skink and Hobie, and if he had been in charge, he would never have recruited them.

* * *

After talking with John, Hyrum Patches turned his wheelchair awkwardly away from the telephone stand. "What kind of fool have I invited out here now?" he muttered to himself as he struggled to maneuver through the tiny, cramped hallway and back into the parlor.

Hyrum Patches was an angry man. After sixty-five years, any quality of patience he had received at birth had withered away to almost nothing. He maintained that his negative outlook on life, to one and all, was the only realistic way to survive in a hostile, uncaring world. He defended himself saying that at least people always knew where they stood with him. It was just honesty, pure and simple. There was no deception, no guessing around. And he didn't need any simpering false concern for himself either. No sir! His was not an attitude designed to win friends, but Hyrum liked to believe it made him a man to reckon with, a man to respect. It was better to have respect, even if people hated you, than pity.

One morning not long ago, he had awakened to realize he was truly alone in the world. He had no friends, no neighbors who gave a hoot, and he had driven his children away. So here he was, forced to hire help to do what he had always done on his own. Always. Fiercely independent all his days, Hyrum had never let anyone do anything for him, except his wife. Let all those do-gooders keep their charity for someone who was too weak-willed to make do without having to be rescued. He had no use for anyone who couldn't take care of himself.

"'God helps those who help themselves,'" he snorted angrily, bumping against the kitchen table with his wheelchair. "So, where is He after all these years that I've helped myself? Humph! I reckon I can still get by on my own. There's no shame in hiring a man to do what I haven't got time to do myself. Never mind about me, God!" Hyrum yelled to the ceiling, shaking a fist. "I'll get by, just like I always have."

With that, Hyrum went back to working on the loose window screen he had been struggling with when the phone rang.

* * *

John covered the three miles from town easily, arriving at Miller's Lane just forty-five minutes after speaking to Hyrum. His denim jacket was slung over his shoulder, left thumb holding it fast. Cedar trees, still damp from last night's rain, filled the air with their clean, fresh scent as he left the paved county road for the dirt one.

John was content. Enjoying the moment, each moment, as it came, he always looked for the good life had to offer. John was grateful for what he had and didn't worry about what he didn't. This perspective had served him well for many, many years.

As he traveled further down the lane, the trees grew closer together, as if he were entering a forest. *You'd never know from this vantage point,* he thought, *that you were only a few miles from town.* Breathing deeply, he drew in the deep peace and quiet of the place, letting it soak into his pores.

The Pacific Northwest always amazed him with its abundant growth and tremendous resilience. He thought it was one of the most beautiful places on earth. Surely the garden of Eden had been much like this.

John had visited most of the world, at one time or another, but this part of it held a special place in his heart; it was so different from the Middle Eastern desert where he had been born.

John passed a tired-looking house with moss growing on the roof, and chickens scratching in a crazily built pen beside a decrepit hen house. A dog raised its head and watched him pass by, but didn't bark. A man's legs in coveralls stuck out from beneath an ancient, rusted pickup truck set up on blocks, a radio nearby blaring country music. John heard the sounds of metal clanging on metal, followed by some mild cussing.

John slowed and considered stopping to lend a hand, but just then another man stepped out of the house. Letting the door bang closed behind him, the man walked over and leaned down to talk to the man under the truck. John moved on, realizing he was not needed.

Another mile on, the road narrowed and curved just past a swampy pond, the abundant weeds around it creeping out into the road. Sharp rocks jutted up from the dirt as the road thinned down to little more than a footpath. Plainly, this part of the road wasn't used very much. A few flies buzzed lazily around John's head. The smell of damp decay was everywhere.

Rounding the next bend, he came upon a faded blue farmhouse set back among the trees about fifty yards, its peaked roof all that was visible behind the thick brush. The path he traveled came to a dead end in the gravel area in front of the house, and his steps roused two large, mixed breed dogs that dozed on the porch. As John approached the house, the larger of the two dogs raised its head and began to snarl, its hackles rising menacingly. The other dog leapt to its feet and dove off the porch, hitting the ground at a run. In short order both dogs were before John, teeth bared menacingly as they growled, eyeing him for any weak spots to attack.

Squatting down to their level, he held out his hands, palms up. He spoke quietly. "Hey there, guys, how you doing?"

With a low, rumbling growl, the larger of the two walked slow and stiff-legged toward John, who held his position, still talking softly.

Inside the farmhouse, Hyrum had heard the dogs growling. Surprised when the dogs didn't follow up with their usual cacophony of barking as he had trained them to do, he pulled back the curtain from the window. Near the road was a slender man of indeterminate age, medium build and broad shoulders, kneeling before the tail-wagging dogs, his hands held out toward them. Hyrum was puzzled. Why weren't his dogs barking? Those two were supposed to keep any visitors at bay until he released them. He had no use for "friendly" dogs.

The wood-framed screen door banged loudly as Hyrum wheeled out on the porch in time to see his dogs sit at the stranger's feet, looking up at him as if *he* were their master. Hyrum had never seen anything like it. Not those dogs!

"Hey! You! What have you done to my dogs?" he yelled.

"Mr. Patches, I'm John," called the man, as he approached the house, the dogs following along behind. "We spoke on the phone." John moved up the steps toward Hyrum, his hand outstretched, almost exactly as he had done to calm the dogs. Hyrum ignored the hand, and after a moment, John tucked it back into his pocket.

"At least you can follow directions all right," concluded Hyrum, looking into John's eyes and finding nothing to criticize. He ran his gaze over John fiercely, seeking any hidden flaws that would confirm his suspicions and justify sending him away. Finding nothing remarkable, he grunted and grudgingly looked up to meet John's eyes. "You look strong enough. You from around here somewhere?"

"I'm new in town, but I sure like the area," John replied, unoffended by Hyrum's frank skepticism. "Where would you like me to start working?"

"Not so fast there, I'm not done checking you out. A man's got to be careful who he hires these days. You might do more damage than good, and I don't need that. Running from the law, are you?"

John smiled and shook his head no.

"You just getting out of jail or prison?"

Another shake.

"Got a family that needs you nearby?"

"No, sir, my family are all dead."

Hyrum thought briefly about the last answer, then said, "You hang out with women, drink, smoke, use drugs, or gamble?"

"No, sir, I do not. Is there anything else I can answer?"

Hyrum hesitated. He couldn't find anything wrong with this one, and it bothered him. As a retired police detective, Hyrum felt that if you dug deep enough, you'd find *something* on anyone.

"Don't like women, huh? You gay?"

"I was married once."

"What happened?"

"She died."

Hyrum saw the touch of sadness in John's eyes. Missing a dead wife, that was something he could understand. "Sorry," he mumbled in acknowledgment. "You aren't all messed up because of it, are you? My wife died, too, but I don't let it get me down. Can't afford to hire someone who's all wacked out inside."

"Most of the time I'm all right with it," said John. "I have no doubts I'll be with her again."

"You mean like reincarnation?" Hyrum scoffed. "You aren't into some weird religion, are you? I don't want any strange chanting going on here all day!"

"No chanting, Mr. Patches." John smiled. "What I mean by seeing my wife again is just what Jesus taught; there is a life after this one. My wife and I are sealed together, forever. Death cannot break that bond."

The left side of Hyrum's upper lip crawled upward. "*Sealed*, huh? You're one of them Mormons, aren't you?"

John started to reply, but Hyrum cut him off. "Never mind. All right, I'll take you on your word, for now. You work for me for free the next four days. If I like your work, you stay and get room and board, and a hundred a week starting from now. If at any time in those four days I decide you're not what I want, for any reason, or no reason at all, you're out of here. And I mean it. I don't owe you nothing! Got that?"

"Yes, sir." John held out his hand again to shake, and this time Hyrum took it. "While I'm here on trial, would it be okay with you if I slept in the room in the barn? I won't ask for meals or anything else, but it would be faster and more efficient for me to get started in the morning if I didn't have to walk out here from town every day."

Having John ask him for something made Hyrum feel better, as if he had somehow scored a point, and, feeling better, he became generous. "That would be all right with me. Besides, I was going to have you start working on the barn, anyway . . . It needs a new roof. What—"

Suddenly, Hyrum became confused as full understanding of John's request sank in. "How did you know about the room in the barn?" he asked.

John blinked, and blinked again. "There's a curtain on the window," he finally said, jerking his thumb toward the old barn. "I didn't figure it was there for the mice."

"Humph!" replied Hyrum, not completely satisfied with the answer, and his suspicious nature snapped back to life. "You can start now. You'll find what you need in a toolbox in the tackroom. The ladder is right where you can see it plain enough, there by the door. Everything's in there, all the supplies; just look around. If you got eyes to see, you'll find it. I'll be out in a while to check on you." Without another word, Hyrum whirled his wheelchair around and back into the house, waving off John's attempt to help him with the door.

At the bottom of the porch stairs, John thoughtfully scratched the ears of the larger dog as it leaned against him. Shaking his head, John thought how hard it must be to live as Hyrum did. He could feel the man's pain. Transformed into hostility, it emanated from him in an angry, miserable wall against others. *What a waste of energy and life,* John sighed.

After giving each of the dogs a final pat on the ribs, he started for the barn. Surveying the job, he grinned to himself, thinking, *You sure have your work cut out for you this time! So what else is new?*

Besides, there would be help, as he needed it. There always was.

John started for the barn, he was thinking he might head back into town at the end of the day. There'd been a promising-looking burger joint he'd seen earlier, and he was a sucker for a good burger.

# CHAPTER TWO

The smell of warm cinnamon and ginger pulled Lacey Taylor out of her daydream and back to the reality of her kitchen. "Oh, shoot! I nearly forgot the cookies," she exclaimed, reaching for a hot pad with one hand and pulling open the oven door with the other. Her first grab for the hot pad missed, but the second was successful. She grimaced, frustrated with her diminishing vision.

The sudden blast of hot air against her face made her eyes water. Blinking rapidly, she leaned back to let the heat dissipate. The aroma was heavenly, and she knew by smell more than sight that the cookies, their edges a slightly darker shade of brown than the center and beginning to split across the top, were done. Nodding with satisfaction, she reached in and wrapped the hot pad firmly around the edge of the cookie sheet, then pulled the pan out, placing it on top of the stove to cool. Then she slid the next pan of cookies into the oven.

Her husband, Kevin, said he worried about her using the stove now, but she would show him the cookies when he got home. She might be going blind, but that didn't mean she was helpless, for heaven's sake! It was endlessly frustrating for her to still be so young and yet going blind. She had children to raise, a family to care for. She wondered wryly if it would bother her less to go blind if she were old and frail. *Probably not*, she thought to herself.

Though it was only late spring, it was uncommonly warm in the house and she wiped a sleeve across her forehead, feeling the combined heat from the oven and the sunny day outside. She shook her head, hoping silently this did not mean that a long, dry spell of weather was coming. One of the reasons they had moved to the coast was to escape the hot, dry summers and extremely cold winters so common to their native Utah.

Deftly she scooped up hot cookies with her spatula, shifting them to the rack to cool. In the middle of the motion, she paused at the window over the sink and looked outside, seeing merely blurs of color and movement. As she listened to to her five-year-old son playing quietly in his sandbox, she could hear his high, little boy voice making motor noises as he pushed his toy trucks in the sand. Nodding contentedly to herself, she turned back to the job at hand.

There was another fireside tonight at the ward, and she was in charge of refreshments. And the music. In a ward as tiny as theirs, everyone with any testimony at all or willingness to serve always had more than one calling. There just weren't enough active members for anyone to do just one thing. Even if everyone on the membership rolls had been willing to do something, which they weren't, there probably would have been some gaps to fill.

In their last ward, in Utah, there had been so many people she had never learned all the names, even after four years. That ward had so many active members, at least in body count, that not even all the worthy, willing souls had callings, except to home and visit teach, of course. It had been a totally different world there. Not necessarily a better world, but definitely different. Here active, willing members were like gold nuggets. She knew of bishops who scrambled to find a place for new families to live within their boundaries just so they could gain another precious active family. She grinned, remembering when the house in Burns' Point they had been renting was sold out from under them, and three bishops called to say they had leads on houses in their wards. It felt good to be wanted that much. And boy, oh boy, did you ever know you were wanted here!

The Burns' Point Ward, membership 563, usually had a sacrament attendance of 160 members. Located on James Island, population 11,000, the local Saints were definitely a minority. The Burns' Point ward, except for the branch out on San Juan Island, was the westernmost group of Church members in the Mount Placer Stake, with most of the members located in Mount Placer, seventeen miles

westward, on the mainland. Lacey had found that living in
Washington state as a member of the Church was radically different
than living in Utah, where wards were often made up of people who
lived within a few blocks of each other. Church members within the
same stake were seldom more than a few miles from each other.

Taking several steps toward the large clock on the wall, Lacey
realized it was time to get that last pan of cookies out and be on her
way. Time was pressing in again. There was too much to do, in too
little time. Kevin would be calling from work soon, to let her know
what time he would be coming home. The girls were picked up at
school by a neighbor, but Lacey needed to go get them and bring
them home. And there was still little Davey's Sunday School talk to
work on.

Doggone! She wished Primary teachers would call and ask
parents first before they assigned these little kids talks. At five, Davey
couldn't read and had to memorize his talks. This was really a bad
week to have to take the time to help him. Ordinarily Kevin might be
able to, but he was gone so much these days.

Lacey had a momentary pang of sorrow over not being able to
help Davey learn to read as she had his older sisters. These days she
could barely read for herself, practically holding the books right up
against her face. Pretty soon she would have to depend on Braille for
anything written down.

That was something else she would have to make time to do,
soon—learn Braille. The thought overwhelmed her. It might as well
be another language. Shoot, it *was*.

Again she sighed. Oh well. She was glad Davey was even willing
to give a talk. Some day he would make a great missionary, she was
sure, all because he learned to be a competent public speaker at the
tender age of five, no doubt.

Lacey turned off the oven, pulled out the cookies, and wiped
her hands hurriedly on a dish towel. The dirty dishes stacked on the
counter would have to wait until after dinner.

"Davey, honey, put away your toys and come in now," she
called through the window. "We have to give you a bath before it's
time to go get the girls."

"Aw, Mom!" came the reluctant cry. But listening carefully, she could tell that he had nevertheless started to gather his toys. She wondered when she would manage to fit in her own shower before taking the cookies to the church.

The phone rang, and she trotted across the kitchen to answer it. "Hello?"

"Lacey? This is Gayle. How are you?" Gayle was the Relief Society president, as well as Lacey's friend.

"Oh, Gayle! You caught me by surprise. I was expecting Kevin to call."

"Well, I'll tell you why I called, then I'll shut up and get off the line. Sister Nurdlinger is having some real emotional difficulties, and her husband called and asked if the Relief Society could help out. I'm trying to find volunteers to take dinner in to them, and somebody to help watch their children for a few days while they try to sort things out. Are you available at all?"

Thinking fast, Lacey did some quick mental computations. "If I throw in an extra pound of hamburger, and have Kevin drop it off on the way to the fireside . . . sure. I was making sloppy joes tonight for dinner, and I can add enough to that to take some over for them. I have plenty of green salad, but nothing for desert . . . I made several dozen cookies today, but I need them for the fireside tonight. Maybe I can make something up or get Kevin to grab some ice cream on his way home. And I could take their two youngest tomorrow from about 8:30 to 4 in the afternoon."

Gayle sounded relieved as she answered. "Lacey, bless you. I knew I could count on you. I'll let Brother Nurdlinger know you're coming tonight, and I'll take care of the rest."

"Gayle, what exactly is wrong with Sue, anyway? Or shouldn't I ask?"

"Oh, Lacey." Gayle sounded uncomfortable talking about it, and Lacey wished she hadn't spoken. "It's not clear. The most I've learned is that she's feeling stressed and overwhelmed. She just needs some time."

"I can sure relate to that." Lacey hoped she sounded light and reassuring for Gayle, who seemed burdened herself. "I'm happy to do what I can. If there's anything else, let me know. I'll just take my Valium and pitch right in," she joked.

They laughed together, said their goodbyes, and hung up. Lacey grabbed another pound of hamburger out of the freezer and pulled an extra can of stewed tomatoes out of the cupboard, as she silently thanked Gayle for still treating her like a normal person. Since word had gotten around about Lacey's progressing blindness, people had been acting as if she were incapable of doing *anything*. A quick look at the clock again sent her adrenaline soaring.

"David Michael Taylor! You get in this house, RIGHT NOW!" she hollered out the back door.

A little boy appeared magically in the doorway, all innocence and large brown eyes. "Okay, Mommy, I'm here! You don't have to yell!"

She sighed in exasperation. "All right, little man, I'm sorry. Now hustle yourself down to the bathtub, *pronto.*" She followed him, shaking her head to herself. *Just another day in the life of a faithful "Saint,"* she told herself with a grimace, *trying to "endure to the end"!*

* * *

Bishop Martin Davis leaned back in his chair and propped a foot on the opposite knee. Drumming his pencil absently against the desk top, his gaze blurred as he faced the wall in front of him, and his thoughts wandered, as they were wont to do these days.

As far as he knew, he was the only one in the entire building, which was precisely why he was there. The fireside wasn't due to start for an hour, which meant he would have this blessed quiet time to himself for at least another half hour or so before people began arriving to set up for the meeting. Moments of absolute quiet were becoming more rare all the time for him, and he cherished each one he could get.

With a thump, he dropped his foot to the floor, slid his chair back up to the desk, and returned his attention to the list in front of him. He groaned and shook his head. President Higgins had been as honest as possible with Martin when calling him as bishop of the Burns' Point Ward. Although the stake president had explained the depth of the problems the little ward struggled with, nothing he'd said had fully prepared Martin for the reality of what he now faced.

Neither he nor his wife, Jan, had come to know very many of the ward well since moving to James Island just a month and a half before. They had been members of the Burns' Point Ward barely two weeks when Martin received the calling. Although he had spoken in the ward as a member of the high council when he was living on the mainland, he didn't know many ward members, and they didn't really know him.

When Martin had voiced his concern about being unfamiliar to the people of Burns' Point, President Higgins had assured him that not knowing the ward might very well be a positive point. Besides, the Lord wanted him in the calling, and as far as President Higgins was concerned, that was the end of speculation. Martin had left the president's office that day wondering, but now he was beginning to understand. Being a relative newcomer to the ward meant he wasn't tied to any of the old ways and long standing "traditions," particularly those traditions that were neither Church doctrine nor the gospel.

Among the other bishops of the Mount Washington Stake, it was a standard joke at their monthly meetings to ask Martin, "So, Bishop, got a fire lit under your members yet?" He would smile weakly, understanding they were supportive of his efforts, and at the same time glad not to share his challenges.

At sixty years of age, Martin had been a member of the Church for only eight years, and he and Jan had moved into the stake six years before. They both loved the coast. It was such a change of life from Detroit, where they had lived for the first twenty-three years of their marriage. Everything about the Northwest appealed to them. The people were more open and less hurried than in the East. The weather was more moderate and gentle.

They took up sailing, crabbing, and beach combing, feeling like they had finally come home. When their daughter married in the temple and moved just forty-five miles away with her new husband to begin their family, Jan and Martin were thrilled. Life seemed full of joy and promise, the years ahead of them rosy and bright.

A few months ago they had moved to James Island. Mount

Placer on the mainland had been green and beautiful, but James Island was another world. They felt called here by God, and blessed beyond their greatest hopes.

Martin laughed to himself; he should have known. He did know. The Lord never answered just one prayer to the benefit of one person. Nearly everything He did, Martin believed, was for the benefit and growth of more than one person at a time. Like ripples in the waters of a pond, all actions and reactions moved outward in ever widening circles, touching many lives, in many ways.

The seemingly small and individualized answer to a young man's prayer for guidance could result in an increased faith and testimony of the gospel, which resulted in a future missionary, which resulted in conversions, which resulted in . . . it went on and on. Martin had seen it work too many times over the years to doubt anymore. The wisdom, clarity, and beauty of God's workings were awe inspiring.

According to President Higgins, he, Martin Davis, was an answer to the prayers of the stake presidency over the needs of a troubled ward. At that memory, Martin groaned aloud. He wondered if this calling would be the death of him. His wife, Jan, tried to buoy him up, assuring him with a smile that it would surely seal him a place in the Celestial Kingdom. Even if it turned out to be true, Martin wasn't sure there would be much left of him to enjoy it by then.

A knock on the office door interrupted his ruminations. The door opened slowly, and a white-haired, wrinkled head stuck itself around the door frame cautiously. "Bishop?" inquired the elderly man, his Eastern European accent immediately recognizable to Martin. "I wasn't sure if you were in here, it was so quiet, but the light was on so I thought I'd better check. You okay?"

Checking the clock on the wall, Martin was shocked to see the time. He had been sitting in his office like a zombie for the past half hour, and now his precious "alone" time was used up, with no progress to show for it.

"Yeah, Crayle, I'm okay. Just going over this list of less-active members. Sure are a lot of them."

"No kidding! Bishop Mackie finally gave up on 'em. Too many

to worry about, if you ask me."

"Wish I could, Crayle, but I think I had better try and track them all down, just so I know for myself who they are and what their story is. President Higgins asked me particularly to check everyone out."

Crayle Eskra shook his head doubtfully. "Well, if President Higgins asked you to, I guess you have to try at least. But it seems like a waste of time to me. Those folks aren't going to change. Leastwise, they haven't all these years. Seems to me like the active folks got enough needs to keep us all plenty busy." He shrugged. "You coming to the fireside tonight, Bishop? I hear this seminary teacher's a real hot shot speaker."

Martin slid his list of names back into the desk drawer. Rising, he pushed his hands into the small of his back and stretched painfully backwards. He felt like he had been sitting in that chair for days, pondering his list of names. Coming around his desk, he put his arm about the custodian's shoulders and reached out to turn off the office light as they stepped out the door.

"I believe it's an institute teacher from Vancouver who is speaking tonight, Crayle, and I could use the spiritual lift. How about you?"

Crayle nodded as he shuffled down the hall with the bishop. "Sure, I guess so. I want to be here anyways, to see everything gets cleaned up afterwards. You can't trust folks no more to do what they ought to, no matter how often I tell 'em. Besides, Sister Taylor is in charge of refreshments tonight, and I sure love her cookies."

Martin laughed as the two of them continued down the hallway together. Now there was a heartening thought, he agreed.

# CHAPTER THREE

Kevin Taylor swung his car around and drove back to pick up the hitchhiker he had passed only moments ago. As the hitchhiker slid into the front seat, Kevin stuck out his hand. "Hi, I'm Kevin Taylor."

"I'm John," replied the stranger. "Thanks for the lift. I'm headed into Burns' Point."

Kevin scratched the balding patch on the back of his head before pulling back onto the pavement. "I don't generally pick people up anymore," he admitted. In fact, he'd been so busy worrying about his physical therapy practice that he hadn't seen John until he'd passed him.

"I understand," John said. "Too bad a few bad apples make it harder for the rest of us."

"Amen to that," Kevin agreed, turning on his wipers as the heavy clouds overhead began pouring rain. "Looks like you got a ride just in time."

John rolled a shoulder and rubbed his neck in an effort to get a few kinks out of his neck.

"Hurt yourself?" Kevin asked, automatically picking up the other's discomfort. It was part of his job to make sense of people's aches and pains.

John reached around for the small of his back. "I . . . did some heavier work today than . . . I'm used to." His face twisted at a twinge. "Guess I overdid it."

"I'm a physical therapist. If you lean forward, raise your arms up, then arch your back while you look at the ceiling, then slowly bring your arms around back, it might help."

John followed the advice as best he could in the small car, and soon experienced some relief. "Ahh, that's better. You really know your stuff. Your clients must love you."

Kevin sighed. "I suppose so. Too bad more of them don't have money."

"The work doesn't pay so well?"

Peering through the rain-splattered windowshild, Kevin thought about his reasons before answering. "It probably would if I did it differently, the way most people do. My wife says I have a soft heart. My partner says the problem is a soft head." Kevin suddenly felt odd, revealing his personal problems to a complete stranger. Just then his passenger spoke up.

"Do you know where I could find the LDS chapel around here? I heard there's one, but haven't found it yet."

As the newest elders quorum president of the Burns' Point Ward—called just two months before—Kevin perked up his ears at John's words. "Are you a member? Or just looking for a church to join?"

"I'm a convert, for a few years now." A voice in the back of John's mind said, *There's a bit more to the story than that, isn't there?* John ignored the internal commentary and continued, "Thought I'd get to know the Saints here, seeing as how I've got me a new job and it looks as if I'll be around here for a while."

"Where are you working?"

"Hyrum Patches hired me to work on his place. Sure is run down. You know him?"

Kevin winced. He could still see the scene a month and half ago on Hyrum's front steps. As the new elders quorum president, he had paid a call on this particular elder to find out why Hyrum didn't come to church anymore. Hyrum's two snarling dogs had forced Kevin to remain in his car until the old man had called them off. Their malevolent stares during the entire visit had convinced Kevin that they were anxious to see what he tasted like. Hyrum had followed one bitter recrimination after another about the Church, God, and the "Mormons," and by the time Kevin had apologetically backed away from the porch and fled in his car, he vowed never to set foot on the man's property again.

Hearing that his passenger worked for Hyrum Patches, Kevin wrestled with his conscience. *I'm a shepherd in Zion,* he thought. *Even Brother Patches is one of the Lord's lambs. Then again, does this John have any idea what he's gotten into? Do I owe him some warning?*

Before Kevin could say anything, John raised his hand signaling him to wait. Both were silent as John listened intently then squinted through the window into the driving rain. Then he quickly turned around to look through the rear window.

"Is something the matter?" Kevin asked, perplexed.

"We have to turn around," John said.

"What?"

"A car went off the road back there. It's down in the trees on the other side of the road. Someone is hurt."

"I didn't see anything," Kevin said, even as he began to brake carefully on the slick road. Slowing down, he made a U-turn and drove until John told him to stop.

As the car rolled to a stop, John jumped out and ran down the grassy hill into the trees. Kevin followed him more slowly, surprised, then impressed, and finally horrified by the deep ruts recently plowed into the peaceful green forest. Whatever, and whoever, had come down this bank must be in deep trouble.

As Kevin caught up with John, he found him determinedly pulling brush and tree branches off what might have been a new BMW that was crushed against a large tree. Wordlessly, Kevin began helping. Along the passenger side, the car was wedged up against the moss-covered boulders; the largest boulder bore a vicious scar across its top where the car had ripped against it, tearing the moss away, grinding metal on stone. Somehow, the engine continued to run.

Inside the car, a woman lay slumped over, her seatbelt holding her upright. An ugly gash on her forehead bled freely down her face.

Kevin groaned. "Oh, God," he said, not in blasphemy but in the most elemental of prayers.

They tried to open both doors on the driver's side, but neither would open. Kevin picked up a heavy branch from the ground and began hitting the front passenger window without any effect. John pushed him firmly aside and smashed a rock the size of a basketball against the window repeatedly until it shattered, spraying the woman with glass splinters, but allowing them entry.

John broke off most of the remaining window glass and reached inside to turn off the engine before they attempted to bring the woman through. The smell of leaking gasoline began to be noticeable.

"We got problems. The gas—"

"I smell it," John said, climbing into the car. "I'll push her through." As John hefted the woman through the window, Kevin took the woman's arms and shoulders. As her legs came through, a flame burst forth from under the car hood.

"We've got to get her out of here, quick," Kevin shouted. "This thing's going to blow!"

Climbing out of the car, John caught his arm on a jagged window piece and blood spurted from the deep gash. Ignoring the wound, John picked up the woman's legs, and with Kevin holding her shoulders, they carried her as quickly as possible up the hill toward the road. Stumbling to the top of the hill, they lay her down as the car below them burned hotter.

The young woman, her expensive clothes bloodstained and dirty from the wet forest floor, blinked as she stared uncertainly at the two men. "Where . . . ?" she tried to speak.

"We pulled you out of your car," John told her. "You're okay, now."

Instead of relaxing, she twisted around to where she could see the burning car. As the bright flames reflected on her face, her eyes widened in shock and she struggled to raise herself. "My baby!" she choked. "My baby's in there!"

Kevin and John looked back in horror at the burning car. John bolted down the hill first, ordering Kevin, "Stay here!"

"Not on your life!" Kevin shot back, his previous fear forgotten, only a few steps behind.

The flames now filled the front part of the car. There wasn't even time to smash the back windows. A terrible helplessness filled Kevin's heart. "I've got a fire extinguisher in my trunk," he yelled, tearing back up the hill.

John let him go, knowing it would be too little, too late. He looked heavenward for a second, then placed his hand on the rear door and pulled.

Kevin, meanwhile, realizing that his puny extinguisher would be no match for the inferno, had turned back. What he saw defied explanation.

Standing with his back toward Kevin, using only one hand, John pulled on the rear door of the smashed BMW. As if it were tissue paper, the door gave way with a tearing, shredding sound. Tossing it aside, John threw himself into the back seat, even as flames billowed out to engulf him. It seemed an interminable length of time to Kevin before John emerged, holding a bundle in his arms. In that instant, the car exploded in a ball of orange and yellow flames, enveloping John and the child, the shock wave throwing Kevin to the ground so hard he saw stars.

Kevin rolled to his feet, shaking his head, and rubbing his ears to overcome temporary deafness from the blast. His unfinished scream of horror when he saw the flames engulf John gave way to dumbfounded surprise at the sight of John laying the child beside her mother. How in the world—?

Before he could form the question to John, a shrill, wailing police car siren broke into Kevin's confusion. Pulling up to the scene, his patrol lights flashing, the police officer barely took time to set his brakes before he leapt out of the car and sprinted toward them. In a short time an ambulance and paramedics were on the scene, and mother and child were taken to Burns' Point Hospital.

* * *

That night Lacey and Kevin lay in each other's arms, pillows stacked behind them on their bed. In their own rooms, the children were already asleep.

"It was so weird," Kevin said, "and I keep asking myself, did I see what I think I saw?"

"And?" Lacey asked.

"And—I don't know."

"Maybe he's one of the Three Nephites?" she offered.

Kevin didn't smile. "Very funny. I don't think so."

"I'm serious," she said. "Why not? Don't you believe what the Book of Mormon says?"

"Lacey, it's not that. You know I believe the Book of Mormon is true."

"Then why couldn't he be one of them?"

Kevin sighed. "Well, for one thing, he was alone. I thought they were a team, like the missionaries."

The cool breeze outside drifted in through their window from the Puget Sound, and Kevin felt the moist air gently soaking into every pore. He loved this place with his whole heart. Come what may, he wanted to stay here forever. He inhaled deeply again, the natural tranquilizers of the land and water beginning finally to relax him. After a deep yawn, he continued his argument, though only half-heartedly, "And since when does one of the Three Nephites need a job? This guy says he just started work here on the island."

"So invite him over for dinner, and let me check him out."

"That might not be so easy."

"Why?"

"The only place where I know to find him is Hyrum Patch's."

"Uh-oh," Lacey said in sudden understanding, "you *do* have a problem. Guess you better start praying." She rolled away from him, out of the bed, and onto her knees in one smooth movement. Holding onto his arm, she swiveled him around to a position half on and half off the bed.

"Hey, I'm still sore from the car blowing up!" he complained.

"Mention it in our prayer—it's your turn tonight."

"No, it's not," he protested, kneeling beside her against the bed. "I did it last night."

"What a fibber you are, Kevin Taylor. I did it and the night before that. Remember now?"

"Vaguely."

"Humph. Sounds like you need to pay more attention, Mr. Elders Quorum President."

"Does that have to color everything I do now?"

"You want the truth?" When he didn't answer, she offered it anyway. "Yes. Everything you do, say, think, and feel, anywhere you go now, anything you dream about, now has to include your calling. It's a very special calling, my love. I read somewhere that after the bishop the next most influential calling in a ward is the elders quorum president."

"The Relief Society president must be in there somewhere," he said lamely.

"No doubt."

After their regular nightly prayer, which had become more involved since his calling, and they were back in bed, Kevin said, "And another thing, that cut on his arm."

"I thought you said it wasn't there when you looked later?"

"It wasn't."

"Could you be mistaken? Maybe he didn't get cut."

"Maybe. And maybe he *is* one of them."

* * *

Behind Hyrum Patch's barn, on a hill thickly covered by interlacing trees, John knelt beside a tree stump. Sunset had come and gone hours ago. Up above the forest canopy, a silver crescent moon cast a feeble light upon the earth so that where he prayed it was darkest night.

He ignored the complaining aches from his body with practiced ease. Long ago, John had accepted the price for communing with his Father in Heaven.

"Father in Heaven," he prayed aloud, "what is it exactly Thou would have me do here? I know someone is planning something terrible, but exactly what that is, Thou hast not told me."

Minutes passed with no answer, and for most people that would have been enough; they would have consoled themselves for a good effort. John's immersion in service to his Lord would not let him do that. He eagerly sought the lessons of Godhood; whatever it took, he would give.

He thought back over his calling, remembering Jesus' hands upon his head as he set John apart as an apostle along with the other eleven that day in Galilee. After praying all night, Jesus had come down off the mountain, his face bright, his eyes like fire. When the Savior's hands had rested upon John's head as he knelt before his

Lord, a quiet sureness filled John's heart and mind, unlike anything he had known before.

That was the moment he had known. He'd known, without any doubt or confusion, that Jesus was the Christ, the Redeemer, the Messiah. Although the feeling would weaken at times during those brief days until Jesus died on the cross, after the resurrection and the descent of the Holy Ghost upon the apostles, all doubt in Jesus Christ had forever fled.

From the time John had been allowed to stay and bring souls unto Christ, any doubts he continued to carry with him through the centuries were his own. No man, not even one schooled in the Spirit for centuries, could pretend himself completely confident in wearing the mantle of an apostle. It was an immortal responsibility, resting upon mortal shoulders.

As the first fingers of dawn crept through the trees around him, John stirred from where he had knelt all night. His bone-deep exhaustion was the price he paid for a knowledge of what was to come to the island and its people. Although there were still some details that it would have been helpful to know, "be still" had been the final answer.

Satisfied that he had learned all he could, John stumbled down the hill and fell into his bed in the barn bunk room. In seconds, sleep overcame him.

# CHAPTER FOUR

Martin drove slowly through Lincoln Park, letting the thick trees and the sound of the nearby water relax him. The park was three square miles of prime land, situated on the point furthest west on James Island. A winding road made its way around the park through thick forest land, often only a few feet from the waters of Puget Sound, which surrounded the park on three sides. Two miles from Burns' Point, Lincoln Park was a short drive along the northern, then western side of James Island. A favorite play spot for year-round residents, as well as the flocks of tourists who found it a perfect example of Northwest geography, Lincoln Park was where Martin often went to rest from life.

Today Martin only knew that he needed to calm down after a day at the car dealership where he worked on the mainland. His job as car salesman was very different from his former position as Vice President of Development for Eastern Michigan Power, from which he had resigned a few years back. After joining the LDS church, Martin could see that his new desires to live more in accordance with gospel teachings would not fit with the corporate life in that particular corporation.

As an executive for EMP, he had always planned his day down to the smallest details, and he had managed to narrow things down to what suited him, even if it meant he didn't grow very much. Thirty years with the corporation had given him a solid confidence of what his life was all about. Yet when the Lord knocked on his door one day, Martin learned he hardly knew anything at all about living.

Martin had come home from work one night to learn that two young men from the Mormon church had stopped by in the afternoon. At his wife's request, they would return that evening. Martin was not eager to talk to them. He believed in God, but it didn't go much further. However, after hearing their message, it wasn't long before his whole world changed.

After they were baptized, Martin and his wife, Jan, had followed a longtime dream, and had moved to Mount Placer, Washington. With their daugter Julie just forty-five miles away, Martin and his wife thought they were in heaven. Julie's husband, Randy, had shown himself to be a good father to Julie's daughter from a former relationship, and now a son had joined the young family. Life seemed full of joy and promise, the years ahead rosy and bright.

Martin sighed deeply and closed his eyes, attempting to ease the throbbing pain of his headache. Trying to make things right with a belligerent customer earlier in the day had pressed him to his limits.

*I should have known,* he thought. *Sell a car to someone LDS, who thinks because you both belong to the same church he should get a discount, and it's bound to come back to haunt you.* Two weeks later, the man had returned, claiming that Martin had cheated him because the car didn't have any power.

"I *told* him *before* he bought that car that a four-cylinder engine wouldn't give him the power he wanted," Martin muttered. "Did he listen to me? No. He comes back and says I *misled* him! *Geez.*"

*It's a good thing they aren't from my ward,* he thought; *bad enough we're in the same stake.* Martin sighed again, rubbing his temples. *Maybe I shouldn't sell to members. So, just how do I avoid that? Throw them out when they walk through the door?* He smiled grimly at the mental picture that brought.

In half an hour Martin was supposed to be at the ward office to go over plans for expanding the Burns' Point building. The church architect was coming up from Seattle to meet with him and President Higgins so they could all discuss the plans. Martin found it difficult to let go of his temporal problems long enough to feel something of the Spirit.

As he came to the park overlook, Martin pulled over and turned off the car. From where he parked, he had an open view of the private marina across the cove. Making sure he was alone, he began to pray.

"Heavenly Father," he began, then paused, thinking first about what he needed, then what he was grateful for. "I'm grateful to Thee that the problem at work didn't get out of hand. Several times during that brother's accusations I felt myself getting angry and ready to lash out, and then Thy hand touched my heart. Without Thee I could not have stayed so calm.

"This meeting at the church is very important, as Thou knowest. I need Thy peace inside me, to be able to understand Thy will for this new building addition. Please make this negative feeling in me go away."

After finishing, he waited for a time, then inhaled and opened his eyes. He felt quieter, if not completely at peace, but at least it was a step in the right direction. Then, he noticed his hands.

Just last week, while working on a sailboat he was repairing to sell, something amazing had happened. Martin relaxed when he worked on the boats; he enjoyed the work and it brought in a little more money. Unlike his church calling, the boats changed in direct proportion to how much time and effort he put into them. Furthermore, the boat work gave him time alone to think.

Thinking now, he remembered what had happened that day. In a hurry to finish a particular job and get home, Martin had absentmindedly put both hands on a hot electrical wire. He should have been electrocuted right then. However, nothing had happened. Coming to his senses, Martin had jerked back, his heart racing, frighteningly aware he should be dead. Yet a kindly heaven had been watching out for a forgetful, preoccupied bishop, and had protected him from his own foolishness. Apparently Martin wasn't going to get out of his calling that easily. Perhaps that was evidence Martin had important work to do in Burns' Point, and that God was mindful of him and preparing the way for success.

\* \* \*

As Martin drove out of Lincoln Park, Hyrum observed John up on the roof of the barn. John worked steadily, tearing off damaged shingles and clearing off moss that had grown thick on the old roof.

Hyrum was debating whether to call John down for some lunch or not. It was way past noon, but John had shown no signs of slowing and Hyrum had not wanted to interrupt John's impressive progress.

Nevertheless, Hyrum finally put two fingers to his mouth and issued an earsplitting whistle. When John looked toward the front porch, Hyrum signalled for him to come around to the back of the house. In a few minutes, John was knocking at the back door.

"Come in," Hyrum commanded, waving him into the kitchen. "Wash up and get your lunch. You've been holding me up for hours. How come you can't eat when everyone else does?" he added, grumbling.

"Sorry," John apologized as he began washing up at the laundry sink by the back door. "I guess I lost track of time. The more I tore out, the more work I found. Is that the original roof up there?"

"Probably," Hyrum said, setting down a plate of fried eggs, hash browns, and sausage on the table. "Coffee?" he asked, partly knowing John would say no, and partly testing him.

John shook his head as he walked toward the table. "Water is fine, thanks."

"Right, you're Mormon," Hyrum grunted, pulling down a plastic tumbler from the low cabinets in his kitchen, especially designed for someone in a wheelchair. "You're one of those people who don't do anything for fun." Hyrum gave John a sideways glance to see how he would react, but John just smiled. *Humph*, thought Hyrum. *He don't rib easy.* No satisfaction to be found there.

As Hyrum plunked the glass of water down on the table, the phone rang. "Eat fast, there's lots of work left on the roof and not much day left." Hyrum wheeled quickly out of the room.

When he came back, John was finishing his meal. "That was the sheriff," Hyrum said. "He said there's no record on you."

"I told you I was honest," John said, grinning.

Hyrum shook his head. "I didn't say 'criminal record.' I meant, 'No record,' period. So what's the deal—you running from something? What's your real name?"

"I told you," John said, rising from the table to carry his dishes over to the counter by the sink. "My name is John."

"Got any ID?" Hyrum asked.

John sighed, as if this was neither a new question nor a new situation for him. He put his hand in his back pants pocket and asked, "What kind of ID would you like to see?"

Hyrum sized him up, then said, "Let's start with a social security card."

John hesitated only briefly, before pulling out a card he handed to Hyrum.

"John Zebedee," Hyrum read out loud. "What kind of name is that?"

"It has Jewish origins," said John, patiently waiting for Hyrum to finish his investigation, so he could get back to his roof repairs.

Hyrum handed the card back to John. "Got anything else, like something with a picture on it?"

"Nope. No driver's license, no nothing. Don't figure to need one," said John as he pocketed the card. "Okay if I get back to work now?"

Hyrum waved him off, pretending indifference, but in truth, he was eager to call the sheriff back to check on the social security number his well-trained detective's mind had quickly memorized. From the first day Hyrum had put on a police officer's uniform, he had set his sights on being a detective, solving crimes, and bringing crafty criminals to justice. Now retired from the police force, he was excited by a new challenge.

John slipped out of the house and was soon back up on the barn roof, fully aware that Hyrum was checking on him again. John chuckled. Hyrum would find out no more than what the card had said. Why couldn't people trust their hearts anymore? The Spirit of God was a more sure check on someone's character than any computer file could possibly be.

\* \* \*

Kevin was completing a treatment form on one of his patients as his associate, Gary Stillman, came into their office at the Burns' Point Hospital.

"Going to make any money today, Mr. Nice Guy?" Gary asked, reaching for a cup of coffee from the pot on the hot plate. "Or are you starting a free clinic?"

Usually Kevin pretended not to hear Gary's jabs, but since being called as elders quorum president, he felt that Gary's sarcasm had increased tenfold, and it had become that much harder. Every day Gary had a new insult, barely coated in mock concern.

Gary was a member of the LDS church by record, but not by intent. He had been born a member of the Church, had grown up in Utah, married a nonmember beauty queen, and through one small step after another, was now one of the many inactive elders Kevin was responsible for in this area. However, Gary was not just a disinterested "less active" member; he was openly hostile toward the Church. Kevin wondered why Gary hadn't asked to have his name taken off the Church rolls.

When Kevin continued filling out the form on his patient without answering the jab, Gary intensified his poking around. "What's the matter, President Taylor, church duties getting you down?"

Kevin swallowed and paused. "Do you want my attention for something real, or are you just bored, Gary? I've got work to do," he said, resuming his writing.

Gary lifted his eyebrows. *"Exxcuuuse* me," he said. "Aren't we touchy these days? Your sense of humor has really gone down the drain ever since you became a management type in your cult group."

Kevin knew Gary was deliberately trying to provoke him. Why, he didn't know. Gary usually gave up before this point when Kevin ignored him.

The Burns' Point Hospital provided office space, support staff, and assorted perks to the two men, who received block rates for hospital personnel and special services. Gary and Kevin managed their own time to meet the hospital contract, as well any other work they personally wanted to do. It was the cost break for office space and support staff that kept Kevin at the hospital and tied to Gary.

More than once during the past months, Kevin had complained to Lacey about Gary, wishing he could afford to go it on his own. The special services he provided out of the office were an attempt to bring in enough income so that eventually he could do this. A small, honest, upbeat office would be preferable to what he had now. He would even do all his own paperwork if he could get away.

Kevin stood up, relieved that his next appointment gave him an excuse to leave. "Good talking to you," he said shortly, stashing the form in a file on his desk and heading quickly out of the office. But as he was going out the doorway, he chided himself for the snide tone he had used with Gary. He knew it wasn't what the Savior would have done.

Leaning back through the doorway, he said, "Gary, I'm sorry, that was rude. I'm sure you're just concerned about me and the different things I'm trying to do with my life. Thanks for noticing and for being my friend."

Gary's face turned to stone but he didn't say any more. Kevin walked down the hallway and out into the parking lot, wondering if his tongue was going to fall off for stretching the truth that far. Gary was far from being his friend, but more important, Kevin thought, I'm *not being* his *friend.*

\* \* \*

Twenty-five minutes later, Kevin was still chewing on this as he crossed the long road that connected James Island to a small island just east of the larger island. Pulling to a stop at the security gate by the oil refinery, Kevin leaned out his open window as the security guard stepped toward his car.

"I'm here for an appointment with Mr. Howks," Kevin said. The appointment confirmed, he drove into the parking lot he was directed to, looking around at the Maxwell Oil complex, the area's single largest employer. Kevin had often watched the tankers loading and off loading at the offshore docking area and speculated that it wouldn't take much to turn this area he loved into an ecological nightmare.

Asking directions as he went, Kevin was soon sitting in the waiting room of Mr. Randolph P. Howks, general manager of the refinery. Mr. Howks' secretary peered at him over her typewriter as she worked. Her eyes held the clear message that Kevin didn't look like most of the people who came to see her boss.

The intercom buzzed on the secretary's desk, and Kevin heard a muffled comment from someone on the other end of the line.

Turning to Kevin as she hung up the phone, she said coolly, "You can go in now."

Kevin thanked her, but she was busily typing again, having already dismissed him as unworthy of further notice. Feeling unsettled and out of place, Kevin entered Mr. Howks office.

"Come in," a voice called. The office was enormous, with a wide variety of plants, paintings, sculptures, and tropical fish in several tanks around the room. Large windows covered one side of the office and expensive leather chairs sat scattered around the room with elegant side tables. A large rosewood desk with an inlaid top was arranged at the end of the room so that anyone sitting behind it had both a view of the entire room and a complete overlook of the stunning vista offered by the windows—the bay itself, which shone a deep, serene blue out past the refinery, a few tiny islands sprinkled across the water, and the snow-capped mountains on the mainland behind. Kevin was very impressed.

A plain-looking man in a white shirt, tie, and slacks, stepped out from behind a wet bar with a glass in each hand. "Here, I think you'll like this," he said, handing Kevin a tall glass filled with a sparkling reddish liquid.

As Kevin politely took the drink, he introduced himself. "I'm Kevin Taylor, Mr. Howks. We talked on the phone about physical therapy services."

"That's why we're here," said Howks as he retreated around behind the bar. "Go ahead, take a swig, and tell me what you think."

"What is it?" Kevin asked.

"Something I made up, from a couple of recipes I talked out of a bartender in Hong Kong last year. It's better than the originals. Drink up."

Kevin thought over all the ways to politely decline the offer and still not offend his new client. This was a valuable contact and Randolph Howks was willing to pay generously to have Kevin come to him, to save him from having to go to Kevin's office.

"I don't drink, but thanks, anyway."

Howks drank his own glass down at once and set it down with a sharp rap on the glass bar top. "Everybody drinks sometime. It's okay.

Most of that is sweet rum and ginger ale. It won't tip you over like some things I mix. Go ahead."

"Really," said Kevin, setting the glass down on the bar, "I don't drink. Ever. I'm a member of the LDS church; some people call us 'Mormons.' It's against our beliefs to drink alcohol, or use tobacco, but I thank you for the thought."

Howks took the drink and downed it himself, before sliding the glass up against the other one with a clink. He smiled at Kevin as he came out from around the bar and took his hand. "You pass."

"I don't understand," said Kevin.

"I already knew," said Howks, "that you—let's go sit over here—that you're Mormon." He took a seat in one of the four plush chairs arranged around a handsome crystal coffee table and signaled Kevin to do the same. "I know all about you; that's why I checked you out with the drink. I don't have time for phoneys. If you had taken the drink, our appointment would have ended immediately— and without a cent from me, I'll add."

Kevin smiled uncomfortably. "Do you test all your appointments that way? Finding a doctor must be hard for you."

Howks laughed loudly. "In fact, it is. They all like what I pay, but they hate what I expect. Most doctors like being in charge, and that's one too many bosses in the room when I'm around. I have this habit of running things, including when I'm sick. Which brings me to what we talked about on the phone."

"You said you hurt your shoulder skiing last year," Kevin prompted.

"At Park City, Wolf Mountain," Howks said. "I hit this side slip area wrong and went down end over end. My doctor said I was lucky not to get more from it than a problem with my, what is it? Rotator cuff, I think it was. But," he rubbed his collarbone, "this bone aches all the time, and none of those fancy, high-priced quacks can find anything. So I thought I would get some help from you."

Kevin felt no small pressure, and he wondered if he was getting into something that would just add more stress to his life. Howks appeared to be a very determined man, one who was used to getting his own way, no matter what. The kind of pain he was describing was often extremely resistant to any kind of treatment. Was this the kind of person who would be patient waiting for results? Kevin didn't think so.

"I'm not sure I—"

"You'll do fine," interrupted Howks as he reached over to a box on the end table beside his chair and pulled out a cigar. Smelling it deeply he said, "Martin Davis recommended you. Anyone who knows cars like that man does, I'll believe what they have to say about anyone. Davis knows the difference between real cars and the junk being sold these days."

At the mention of his bishop's name, Kevin was taken aback. How did Howks and Bishop Davis cross paths? "You know Martin Davis?"

"Sure do. He sold me my new Cadillac, and a good deal we made, too. It was nice to work a deal with someone who is older than my kid for a change. Turns out Davis and I have some mutual friends back in Detroit. He and I grew up only a few miles from each other."

Kevin was at a complete loss. "Oh," was all he said.

Howks popped his expensive cigar back into its box and hopped up out of his chair. "Get yourself set. I'll be back in a second after I change into some sweats."

As Howks disappeared into a bathroom, Kevin attempted to organize his thoughts into some kind of professional perspective. This man was going to be an experience, of one kind or another. Kevin was going to earn his large fee—no doubt about it.

＊ ＊ ＊

As Kevin began treating the general manager of the refinery, a man stared at the administrative building from under his yellow hard hat. Known as Vincent Corrilo by his fellow refinery workers, he had been employed there for the past four months, doing a fair job of maintenance on the electrical machinery. His supervisor had only one complaint. He felt that sometimes Vincent didn't seem like he was quite "all there." He was slow to respond when called, often acting like he didn't know his own name. The truth was, Vincent didn't often respond to his name because he had been born with another one.

Using the pay phone by the lunchroom, Vincent dialed a number, looking around him to make sure no one would overhear him. As his call rang through, he played with the large collection of keys hanging from a clip on his belt. With the keys he needed to do his job, he could enter most parts of the refinery to fix the machinery.

"Holtz?" Vincent spoke sharply. "Did you get it?"

"Yeah, I got it." Holtz yawned into the phone. "What's your problem? I always get it, don't I?" At one time Holtz and Vincent had worked as equals in the group, but after a while Holtz ended up as second-in-command, as far as rank went in the loosely organized group. The distinction was a sore point between them. Holtz could remember very well how things had been before Vincent had found allies in a Middle Eastern terrorist group, who supplied him with money in return for hitting certain targets they designated. Every day, Holtz made new plans to take off on his own. And someday, he swore to himself, he would, too.

"Saturday," said Vincent, "we do it a week from this Saturday."

"That's too soon," complained Holtz. "Everything is set for the nineteenth—"

Hearing voices, Vincent interrupted Holtz. "The plans have been changed."

"You can't—"

"Do it!" ordered Vincent. "It all goes down a week from this Saturday, and— Gotta go, someone's coming. Call everyone together for tonight."

Vincent slammed the phone down in the holder, then hurriedly found a couple of quarters in his pants pocket. He shoved them into the pop machine next to the phone just as two men in yellow cleanup crew uniforms appeared from around the corner of the building.

"Hey, Vincent, how you doing, buddy?" the smaller of the two men yelled. "Where's the ten dollars you owe me from the Trailblazers' game? I want my money."

Vincent mumbled, "Pay day," and hurried away with his can of pop.

"Weird dude," the tall, skinny man commented, as he put his own money into the machine.

Vincent would have seemed different even if the two men had known more about him. The son of a wealthy family, educated in the best schools, and thoroughly indoctrinated in fundamentalist religious beliefs, he had rebelled enough to ignore the laws of society, but not enough to completely shake off his upbringing. Part of him wanted to be a hell-raiser, but he was never able to overcome his guilt about going against authority. Vincent could set off explosive charges that would destroy the hopes and dreams, not to mention lives, of many. At the same time, he was uncomfortable drinking anything but soda pop.

If Vincent had not commanded such destructive force, he would have been an object of pity. Instead, with his unleashed tendencies to violence, he was definitely someone to fear.

# CHAPTER FIVE

Lacey's prayers, petitioning God for a little more time, did not slow her blindness. The darkness about her was closing in. She reached out into the blur, to the bit of light that shrank a little more each day. Moment by moment she had to depend more upon the Spirit to hold her emotions together, to keep her from screaming out in fear and anger. Each day she found some new bit of pride within her heart she had never known was there.

She *wanted* to submit herself to total trust in God, and His ability to care for her, to help her through everything that came her way, but it was so *hard* to accept that she, a young wife and mother, she, who had always been so independent and active, was going into a world of blindness, dependence, and fragility. How could this happen to her?

Some days she resented that God did not stop her blindness from happening. He was all powerful and knew everything. He could stop it. So why didn't he?

Before long she would live in a world of total darkness, unable to even see the smiles of her children or husband. Soon her blindness would lock the sunsets she loved to admire each evening behind dark curtains of blackness. If Lacey thought about it too long, the fear would grow within her heart, and a cold shiver would race up her spine. At times like this she longed to call Kevin home, so he could hold her in his strong arms until she felt safe again.

After learning two years ago that she was going blind, she had called Kevin home several times from work during those first months, crying into the phone that she needed him. But over time she had learned greater trust in God, because the only way she could overcome her fear and anxiety was to trust that He really was there and that He really would help her and her family. Lately, she had felt a presence when she slowly moved her hand forward into the blur, like someone was touching her. In the touch came peace and comfort.

Lacey had always been "LDS," even before she joined the Church as a teenager with her parents. The goals in her life had required almost no revision as she learned more about the Savior and His plan of salvation. Living as a member of the Church had fit comfortably, as if it were the way she was always meant to live.

Sometimes these days she felt her spirit expand until she seemed able to touch everywhere in the world at once. The differences and boundaries between her heart, God, and all His children who ever had lived or would live upon the earth, dissolved. At times like these she remembered about the doors in life; that as some closed, others opened. And yet, this comfort and peace wasn't always in place. Darkness often closed in about her and overcame the growing strength in her spirit.

A trickle of fear and despair crept along the edges of her heart, and she reflexively wrapped her arms around herself. "My Lord," she cried out. "Hold me, please! I'm frightened again."

Heedless of the stream of tears flowing freely down her face, Lacey rocked back and forth as she sat on the living room couch, struggling not to let go of her Savior's hand.

Davey, just off the school bus, burst into the room, full of wonderful things to share with his mommy about kindergarten. As he found her crying, his face grew serious and his own eyes reddened. Hugging her, he said softly, "It's okay, Mommy. Jesus loves you."

Lacey swallowed with difficulty and pulled her young son closer, and before long both of them were crying together. "I know, Davey. I know He does. He's right here with me. Thank you."

The gratitude in her heart for all that God had blessed her with encouraged more tears. Yet this weeping brought healing instead of sorrow, hope instead of despair.

Taking a breath as large as the sorrow only moments before, Lacey stepped up to the next level of understanding. *Line upon line, precept on precept,* she thought, kissing the top of Davey's head. *That is how He lifts us, That is how He teaches His children,* just as the song said.

* * *

John walked along the road, listening to the birds singing, knowing that in only seconds the rain would begin again. He had finished working for Hyrum Patches and now that Friday had come, John had business in town that needed his attention.

"'Afternoon," John said to a black and yellow cat as it hurried across the road in front of him, stopping in midstep at the sound of his voice. Sitting in the middle of the road, it watched him as he came closer.

"How are your kittens this day, Mama cat?" John asked. "They must keep you busy, finding food for them. Wouldn't you rather go back and live with the little girl in town who misses you instead of being out here in the woods all the time?"

The cat looked away from him, purred a moment, then leisurely moved off into the brush.

"Think about what I said," John said over his shoulder as he walked on. "You might be freer out here, but you ate better in town."

The expected rain dropped several large drops of water about him, then paused before beginning in earnest, washing steadily down on the already damp island. John pulled the collar of his denim jacket up about his neck. Smiling, he looked behind him back down the road, as if expecting someone.

A lone white car came around the bend toward him, headlights glowing through the sheets of rain. John stopped walking and waited patiently by the side of the road.

The car slowed to stop beside him, and the driver waved him in. As John slid inside, he said, "I was hoping you would get here *before* it started raining. But I'm glad you're here anyway."

Kevin Taylor pulled back onto the road and drove on. "You sound like maybe you *knew* I was coming. What have you got, an inside line to God?"

John shrugged. "Good intuition," he said mildly. "People who walk a lot in the rain get good at telling when a ride is coming along."

Seeing John, Kevin suddenly remembered something. "Finding you here is going to save my neck. My wife asked me to invite you to dinner, and I completely forgot it until now. How are you fixed for tonight? We're having lasagna, but it's meatless. Are you someone who has to have meat at every meal?"

John chuckled. "No. The way I understand the Word of Wisdom, it says meat is something you eat very sparingly. 'Yea, flesh also of beasts and of the fowls of the air, I, the Lord, have ordained for the use of man with thanksgiving; nevertheless they are to be used sparingly; And it is pleasing unto me that they should not be used, only in times of winter, or of cold, or famine.'"

Kevin nodded. He was liking John more all the time. "Doctrine and Covenants eighty-nine, verses thirteen and fourteen I believe. No, twelve and thirteen . . . that's right. You know, that's something I believe in very strongly. I gave up eating meat a few years ago after studying that scripture, and realizing that the Lord really meant what he said in there. All the studies these days say a low-meat or meatless diet is the best way to go."

John nodded in agreement.

"Anyway, my wife will be glad to see I finally followed through and invited you home. She's anxious to hear your side of what happened when we found the car that exploded. I think she believes I've embellished it a bit."

"Don't you need to check with her before bringing someone home first?" John asked, shifting the conversation. "My wife never minded much, probably because she grew up with a house full of brothers, but some women do."

Kevin shook his head. "Honestly, Lacey doesn't mind. She grew up in big family, too. I'm the one who has trouble with people showing up unexpectedly."

For a few moments neither man spoke, as the rain and the wipers moved back and forth.

"You married now?" Kevin asked, making conversation, but also curious.

"She died," John said evenly, looking out the window beside him.

"I'm sorry," Kevin offered.

"She lived a good life, and I know she's happy now," John responded. "I plan to be with her again someday."

It was only a few miles more before Kevin pulled into his driveway, after stopping by the curb because of the bikes and toys that blocked his way. "My kids have been busy," he commented.

"Enjoy them while you can," John said. "They'll be grown before you know it."

"Honey, I'm home," Kevin called, as he and John came through the front door. "I brought home that certain someone you wanted to meet." Kevin winked at John as he put both their wet coats on the hooks by the door.

Lacey came around the corner and down the hallway toward the two of them, wiping her hands on her apron.

"Hello," John greeted her. "Your lasagna smells good."

Lacey smiled, squinting at John.

"I found him along the road again. We seem to have a pattern going," Kevin said as he kissed Lacey on the cheek. "Lacey, this is John. John, this is my beautiful and 'smarter than I am' wife, Lacey."

"It's very nice of you to have me over for dinner," John said as he took Lacey's outstretched hand.

"Oh shoot," Kevin exclaimed. "I just realized something." He slapped his forehead. "I never actually asked you if you *wanted* to come here tonight."

John smiled. "What, and turn down a free meal? Especially when it's the best lasagna in Washington?" There was no point in telling Kevin that meeting up with him "by chance" had been John's design all along.

\* \* \*

John insisted on helping clean up after dinner and dried the dishes while Kevin washed. Lacey gave the children their baths and helped another child with a school project that was due Monday and had been put off much too long.

"Lacey's adjusting well to losing her sight," John said thoughtfully, thinking about what she told him over dinner. Kevin had brought it up, remarking how incredible his wife was in continuing to do all she had before, in spite of the tremendous challenge.

"I couldn't do it," Kevin said as he slid the rinsed dishes into the drainer in front of John. "Being without my sight would be too much for me. It's bad enough I always forget things. Lacey says if I didn't have her around to remind me, I would probably forget to get dressed in the morning."

"That would wake people up in church on Sunday," John joked, enjoying his own humor.

Kevin laughed, too. "We could use you in the quorum to lighten things up—which reminds me, do you need a ride to church this Sunday? I'd be happy to come out and get you." Even as Kevin spoke, he thought of Hyrum and winced, then tried to set his spirit in the right direction. "While I'm there, I could check in on Brother Patches again. Maybe he'll be in a better mood this time."

"He's not a bad man," John said. "Just a lonely, frightened one."

Kevin nodded and shrugged. "I know. I . . . it's just hard for me to get used to selling the gospel to someone. No, I don't mean sell. It's—"

"Hard to keep ministering to someone who takes offense when you do?" John suggested, understanding exactly what Kevin was talking about.

"Exactly. I joined the Church for the principles, not the people, so I haven't been all that bothered if people didn't like me or weren't very friendly. Now, Lacey, she really likes people, and it hurts her to be at odds with someone. My calling as quorum president . . . I don't know. It takes all I have sometimes to keep a smile on my face and keep working with some brethren. It would just be so much easier to say, 'Okay, that's fine, have a good life. You do your thing, and I'll do mine.'"

"'How think ye,'" John quoted softly, "'if a man have an hundred sheep, and one of them be gone astray, doth he not leave the ninety and nine, and goeth into the mountains, and seeketh that which is gone astray? And if so be that he find it, verily I say unto you, he rejoiceth more of that sheep, than of the ninety and nine which went not astray. Even so it is not the will of your Father which is in heaven, that one of these little ones should perish.'"

Kevin weighed the words of the Savior, feeling their truth soften his heart toward Hyrum Patches.

John continued. "He saith unto you, Kevin, 'Lovest thou me?' And you say unto him, 'Lord, thou knowest all things; thou knowest that I love thee.' Jesus saith unto you, 'Feed my sheep.'"

As he scraped the lasagna pan, Kevin pondered John's last words. A picture came to him, of the eleven apostles and Jesus, sitting around the fire on the beach beside the Sea of Galilee. After everyone there was well fed from their meal of fish, the Savior taught Peter a powerful lesson about love, saying, "Feed my sheep," meaning we are to love all God's children, not just those we like. A quiet, peaceful strength lifted Kevin up and fortified his resolve to reach out to the lost sheep under his care.

As he worked free the last of the baked-in lasagna from the pan, Kevin remembered something else. Near the end of that last chapter, in the book of John, Peter had asked about his fellow apostle, John. In reply, Jesus had questioned, "If I will that he tarry till I come, what is that to thee?"

Lacey's remarks that first night after the accident, just yesterday, came back. What if John wasn't one of the Three Nephites, but was John the Apostle?

Kevin turned toward John impulsively, the question on the tip of his tongue, but he found himself alone in the kitchen. John's dish towel hung neatly on the rack. Surprised, Kevin looked out into the living room and found John there, reading a bedtime story to little Davey.

"And the big bear said, 'That's my motorcycle. How come you're riding it when you didn't even ask?'" John read with a deep voice for the bear. Then in a little voice, "'But I didn't know it was yours,' said the little boy, kicking at the dirt with his toe. 'I'm sorry. Really I am.'"

Davey said, "Sometimes I get in trouble like that. I use my sister Valerie's hairbrush when I can't find mine before church on Sunday. She gets really mad at me."

"I used to tease my sister," said John. "My mother told me I was a pest."

Davey nodded in understanding.

Back in the kitchen, Kevin finished off the pans, drained and cleaned out the sink, and was wiping off the counters when Lacey came up behind him.

Rubbing his back, she said, "Good job, Mister."

"How would you know, blind woman?" Kevin kidded her gently, as he often did.

She ran her fingers along the counter, and then on the pots and pans in the drainer. "I can't see all that well anymore, but I can still feel and smell. You missed some crumbs by the toaster, by the way."

"Oh, no," he complained. "Now she's going to be sniffing after to me to see if I dusted the piano."

"Don't have to smell that one, I can feel it. Besides, you never dust. You always say, 'That's what kids are for,' or 'Dust is a protective coating for things, so we should leave it alone.'"

As if on cue, someone began playing their old piano in the living room, a flowing, haunting melody that both of them knew couldn't have come from their daughters, no matter how much they had been practicing lately. They listened for a moment before Lacey turned back to Kevin.

"So what do you think?" she asked.

"About what? Whether he's one of the Three Nephites?"

"Yeah. You have to admit, he's not your typical roam-around drifter. The man has more to him than we can see, I'm sure of it." She yawned, more than usually tired out from watching the Nurdlinger kids all day. Those twin girls would wear anyone out.

The piano music instantly changed into a Scott Joplin ragtime tune, accompanied by clapping from the kids.

"I don't know," said Kevin, overwhelmed by the thought. "I mean, really, how could he be? It's just so impossible."

"Is he coming to church this Sunday?"

"I guess so. I offered to give him a ride in."

"Going to brave the ogre under the bridge again, are you, Billy Goat Gruff?"

Kevin smiled thinly, his former fears beginning to return. "If I go on an errand from God, I should make it back alive, right?" He was only half kidding.

# CHAPTER SIX

Hyrum was secretly delighted with how his new hired man was working out, though no one would have known it by the scowl on his face whenever he watched John. During the past three days, John was making short work of the many repairs the old place had needed. Nevertheless, as Hyrum watched the progress, he was angry, his pride offended that someone else had to do the work for him.

As John came out of the barn, after putting away the paint and brushes he used on the old barn planks, Hyrum wheeled down the ramp by the front door of the house. Flipping a set of keys at John as he approached, Hyrum ordered, "Go get my van. We need to run into town and get what's needed for your next project."

John caught the keys, smiled, and saluted before walking off to get the van. Hyrum snorted after him, uneasy with how much he was coming to trust John. Trusting anyone these days wasn't wise.

As the two of them rode along the road to Burns' Point, John stuck his right arm out the window, enjoying how the air felt as it flowed over his skin.

"Better pull your arm in," Hyrum grumbled, squeezing the steering wheel tighter. "It's against the law to do that in this state."

"Sorry, officer." John retracted his arm but left the window down enough to feel the breeze on his face. "So, what did you find out about me when you checked on my social security number?"

Hyrum eyed his passenger for a moment before looking ahead at the road again. "Just what you knew I would—nothing."

John grinned. "Well, maybe that's because there isn't any deep, dark secret to find out about me. Maybe I'm just what you see. Some people are pretty simple, you know."

"Maybe," Hyrum snorted. Then lighter, "Sometimes."

In a few minutes, the two of them pulled up outside the hardware store. "Talk to the owner, Bill Gibson," said Hyrum as John stepped out of the van, "I called and told him you would be in to pick up my order."

John began to ask a question, but Hyrum was already driving off, without a word about when he would be back or where he was going. Shaking his head, John entered the hardware store.

A slim, white-haired older man with sparkling eyes and an easy smile greeted him from behind a counter. "Morning. You John?"

"You Bill?" John asked.

"Patches said you were coming. I've got most of what you'll need all set aside in the back. There's a couple of things he didn't mention, so you can decide, now that you're here."

Getting all the supplies for fixing the plumbing in Hyrum's house took no time at all. While John waited for Hyrum to return, he visited with Bill Gibson, who turned out to be a walking history book about Burns' Point.

"My wife and I came here long before it turned into a refuge colony for those people running away from California earthquakes," Bill said. "My wife is a part-time nurse at the hospital here. Yeah, Janet loves working with those babies in the nursery. She says it gives her a reason to keep going now that our kids are grown and gone. I used to work at the veterans hospital in Seattle, running the equipment repair department until I retired." He made a face. "Sitting around made me crazy. Next thing I knew, I owned this place."

John surveyed the neat, orderly store. "I would guess you like it," he said.

Bill nodded. "I do, but I like to pretend I don't. Guess that's one of those old men things." He tapped on the counter, "Where's that boss of yours?"

* * *

It didn't take Hyrum long to drive the short distance from the hardware store to the little house among the pine trees by the water. As he looked out over Puget Sound toward nearby Gomez Island, the setting was very restful. Unfortunately, it was lost on Hyrum, who was too consumed with his own thoughts.

He transferred himself from the van seat to his wheelchair, then set the lift in motion. As soon as he was outside of the van on the dirt driveway, he slowly made his way up the ramp by the front door. After a moment, he pushed the doorbell and waited.

The door opened and a cheerful, elderly woman said, "Good morning, Mr. Patches. Thank you for coming. Now that you're here, Melinda will rest easier."

Hyrum nodded, and wheeling himself inside the cottage, followed the old woman through the house until he was at the bedside of a pale, fragile-looking little girl. With so little left of her she barely made any mound at all beneath the flower print quilt.

"Melinda?" he called, so softly in just a whisper. "Melinda?"

Gradually a tiny face moved out from beneath the covers, much like a turtle awakening, the eyes fluttering, wakefulness returning piece by piece. Hyrum swallowed back sorrow at how much weaker she was from his last visit just a few days ago.

"Good morning, Melinda," he said gently.

Melinda gave a thin smile and Hyrum ached even more for her. For a fleeting moment he wished never to have known her rather than witness her gradual death. The thought passed quickly and was replaced by gratitude to have her in his life for any length of time at all.

An hour later, Hyrum wheeled down the hallway to the living room, where Melinda's grandmother was sitting on the couch, crocheting something with yellow yarn. Hyrum came to a stop nearby, hurting too much to say anything but not wanting to be alone with his grief.

Melinda's grandmother looked up at him. "You are an angel from God, Mr. Patches," she said. "Since her mother died last year, I don't know what I would have done without you to help me with Melinda."

Melissa's young father had been Hyrum's friend from the police force in Seattle. A punk's gun had caused his senseless death nearly five years ago. Melissa's mother had died of cancer just two years before, leaving this nine-year-old girl, who was now herself dying of AIDS. A hemophiliac, she had received blood that was supposed to be safe. It wasn't.

Melinda's father had been like a son to Hyrum; the older man had taught the younger all there was to know about police work. A bond had grown between them, bringing something Hyrum had never known with the children of his own flesh. The young man's death had ripped Hyrum's heart in two.

Hyrum's eyes watered from unshed tears, and he awkwardly brushed them away. The tough, gruff, old man most people knew and feared was absent. A dreadful emptiness filled his heart, especially when he looked ahead toward the time when Melinda would be gone. Hyrum could see so much of her father in her. Ever since his friend's death, Hyrum had taken it upon himself to look after this family as their lives had steadily gone from bad to worse.

"What did the doctor say?" he asked. He knew what the grand-mother had said over the phone last night, but he needed to hear it again. Could there be something the doctors had missed?

"He said she'll probably be gone within two weeks."

Hyrum looked at the old woman, who continued her knitting, not looking up at him. Although she appeared calm and composed on the outside, Hyrum noticed a slight tremor in her hands that had not been there the last time he had visited.

"Would it be all right if I came back tonight?"

Her eyes met his briefly. "Of course, you know you're always welcome."

As Hyrum drove away he fought a mammoth battle against the tears inside, refusing to let them out, knowing that once he did, he would be unleashing a torrent.

\* \* \*

"So where's my stuff?" Hyrum asked. "You had long enough. I expected it to be out here at the curb."

John climbed into the van as he answered, "Around back, as usual. Bill said that's where you always pick things up."

Because Hyrum's thoughts were still with Melinda, he was uncharacteristically quiet, and John watched him closely. When the supplies were loaded and the van headed back to Hyrum's place, John said casually, "So you and Gibson are old friends?"

"Used to be," Hyrum said curtly.

"Mind if I ask why not now?" John asked.

"Yeah, I mind. It's my own business." Hyrum paused. "No . . . I . . . it was a bad time."

"Okay. So how come you aren't friends now?"

Hyrum felt something touch his heart. His grief over Melinda had opened things up inside. His past sorrow for his wife, which he usually kept locked away behind all the anger, unexpectedly stepped out on its own and starting talking.

"Bill and his wife were in an accident about the same time my wife and I had ours. We were all in the hospital together, his wife and mine in one room, and he was in mine." Hyrum made a halfhearted attempt to stop talking, but he genuinely felt better telling John about it, so he continued. "We were all down in Seattle, there at the University hospital."

Hyrum stopped as intense grief engulfed him, catching in his throat and tightening his chest so he couldn't breathe. He felt dizzy and lightheaded all at once.

"You okay?" John asked, seeing how quickly Hyrum had changed. "Do you need me to drive?"

"No," Hyrum croaked, struggling to regain his composure. "We're almost home."

John looked out the window and recognized the man he had seen working on his old car the first day John had walked out to Hyrum's. In place of the old, broken down vehicle he had been working on that day, he was now waxing an expensive-looking, new car. Hyrum shook his head and John caught the look on his face.

"True happiness is not found in getting something," John said quietly. "True happiness is found in becoming something."

Hyrum looked at John in surprise. "What?"

"One of the apostles of the LDS church said that," noted John. "Sound familiar?"

Hyrum grunted as they pulled up to his house. "There's plenty of day left. You can get busy on the pipes under the house." Hyrum turned his seat around, moved into the wheelchair lift, and lowered himself out of the van.

"Okay, boss," said John. He was sorry that Hyrum had closed up again. John found it sad how much the tired old man needed to talk and how much he fought the inclination.

After unloading the supplies, John crawled under the house in the narrow area between the floor and the dirt, looking carefully around for spiders, and anything else that lived under there.

"There's nothing to be worried about," he told himself. "All the years you've lived, you'd think you wouldn't be afraid of spiders anymore."

"I'm not afraid," he responded, as if he were talking to someone else. "I'm just *very* respectful."

A huge spiderweb blocked his path along the pipe he was tracing. In the center of it was a spider that would have given King Kong second thoughts.

"Oh, yuuck!" groaned John, saying a silent prayer.

* * *

Kevin and Martin stared at their copies of the ward activity report for the past three months. The numbers were discouraging. Attendance at sacrament meeting had dropped even lower than its usual dismal basement percentage, correlating with the drop in home teaching and visiting teaching efforts. Gayle Shumato, the Relief Society president, wrote a note to herself in her blue planner. Jose Riveria, the high priest group leader, had to work this Saturday morning and couldn't attend the unhappy meeting.

"I know it looks hopeless," Gayle said, her usually unreadable face betraying her own heaviness over the ward's troubles. "But I've lived here for over fifteen years now, and it won't get any worse than this, at least. It's a seasonal thing. The weather gets good and everyone goes out to play. I can't believe it won't improve come fall."

Kevin spoke up, conscious of his responsibility as elders quorum president. "Bishop, we've played it pretty soft and gentle until now. Don't you think we might start being more straightforward with the members now? I mean, after all, can they get any less involved than they are?"

Martin sighed. Corporate management had been so much easier. Employment was dependent on performance; there, you either did the job or were gone, no matter how good a person you were. Volunteer organizations like the Church were another matter altogether. While numbers on a sheet of paper weren't the true measure of how things were going, they did reflect something about the members' spiritual level and growth.

Martin smiled slightly at Kevin. "Think we ought to get out the whips and cattle prod, do you, President?"

Gayle shook her head. "I've already thought about that one and decided bribes might work better."

Martin chuckled. "You two are good for me. Besides being good counselors, you two are gifts from God above. I don't even want to think what it would be like around here without you. We may not win the war, but we'll give it a good effort. Thank you, both."

The meeting broke up a few minutes later, with everyone promising to fast and pray over the problem. They would meet again Sunday morning at ward council.

Kevin stayed to talk with Martin. "I'll be bringing someone to church Sunday I know you'll want to meet," Kevin said. Placing his church papers in his planner, he snapped a big rubber band around it; the zipper was broken, and he didn't want to spend the money for a new one.

"Are you talking about the man who helped you rescue the woman and her child from the car accident?" Martin asked.

"How did you know about that?"

Martin chuckled. "Burns' Point isn't that big. News travels fast. I heard about it that night from Jose, who heard it from a nurse at the hospital and from a police friend of his. Pretty amazing what the two of you did."

Kevin shook his head. "What I did was nothing. What John did . . . well, that was amazing. This guy, John—he's the one I'm bringing to church Sunday—he walked out of the explosion without a mark on him. Now you tell me, Bishop, isn't that a bit strange?"

Martin tilted his head to one side. "Maybe it just looked like that. You were probably pretty stressed at the time—"

"No." Kevin was adamant. "I know what I saw. You know what Lacey thinks? She thinks this guy is probably one of the Three Nephites. When he was over at our house for dinner last night, he . . . well . . ." Kevin paused a moment, not sure how to put last night's feelings into words. "When he talked to me about Hyrum Patches, I felt like I was talking to the Savior, face to face. It felt that powerful. I didn't much like what he told me, since it means I have to face Hyrum again, but . . . I don't know. It's weird."

Martin leaned back in his chair, put his hands behind his head, and stared up at the ceiling. He sat quietly for a few moments, checking his heart, feeling for what Kevin was telling him. "Let's make sure I get to talk with him a bit tomorrow. You know how it gets around here, everybody all over the place. I hope people eventually get the message that an executive secretary serves a useful purpose; there is an order to things. Now if Dee Calton can only learn that he's supposed to be a gatekeeper for me, then maybe things will stop looking like a circus around here."

Kevin laughed. "You do look like a ringmaster sometimes. I can almost imagine you in a red coat with long tails, big, black, knee-high boots, and a whip."

"Being a clown might be more fun," Martin said ruefully.

The affection the two men felt for each other was evident. Neither of them were comfortable in their callings, neither enjoyed having to be as firm and tough as their callings at times required as they attempted to reorganize the ward into something resembling what the Lord wanted. The bishop was grateful he had someone with whom he could talk honestly about what went on in the ward. Without Kevin, it would have been very lonely. The bishop's counselors were good men, but they were different from Martin in how they thought. Kevin and Martin were more alike.

"How's your beautiful wife adjusting these days?" Martin asked.

"Lacey is a wonder. I couldn't do what she does. I wouldn't even want to try. To be going blind . . . her world gets darker every day. I know she struggles with it all sometimes, but you wouldn't know it from her energy level. She still does more than three of me."

"My wife always says it takes three men to do what one woman can," Martin agreed. "Lacey is a remarkable woman no matter how you slice it. I feel very sure that God planned all this change long ago, before she came to earth. Lacey is someone who will use it as a stepping stone, rather than whine about what a big stumbling block it is. She's an inspiration to a lot of us."

Kevin looked at his watch. "I've got to go. I have an appointment in a few minutes. You know Mr. Howks, the general manager at the refinery. He said you sold him a car a while back."

"Enjoyable man," said Martin as both men left the office. "Knows his cars, too. I wish more people were like him. He could be a real asset to the Church if he got straightened around and joined up. Maybe you could be the one to bring him in from the cold."

Kevin rolled his eyes. "Me? I don't think so. He's— I feel like a little kid around him most of the time. If he wanted to, he could probably chew me up and spit me out without breaking stride. I'm amazed he likes to talk to me, but he does. We spend most of his appointment time shooting the breeze about things."

"God works in mysterious ways," commented Martin as he locked the office door behind him. "See you tomorrow, President."

"So long, Bishop, rest up tonight. Tomorrow will be fast and furious."

\* \* \*

At the refinery gate, Kevin found that the sticker Mr. Howks had given him for his car bumper guaranteed instant entry into the facility. The security guard just waved Kevin through, as did the security guard at the entrace to the administration building.

As Kevin entered the general manager's waiting room, Howks glanced at his watch and said, "Right on time, two points for you. Let's get started." Kevin smiled nervously, wondering what Mr. Howks had planned for this meeting. With some people, you just never knew what they were going to do next.

When the two of them had entered the inner office, Howks handed Kevin a drink in a tall glass. "Try it," he commanded.

Kevin held the glass up to the light coming in from the large picture windows behind Howks' desk. The cherry color was appealing, though he wondered what this one was. "This isn't another test, is it?"

Howks laughed heartily. "No, no, this is safe. It's fruit juice and ginger ale. Even you can drink it safely. No more tests, my friend, you already passed. So relax."

Kevin downed the drink in one long swallow, dry from his previous meeting at the church. "Ah, that really is good. I'll have to get the recipe for this one. My wife likes to make blender drinks. Maybe we can add this one to our list of Mormon drinks."

"You do that," said Howks, already heading into his bathroom to change into a warm-up outfit for his appointment. "Oh," he stopped abruptly by the couch, "that pile there is for you. It's a warm-up outfit and some running shoes. You and I are about the same size so I know the outfit will work. I had to guess on the shoes, so if they don't fit, you can take them back to Mortenson's Athletic Store in Mount Placer and exchange them. I thought next week, you and I might start walking and running together as part of my recovery program."

Howks was gone before Kevin could protest. Rubbing his over-weight belly with one hand, Kevin thought, *Howks is full of surprises, all right. I do need to get into shape, but running with Mr. Dynamo wasn't what I had in mind. Then again, maybe this could be the way the Lord would have me gradually fellowship a prospective investigator.*

Kevin sighed tiredly.

# CHAPTER SEVEN

Lacey locked the front door of her house, rattling the doorknob to make sure it was shut all the way. She hoped Kevin would notice the note she had left for him on the kitchen table. Carefully following the line between the grass and cement, she made her way to Gayle Shumato's truck at the end of the driveway.

She still felt warm from the love her brother Aaron had expressed to her on the telephone just a few minutes before. He'd been in the middle of a meeting and felt impressed to call from his bank office in Utah. He said he just wanted her to know how much he loved and looked up to her.

Lacey smiled as she found the handle on Gayle's small pickup truck. *I'm so blessed,* she thought. *I have family and friends who love me. What does losing my sight matter compared to that?* She tried to ignore the tiny voice inside her that whispered, "Who are you kidding?"

"Took you long enough," Gayle teased as Lacey slid into the truck.

Lacey stuck her tongue out at her, enjoying Gayle's playful banter. Gayle never patronized Lacey; no overemphasizing the encroaching blindness, no talking loudly—as if Lacey was going deaf instead of blind. Gayle acted like Lacey was still Lacey, just more fuzzy-seeing than before. It was refreshing.

"How's Calvin?" Lacey asked. Gayle's husband had pneumonia but refused to take any time off from his work at the pharmacy.

"Stubborn," snorted Gayle, as she backed the truck out of the driveway. "The prideful bonehead thinks because he knows all about medicine it gives him some kind of immunity to being sick like everyone else."

Gayle shifted and then continued speaking as she drove out of the cul-de-sac toward the main road. "For someone that talks to doctors all the time, you'd think he would trust them. Far as he's concerned, most of them are witch doctors."

Lacey yawned, tired from being up late last night with her youngest who had been ill. This afternoon, however, he'd been just fine. Kids!

"Have any trouble getting someone to watch your kids for a few hours?" Gayle asked, braking at a stop sign and looking both ways. A dog took its time loping along in front of the truck, and Gayle tapped expectantly on the steering wheel while she waited.

"No," said Lacey, "my neighbor owes me some last-minute favors. I've watched her kids plenty of times. Besides, this won't take very long, will it? Davey's better than he was last night, but I don't trust his stomach. My kids do this back and forth thing before they really get better."

Gayle pulled ahead onto the main road and accelerated, grinding gears as she searched for the right one. "Ah, there it is. I guess I better take this old truck into the shop one of these days, before it falls completely apart on me."

"I'll pray for your truck," joked Lacey, only half kidding.

"Thanks," nodded Gayle. "Hopefully this won't take very long. I only want to check in on Sister Nurdlinger, not fix her whole life. I'd take one of my counselors if I could, but they're both out of town, and the visiting teachers don't seem to get around to it." Gayle growled, "Women. Sometimes I hate to admit I am one."

Lacey patted her on the shoulder.

"You're the only person in the world I would dare talk like this around," admitted Gayle. "If Helen Norman's husband gets that job in California and moves away, I think I'll ask for you as a counselor. That way I could really talk to you about all of this."

Lacey smiled, loving Gayle all the more because she was a strong Latter-day Saint and real at the same time. "You have Calvin to talk to."

Gayle really snorted at this suggestion. "That old grump? Sheez, I'd rather talk to my plants at the nursery than him. When everything stays level and pleasant, he's fine. Let me have a problem, and he's off like a shot. No thanks, I'll stick to my plants. My girls think I'm losing my mind these days, but at least the plants don't ask me where I'm 'going with this line of thought,' the way Calvin does. Some people really change as they get older."

Lacey chuckled, imagining Gayle talking to her plants, but didn't say anything.

"Maybe we better have a prayer before going any further. I'm having a hard time feeling the Spirit this morning," said Gayle as she pulled over to the side of the road. As both women bowed their heads and invited the Spirit of God to be with them, a peaceful atmosphere descended upon them, easing their temporal cares and concerns. As they lifted their heads afterwards, they now felt prepared to minister to the struggling sister.

\* \* \*

Hyrum had changed his mind and decided to have John do some more work on the barn roof instead of the plumbing under the house. John had quickly finished the small project and now lay stretched out on the roof of the barn, soaking up the infrequent sunlight that splashed for the moment over the land. This part of the barn was out of sight of Hyrum's house, so John had no worries about the man whistling at him to get back to work. Most of the roof repairs were done, anyway, and besides, even the Lord had taken time during His three-year ministry upon the earth to enjoy the joys of nature. John let his eyes close, drifting off into a pleasant sleep.

He dreamed of the lost tribes, as the world called them, though their whereabouts were not lost to God, or John either, for that matter. For many years he had been laboring with them, preparing them for the time when they would return and once again be part of the whole. Separated from the rest of humankind by the Lord—the better to be prepared for their work in the last days—John felt honored to teach them the gospel.

John had been given leave to return among the Latter-day Saints, the gentiles, and so-called heathen nations to allow him to rest from his labors with the tribes. As Joseph Smith had so aptly put it, sometimes it's necessary to unstring the bow or it will lose its spring.

During his quiet moment of repose, John thought of Sheena, the eight-year-old daughter of humble parents from the tribe of Asher. Sheena, with her bright and easy manner, had especially tugged at his heart. She never failed to bring a smile to his face when he was struggling with some part of his ministry to the tribes. Sheena's family had always had a place for him at their table, and often he would go there to remember the quieter, more gentle elements of life.

Sheena had fallen ill and suffered from a fever that resisted all the efforts of the healers and the blessings of the elders. John had suffered intensely over the prospect of losing, even for the brief moment that he knew mortality to be, any contact with his beloved Sheena. Many nights he prayed mightily to his God for her life, knowing he must be content with what was His will, and not John's, but it was so hard.

When at last Sheena began to recover, no one was more grateful than John.

\* \* \*

"I'm done," John reported when Hyrum opened the door at his knock. "Looks like I'm also done for the week. Guess I'll see you early Monday morning?"

"Think you got a job, do you?" Hyrum muttered, still trying to appear gruff and in control. "I guess so. You've done all right so far. Yeah, okay, you can have the job. But don't slack off, now that I've said you got it, hear? And I suppose I better pay you now."

John shook his head. "Monday is soon enough. See you later." He backed down the porch and quickly walked across the barnyard to his room. He already had a plan in mind for the weekend and was anxious to get going on it.

\* \* \*

Kevin carted in the pile of running warm-ups that Mr. Howks had given him for their running program, dropping them on the couch as he came into the house. "How do I get myself into these things?" he muttered to himself in the still house.

Wandering into the kitchen, he called, "Anybody home?" before he saw the note on the table. Lacey's handwriting was gradually becoming more unsteady as the blindness progressed.

*Kevin,*

*Gayle needed me to go see a sister with her, so the kids are next door at the Mellons', I didn't tell Sally that you would be by to pick up the kids before I got back, so if you need some time to yourself you can leave them over there. They always have a good time anyway.*

*I love you. There's some leftover apple pie in the fridge. If you don't eat it now, the kids will.*

*See you,*

*Lacey*

*P.S. Don't forget, you're supposed to give the First Presidency message from this month's* Ensign *tomorrow in priesthood. You asked me to remind you, sweetheart.*

As if Lacey were right there in front of him, Kevin nodded, remembering that he did have that self-appointed assignment for tomorrow. So now he could either turn on the boob tube and veg out for a while, or get right down to it.

Which to do?

Kevin went into the bedroom and picked up the current *Ensign* magazine from the top of their waterbed headboard and wandered out into the living room. Stashing the magazine under this arm, he leafed through the TV listing, checking to see what was on this weekend. Finding a movie that might be interesting, he checked his watch and calculated how much time he had before it started. Then, tossing the TV listing back on top of the television, he settled into his should-have-been-retired-and-thrown-out-long-ago recliner.

After a quick prayer for guidance and inspiration—which he guiltily thought should have been done on his knees—Kevin began reading the First Presidency message. The home teachers of the ward were supposed to be taking these words to all the members, but he wondered how many of the messengers even read them? Oh well, at least they got them in priesthood. After that, he couldn't do much about it.

He was asleep, with the *Ensign* magazine across his chest when Davey came charging down the hallway and into the living room.

"Daddy," Davey squealed, launching himself onto his father. Kevin, yanked out of his pleasant nap, nearly dumped his son on the floor in surprise.

"Hey, guy . . . slow down," mumbled Kevin. The girls ran down the hallway to their bedroom, closing the front door behind them with a bang. Davey slid off his father and ran off searching for more active interests.

Kevin's eyes gradually focused on Lacey, who was carrying a bag of groceries that was starting to rip out. As she put the bag down on the kitchen table, the bag completely gave out, and the contents slid in all directions. One can rolled off onto the floor, and Kevin picked it up and set it beside the microwave.

"Thanks, hon," Lacey said. "Get any sleep?"

Kevin yawned. "Just being quiet, checking for leaks in my eyelids. How'd your visit go?"

"Good," Lacey replied. "Sister Nurdlinger seemed genuinely uplifted by our being there. I wish I felt all of my visits to the sisters were so worthwhile. Sometimes it seems they don't even want us there."

Kevin came up behind Lacey, wrapping his arms around her waist and pulling her close. She closed her eyes and leaned into his arms, enjoying his love. Together, they paused for a moment in peace before going on.

"Thank you, my love," she said, then continued putting away the canned goods into the cupboard. "I thought while I was out, I'd pick up some groceries. Gayle needed to talk, so it gave us more time." Kevin folded the grocery sack and stashed it in the space between the refrigerator and the wall where the rest of them were.

"I told the bishop about John, and he wants to meet him tomorrow," said Kevin.

"So, does *he* think John might be one of the Three Nephites?"

Kevin smiled, thinking about how carefully Martin Davis thought things through. Their bishop didn't make quick judgements.

"I doubt he's gotten that far with it, O wife of mine. One step at a time. One step at a time."

Lacey shook her head. "You men! You think you're so wise and rational. We women know it's intuition that makes the day."

"I know, I know," interrupted Kevin and quickly repeated her favorite saying before she could. "The heart knows today what the head won't know until tomorrow."

Lacey put the last can away and wrinkled her nose at him. "Smart aleck! Would you rather have meatless meatloaf for dinner or goulash?"

"Umm, how about Mexican?" he suggested.

"So be it." She pinched his arm as she went to check on the girls, to see if they were getting their Sunday clothes ready for the morrow.

* * *

With the ease of an Indian in the land of his birth, John moved along the narrow, almost invisible forest path, his senses at one with the beauty and stillness about him. His mind was quiet, moving aside so his spirit could fly free. The tread of his boots was almost silent amid the dense foliage and moist ground cover. John could believe that once, long ago, everywhere in this part of the world, it had been like this.

A combination of city, county, and state authorities managed the thick forest on James Island, which resulted in overlapping responsibilities and lagging follow-through. Left to itself, the forest had nevertheless overcome the years since the early days of settlement on the island, returning nearly to its original condition.

A tiny brook, only a foot wide, appeared in front of him, and paralleled his path. Bits of fern leaves floated along the small waterway toward some unknown destination, like tiny gondolas in a forest Venice. John noticed small green beetles attempting to walk across the brook, waiting for the miniature eddies to subside before continuing. A six-inch orange slug intently made its way in the opposite direction on the path.

John breathed in deeply, closing his eyes briefly, then opening them to see even more clearly the intense green all around him. This was what he needed now. This was his balm of Gilead. This, and the spiritual communion with his Lord he planned to have soon.

Searching with that inner eye that comes from growth in eternal truths, John soon found the place he sought. As the forest fell away beside the waters of Puget Sound, a rock ledge appeared, jutting out clean over the salt waters below but for the moss that grew along its edges. John nodded contentedly. This was his place.

Soon he was deep in prayer and communion with the Spirit, kneeling beside the jagged stone that was his altar. An unexpected noise behind him brought him up sharp and broke his concentration. There at the edge of the trees, standing unsteadily upon fragile legs, a young deer gazed upon him. Even before John could rise, it sank heavily down upon the ground.

Examination of the deer revealed a broken-off arrow wedged between its ribs, the wound festering and smelling of disease. John closed his eyes in prayer, before working the arrow out as tenderly as he could, while watching his patient for signs of increased pain. The deer neither moved nor made a sound as John gently worked.

"There you go, my little one," said John, briefly inspecting the arrow, before tossing it off into the brush. "Now, let's see about a blessing for you."

He lay his hands upon her side, knowing how much God loved the innocent creatures. Finishing, he thought for a moment while stroking the deer, then he returned to his prayer on the ledge.

About an hour later, by the position of the sun above, John opened his eyes and slowly rose to his feet. Moving his neck around to ease the stiffness, he took a deep breath, feeling better.

The deer had not moved from her position. Kneeling beside her, John found that she was dead. He cried for her suffering, and more for those who'd hurt her. How ignorant people were to the damage they did their own souls. How many such souls he had ministered to during the past thousand plus years, and how many of his spirit family would be forever unable to know true joy on into the eternities!

Finding a stick and a rock to use as tools, John quietly prepared a grave for his fallen friend there in the forest glade. After burying the animal, he stood beside the grave praying over it, remembering other deaths, other funerals. A quote from Catholic Cardinal Newman came to his lips. "Fear not that thy life may come to an end," he whispered, "but rather that it shall never have a beginning." John knew that this had never been a problem for this pure creature now at rest in the ground before him, as it is so often among human beings.

Nodding, he brushed off his hands, and thoughtfully made his way back.

# CHAPTER EIGHT

Sunday morning came in with drizzling rain and grey skies, nothing unusual for the congregation of members who attended the Burns' Point Ward. To satisfy the ferry schedule from nearby Gomez Island, the first meeting started half an hour later here than did the other meetings in the stake. Only one member, elderly Charlene Gubler, lived on Gomez Island, but she appreciated everyone waiting for her to arrive before starting. Since she came every time, no matter what, the bishops had found it an easy wait through the years.

Kevin and Lacey lived only two blocks from the chapel, and often walked to and from church with their children. This morning the rain was a bit heavier than usual so Lacey decided to drive over with the children. Then she remembered that her eyesight had deteriorated too much to do that safely.

"Oh, shoot!" she complained, stomping her foot, feeling the pinch of her challenge growing tighter around her.

Punching the number for the ward into her phone, she waited, drumming her fingers on the counter. When someone answered, she asked for Kevin, who had gone early for a priesthood executive meeting. In a few minutes he answered.

"Kevin, it's raining too hard for us to walk over—you know how the girls' hair gets when it's like this. Will you come home and drive us?"

Lacey heard Kevin's sigh. "I'm sorry," she said. "I wish I—"

"It's okay," he interjected, "it's not you. I'm upset about the home teaching numbers. It never seems—never mind, that's my problem. I'll be right there."

Lacey tried not to think about how much more dependent upon Kevin she would soon become, nor what burden that would place on him, as she made sure the kids were ready and waiting when he showed up. Some things were better left alone.

*  *  *

"I'll be right back," said Kevin to his second counselor, Morten Glazier, a retired security guard from the refinery. Morten had been semi-active for years, and had responded moderately well to being called to the elders quorum presidency. Morten was older than most elders in the church, but fit in better there than he would have with the high priests.

Kevin sprinted down the chapel driveway as fast as he could in his dress loafers and Sunday suit, looking both ways as he came out on the quiet road and began to jog along toward his house.

"Everybody ready?" he called as he opened the front door.

"We're coming," answered Lacey, shepherding the brood toward where Kevin stood. "I'm sorry you had to come back, hon."

To reassure her, he kissed her and said, "I need to be needed."

"Are you ever in luck, then," she groaned, only partially joking.

As they were backing out of the driveway, Kevin suddenly exclaimed, "Oh rats! I forgot to pick John up."

"I'll tell your counselors to cover for you," said Lacey.

"Sorry to be late," Kevin apologized as he pulled up beside the barn where John was waiting for him. "I forgot."

"No problem," John said easily. "We have time to give Hyrum a blessing, though, don't we? He's been sick and could use one."

Kevin felt trapped. Without any question, the Spirit was telling him loudly in his heart, *Hyrum Patches is an elder in the quorum, which you, Kevin, have consented to minister to. It doesn't matter whether you like each other or not.*

He nodded silently, his stomach doing flips as he imagined Hyrum chewing him out again. Following John up to the steps, he prepared for the worst. John knocked on the door, and Kevin followed him inside.

The home was much nicer and more comfortable-looking than Kevin had expected. Kevin didn't know what to expect, but this homey place didn't square with the type of man he knew lived here.

"He's in the bedroom," said John, before calling, "Mr. Patches, it's John."

"What do you want?" croaked a gravelly voice from the back of the house.

"This way," said John, leading a cautious Kevin down the hallway.

As they entered Hyrum's bedroom, John said, "I brought a friend to help me give you a blessing. I found out you're a member of the LDS church, so here we are, two priesthood brethren to give our brother a blessing for his illness."

Hyrum lay on his back in his bed, covered to the neck in several blankets, shivering from an influenza viral chill. For a moment, Hyrum was stunned at John's boldness—both at bringing a stranger into his house, and for insisting he was going to get a blessing.

"I'll be damned if you will!"

John felt Hyrum's forehead. "It's more likely you'll be damned if you don't. Phew, are you hot! We'll give you a blessing right away."

Hyrum stuck an arm out from under the covers and motioned at some over-the-counter medicines that sat on the bedside table in a cluster. "I already took something for this. That's all I need." His effort to speak obviously drained him, and his usual gruffness was impossible for the moment.

"I know you believe in God, so don't make such a fuss," John said, looking up at Kevin, who still stood in the doorway.

Kevin would have been ready to say, "Forget it, no problem. Maybe some other time," but he knew John was acting the way Kevin should have—secure in the knowledge of the gospel and eager to minister to all God's children. Kevin couldn't get himself to come into the room, but he couldn't leave, either.

Something in Hyrum, maybe the wall he had built around himself, weakened from his illness. A tiny crack into his spirit and heart emerged, and through this opening John was reaching in.

"Betty would have wanted you to," said John.

At the mention of his dead wife's name, Hyrum abruptly paused and his breathing nearly stopped. He hadn't allowed anyone to talk about her for a long time, hadn't even wanted to think about how much he missed her. His guilt over what had happened that day still haunted him. Dazed, unable to put away the sudden flood of missing her, Hyrum nodded slowly.

John waved Kevin into the room. From a vial on his key chain, Kevin anointed and John acted as mouth for the sealing. After the blessing John promised that they would look in on Hyrum after church.

When they were almost to the chapel, Kevin said, "That was very strange back there."

"What was?"

"How it felt to give that blessing. No one has ever shown less interest in the Church than Hyrum and yet when we put our hands upon him I felt . . . I don't know how to describe it."

"Those who need it the most," said John, as they pulled into the ward parking lot, "often seem least likely to accept it. If we look for appreciation from them before we help, we'll always be disappointed. Hyrum doesn't fully appreciate the blessing yet, but God always does." John grinned at Kevin. "And maybe the blessing wasn't just for Hyrum."

As Kevin turned off the engine, John firmly grabbed his shoulder and affectionately shook it. "You did well, President. You did well. Now, introduce me to the ward."

* * *

Priesthood had already split up into groups by the time Kevin led John into the small classroom the elders met in each Sunday. The elder who was supposed to teach the lesson hadn't shown up, so Morten was stumbling through his thoughts on the First Presidency message in the most recent *Ensign*. With a look of relief on his face, Morton said, "Now we'll hear a few words from President Taylor," before he quickly sat down next to John and shook his hand in greeting.

Kevin took a deep breath and launched into the lesson he always kept stored in his head for times like this. "Prepare for the worst, and hope for the best," his mother had always told him.

About this same time, Martin was just finishing an interview with a young single mother who once again could not pay her bills and feed her children. When the sister had wiped the tears from her face, she left the office with a heartfelt, "Thank you."

Closing the door behind her, Martin walked over to the window, where he stared out at the trees. His last conversation with his daughter replayed clearly in his mind.

"I'm sorry, Daddy," Julie had said. "I hope it will only be for a little while. Maybe just until Randy and I can work things out. I don't understand why he blames the Church for all our problems. I know this hurts you and Mom, but . . . I don't know what else to do. I'm afraid if I push at all he won't come back."

"It doesn't make sense. How can our seeing the kids hurt anything?" Martin had asked.

Julie had fumbled around, looking for the words. "Randy thinks since you became a bishop you push religion too much."

"But he's a member now, and you two were married in the temple."

"I know," Julie admitted. "I guess Randy didn't take it as deep as I thought." She began to cry. "Daddy, I don't want to be alone again. I can't stand it."

Stepping away from the window, Martin grimaced. His son and daughter had been good kids. There'd been no drugs, no serious drinking, although when he and Jan had joined the Church, the kids, now grown, had shown no interest in religion. When his daughter's divorce had left Julie a young single mother, she had been humble and open to the gospel. Some time after her baptism, she met Randy, who had seemed interested in the gospel beyond his interest in Julie. Randy had joined the Church then asked her to marry him. Not long after their son was born, a temple sealing had graced their life together. The news of Randy's change in attitude had shocked Martin to the core.

His watch said it was almost time for the break. After ten minutes, Sunday School would start. Was he going to be sitting in a class today, or was there another appointment now?

He knelt beside the desk and prayed intently for his daughter, her husband, and their two young children. When he finished, there was no doubt in his mind his prayer had been heard, though how it would be answered was beyond his understanding.

At the knock on the door, Martin stood up and brushed off his knees. Opening the door, he saw his elders quorum president standing with an unfamiliar young man.

"Bishop, this is John, my partner in saving people," Kevin said by way of introduction.

Martin half smiled automatically, shaking John's outstretched hand. "I'm glad to meet you, John. Welcome to the ward."

"Thank you, Bishop. I already feel at home. There's something about a small ward or branch, something special about the members. It usually feels more like a family than the bigger ones."

"We're pretty small all right. Do you have time to visit for a few minutes?"

Kevin nodded and patted John on the shoulder. "That's a good idea. I have some family stuff I need to check on, and I don't want John to get lost walking around here," he kidded. "I'll catch you two later."

Before Martin could shut the door, Dee Calton, the executive secretary, caught him. "Don't forget you're supposed to be in Jackie Morgan's class to talk about marriage to the teenagers."

Martin had forgotten. "Okay," he groaned, feeling more tired than usual. He hadn't slept well last night after talking to his daughter. "I'll be there in a few minutes."

John hadn't even sat down, and now he smiled broadly. "No problem, Bishop. We can talk some other time."

"You're staying out at Hyrum Patches', aren't you? I haven't been around to see him yet, I'm ashamed to say. How about I come by this evening, say eight o'clock? That way I can see you both."

"Okay by me," John said, shaking Martin's hand. Locking the door behind him, Martin hurried down the hall toward Sister Morgan's class.

# CHAPTER NINE

The rain had stopped but the heavy, grey skies remained. Usually by this time of year sunshine was more in evidence. Looking up, Martin wished the sun would break through as he climbed out of his car in front of Hyrum Patches' home. Another hour and it would be sunset, and another Sunday would be history. Martin rotated his neck around a few times, trying to work out the kinks from a long string of interviews that day. Sometimes it seemed like everyone in the ward had something they needed to talk over with him.

A wisp of smoke rose from a chimney pipe off the barn. According to Kevin's instructions, this was John's place. The dogs were nowhere to be seen as Martin climbed Hyrum's front porch steps. Martin noticed someone had recently replaced the porch rails and some baseboards at one end. Either Hyrum was healthier than Martin had heard, or this man John had been doing a good job as handyman around there.

Martin knocked twice before he thought he heard someone answer. Opening the door a crack, he called, "Hello, Brother Patches, it's Bishop Davis. Are you home?"

"Come in," a deep, croaking voice answered.

As Martin entered, he found Hyrum laying on the living room couch under a flowered quilt, with two pillows under his head. Nearby on an end table was a half-eaten bowl of soup and a mug of something.

"I'm sorry you're ill, Brother Patches. Is there anything I can do for you?"

Hyrum fussed with the quilt for a few moments, while Martin

waited uneasily. "Have a sit, Bishop. I heard they plugged you in as the new man, but thought you'd take longer to get out here. They all come, eventually. Still like the job?"

Martin found himself a comfortable place to sit in a brightly-flowered easy chair nearby, thinking Hyrum's wife must have picked out the furniture in the room since most men didn't have much interest in such things. "I'm doing well with it," replied Martin. "Being bishop isn't something I looked for, but it has its rewards."

"That's what they all say about now," observed Hyrum. "It's what you guys don't say about the job after a year or so that worries me. People eat you up if you aren't careful. I always said if I was bishop I wouldn't be as available as some men are. People need to work their own problems out most of the time."

Martin nodded. "I couldn't agree with you more."

There was silence between the two men for a moment before Martin asked, "So how is this John fellow working out for you? Your porch looks like someone has been working on it."

Hyrum curled his lip. "He does good work. Kind of pushy sometimes, though. Him and that elders quorum president of yours came right into the house and pushed a blessing on me. I never asked them to do that."

"Kevin Taylor insisted you have a blessing?" Martin asked, thinking that wasn't the man he knew.

"Nah, not him, he just tagged along. It was that John fellow. Got real pushy about it. If I wasn't feeling so sick, I would have fired him on the spot. Guess I'm a softy for young people."

Martin didn't know what to think about all this. Being a softy wasn't something he had *ever* heard about Hyrum Patches. Who was pulling whose leg here?

The rest of the visit turned out to be very pleasant, and by the end the men were laughing over a story Hyrum had shared from his days on the police force. Martin would be going away with a different impression of Hyrum Patches than anyone else in the Burns' Point Ward had ever gotten.

"All right," said Martin, "I'll stop by later in the week to see how you're getting by."

"I'll either be dead or glad to see you," joked Hyrum.

"Take care. While I'm here, I think I'll go look in on your hired man," said Martin as he let himself out the door. Walking over to the barn, Martin tried to sort out his visit with Hyrum. A lot of things didn't add up. Martin's own observations of Hyrum didn't square with the reports others had given him. How could things be so different from what he had been told—unless, perhaps Hyrum was coming to a point in his life where the Spirit was getting through? Martin thought that someone with the right balance of love and directness might make a difference.

The sun behind the thick clouds had nearly dropped below the horizon as Martin opened the door and stepped into the barn. It smelled like well-kept barns always do—of tools, straw, supplies, honest labor, and the scent of clean dirt. A doorway was outlined in light at the far end of the large open area and he made for it. "Come in, Bishop," a voice from inside called.

Martin pushed open the rough-built wooden door and entered a room that was no more than ten feet square. A small wood stove radiated out more than enough heat, while cooler air came in from a partially open window in the corner. A neatly-made bed was built into another corner, where John lay, reading.

"Want some company?" Martin asked.

John put his book down and hopped up to shake Martin's hand. "I'm glad you could stop by, Bishop. Here, take the chair," he suggested, motioning toward the rocking chair.

As Martin sat, he saw the clothes hung on nails along the one wall, and an old picture of the Salt Lake Temple.

"So," began Martin, fighting the desire to sleep as the tiredness in him mixed with the heat from the stove nearby.

"So, you want to know about me," John jumped in, sitting back on the bed, up against the wall. "Where do I come from, how long have I been a member of the Church, do I plan on sticking around here long?"

This woke up Martin, who narrowed his eyes in concentration, evaluating if this John was upset, a smart aleck, or just used to the routine. Also, if he was used to the routine, then how many towns *had* he drifted into?

John seemed to know his thoughts. "Excuse me, Bishop, but I've been at this point before. I move around a lot, and the questions are usually the same. I thought I might save us some time. No offense."

Martin nodded. "None taken."

"Before I came here," John began, "I was down in San Francisco briefly, and before that, up north."

"North?"

John grinned. "Way up north."

*Alaska or Canada,* Martin decided and left it at that.

"I've been a member of the Church since I was twenty, though my family was always interested in God and things of the Spirit. Finding the gospel was the best thing that ever happened to us. As far as how long I'm going to be around here?" John shrugged. "Until it feels like it's time to move on."

Martin wondered about what John said but didn't want to pry. It wasn't up to him how people lived their lives, and if John wanted to wander around, what did it matter? Young men often drifted until they found themselves.

"Hyrum Patches says you insisted he get a blessing for his flu."

John smiled. "I did. He needed it and it helped him. When Kevin and I came back here after church, he was doing better in spite of himself. That's why I moved him out on the couch. A change of place often helps you feel better."

Martin moved his chair a bit further away from the stove. "That little thing really puts out the heat."

John jumped up to open the stove door and poke around inside with a metal bar that he kept behind the stove. "This little room is too small for the stove." He shut the stove door with a metallic clang. "Whoever put this stove in here didn't know much about heating. I'll bet I could put this old thing out in the main barn area and heat the whole place if I got it really stoked up."

Martin was thinking about leaving when he noticed the Book of Mormon on the bed. "Getting your daily scripture study in?"

"Good stuff, daily spiritual vitamins." John nodded his head agreeably as he sat back down on the bed. "Counsel with the Lord in all thy doings, and he will direct thee for good—"

"Yea, when thou liest down at night lie down unto the Lord," Martin added, "that he may watch over you in your sleep; and when thou risest in the morning let thy heart be full of thanks unto God—"

"And if ye do these things, ye shall be lifted up at the last day," John finished.

"Alma 37:37," Martin commented. "That's one of my favorites."

"Me, too," John agreed.

Standing to shake John's hand, Martin said, "Welcome to the ward, John . . . I don't know your last name?"

"Zebedee. It's of Jewish ancestry," John quickly added.

"That's interesting. I'll see you next Sunday?"

"Probably so. Drive careful, Bishop."

"Oh, before I forget, congratulations on saving that little baby girl in the car fire," Martin said. "Kevin Taylor told me it was pretty amazing how you came out of the fire without being hurt."

John squirmed only a moment, but Martin caught it.

"People's eyes trick them," John said nonchalantly. "Everything moves so fast at times like that. I hardly remember what happened."

"Still, I imagine that young mother is glad you were there."

John gave a half smile, and Martin said goodbye and left.

Forsaking his usual habit of listening to the radio news, Martin drove home in silence. He looked forward to his long overdue evening meal and a hot shower.

.

# CHAPTER TEN

The man who called himself Vincent watched Randolph Howks jog out the front gate of the refinery around noon. He wished he could just snatch the fat old man now and be done with it. How hard could it be to force Howks into the van in some out of the way turn of the road? But plans for the operation were set for the coming Saturday, so everything would have to wait until then.

Vincent spit onto the cement floor from habit, and returned to repairing the overhead winch wiring in the east machine shop. The plans were set, the timing practiced so often he could do it in his sleep.

"Man, when you going to get that done?" Vincent looked up for a moment, seeking the face to go with the voice that had yelled at him. It was a machinist from across the shop. "We got work to do— unlike some people."

Vincent ignored the sarcasm and the implied put-down. He didn't care that the other men at the refinery didn't like him. He didn't like them either. Vincent couldn't honestly say he liked anyone.

Although he had been listed as a terrorist on the FBI Most Wanted list six months ago, Vincent didn't see himself as one. Five years ago he had dropped out of college, and after participating in a number of anti-government radical political groups, he had finally come to lead his own loosely ordered collection of misfits. Over time the group had managed to rob five small town banks, and even blow up a power station relay. The regional phone company computer center, handled just two months ago, had been easy. Still, communication within the group was clumsy, and at times critical information was faulty. Otherwise, they would have seven bank holdups to their credit by now.

The kidnapping and refinery bombing was their biggest project thus far. The effort to keep everyone on track had pushed Vincent to the limit of his patience. Although his people were dangerous and capable of great destruction, he saw them as small-minded, unable to see the bigger picture.

None of them knew where Vincent got most of their money. Starting with an Internet contact, Vincent had met a man with Middle Eastern connections. Within a year, Vincent was carrying out small jobs for his money source, nothing all that big, but apparently important to them. Vincent knew he was just part of a bigger plan to disrupt the workings of the United States, but he didn't care. He could use them just as they thought they were using him. And after all, money was money.

Vincent enjoyed feeling powerful. Of course, there were some vague hopes that what he did was making room for something better. Once the old society fell apart, a better one would naturally spring up. Where that would leave him, he hadn't quite figured out yet. Meanwhile, his group of eighteen men and two women, self-proclaimed as the Free Earth Revolutionary Army, would do what they could to tear down the old, hateful, ineffective system.

The last wire in place, Vincent dropped his needle nose pliers into the tool box, snapped the box lid shut, and left the shop without a word to anyone.

"Hey, man," a machinist called after him, "Anyone ever tell you not to talk so much?"

The insulting laughter that followed Vincent made it that much easier to think about blowing the place up. People like that didn't deserve jobs. Would they be laughing so much if they knew about the explosive charges Vincent's group had planted around the island? Probably not. To make sure things went as planned, Vincent had arranged for key places on the island to come tumbling down if the police, or money people, didn't do what they were supposed to.

Vincent smiled to himself. They would see who had the last laugh.

* * *

Lacey knelt in the dirt along the back fence, pulling weeds out of her flower bed, making room for yet another rose bush to join the other members of her flower brigade. She never claimed to be an expert on roses, only a devoted admirer of the delicate yet pointedly defensive plants. These days she couldn't look out her bedroom window and see the roses along the backyard fence, but their fragrance still came in the window when the breeze was right. Even now, only inches away, Lacey could only see the rose plants in a blur.

The shy Washington coast sun was out today, reigning supreme over a cloudless sky. The warmth felt delicious on Lacey's back. She paused from digging ferociously with the three-pronged weed digger in her gloved hand, and wiped the sweat off her brow with a shirt sleeve. Her aching back reminded her she didn't exercise enough these days.

Not being able to go for walks whenever and wherever she felt like it had been one of the hardest things for Lacey to give up. When he could, Kevin took her out along her favorite country roads and forest paths, but it was never enough to satisfy her longing. A part of her was never alive unless she could sometimes be alone, among the wild places.

By chance, Lacey's hand grazed up against a slug that was struggling to move across the dirt toward her rose bushes. "Gotcha!" she exclaimed, grabbing the potential assailant and rising with it clutched in her grasp. The slippery, six-inch dark-blue creature wiggled slowly in her hand as she opened the gate to the four-acre field behind their house. After several steps she deposited the slug gently on the ground.

"You stay out here, and leave my flowers and garden alone," she declared. Kevin kidded her about being so kind to the slugs, since they always came back anyway. He had told her to pour some salt on them, and then flip them over the fence into the field. That way they wouldn't ever come back to bother her plants.

"But that kills them!" she had protested.

"That's the whole idea," he insisted. "That's what they want to do to your roses."

"Well," she said, "they're only simple creatures, but we're supposed to be like Christ. Would He put salt on them and flip them over the fence like that?"

As Lacey continued her weeding, she closed her eyes, pretending she was already completely blind to prepare herself for that time. It wouldn't be long now, according to her doctor in Seattle. Usually she was able to shrug away the fear of being in continual darkness, unable to see anymore the faces of her family. This time, alone, kneeling in the dirt, it reached out and held her tight.

"It could be worse," she said aloud, trying to distract herself. "I could be like Aunt Laurie, with that weird allergy problem where she just up and stops breathing." That would be worse. How many times had she been rushed to the emergency room?

Her aunt had told her more than once how much she admired Lacey's strength and courage, because although she might herself "drop dead" from time to time, at least she wasn't going blind. During their last phone conversation, Laurie had said, "If I'm dead, I'm dead, and God will handle things. Between times, I'm dandy, so who can complain?"

Lacey's fear retreated only slightly, as if still determined to draw Lacey out of the circle of light, truth, and Spirit—gifts that had been given to her as her sight slowly diminished. When Lacey stayed inside that circle, no matter where it led, she was all right. In it was peace and hope. Hurt could still get to her sometimes, but healing was quick and sure.

Lacey opened her eyes as she tugged at a particularly stubborn weed and gasped in terror. Everything about her was as black as if her eyes had remained closed. She forced herself to breathe slowly, and deeply, then closed her eyes again, and sat back on the grass, feeling the blades between her fingers. Listening to the birds singing nearby, Lacey talked to herself. "You're still here in your own yard. Don't panic. Be still and trust God. He hasn't forsaken you."

When she opened her eyes a few minutes later, she almost wept for joy to see the blurred images around her.

*I guess this means it really won't be long,* she thought. *Kevin thinks I need a guide dog in the house. Am I being silly, not wanting one? I just don't want to give in yet. I want things as they are, for just a little longer. Once it changes, it's changed forever.*

A few minutes later the rose bush was safely planted and Lacey was back in the house when the phone rang.

"Hi babe, how you doing?" Kevin asked.

The words caught in her throat. "I opened my eyes this morning, and there was nothing," she told him. "That's never happened before."

"I'll come home," he said quickly.

"No, it's all right," she reassured him. "It's better now. It just scared me for a moment."

"Are you sure you don't want me to come home? Honey, that must have been awful. We knew it was coming but . . . I don't know, I thought it would be more gradual."

"Me too. I—" Lacey ran her fingers over the file box on the kitchen counter where she kept her scriptures and quotes to memorize while she washed dishes. In odd moments she had memorized hundreds of useful and uplifting thoughts over the years. "It'll be okay. We've been through other tough times. We'll get through this. Remember what G. K. Chesterton said?"

Kevin chuckled. "No, hon, I'm not the one who remembers all those quotes. You tell me."

"Faith means believing what is incredible, or it is no virtue at all. Hope means hoping when things are hopeless, or it is no virtue at all."

"I remember now," he said. "You've told me that one before. You know, I understand what it means better now, but I like it less."

"Trust in God, President Taylor."

"Okay," Kevin sighed. "You, too, and call me if you need anything. I love you. Bye."

Lacey hung up the phone and felt the fear return. "I'm going blind," she said quietly. "I'm going blind." Lacey's younger sister, who was a social worker, had told Lacey to say it out loud frequently, to help her adjust and diminish the shock.

Forcing herself to be quiet, Lacey sat motionless at the kitchen table for a long time, listening to the air move in the room, until her own heart beat sounded like drums.

* * *

Kevin hung up the phone at his desk and thought about his wife, their life together, what was likely to change in the future. He pondered over his children and their needs, particularly how they would be affected by their mother's blindess. He was still thinking, when Gary walked into the room and sat at his own desk. He appeared so absorbed in this particular patient file that he didn't speak to Kevin for several minutes. When he looked up at last, his cynical expression warned Kevin that he was about to make a snide remark, no doubt about Kevin's church calling or about the Church in general. Then, as if realizing that Kevin had been more quiet than usual, Gary apparently reconsidered. "You okay?" was all he said.

Kevin had been so wrapped up in his thoughts that Gary's words took a moment to register. Considering the offer only briefly, Kevin shook his head. He hardly thought that opening up to Gary was a good idea. The two of them weren't exactly best friends. "Just something at home," he said shortly.

Gary swivelled around in his desk chair and gave Kevin a careful look. "You're worrying about Lacey, aren't you?" Not waiting for an answer, Gary sighed. "Having your wife go blind has got to be hard."

Kevin felt torn. Although he didn't feel like talking about his feelings, he felt a prompting to open up to Gary. "Let him in," the Spirit whispered.

Kevin leaned back and looked up at Gary. "Lacey had an episode this morning, where all her vision was gone. I knew it was coming, but . . . I guess you're never ready for it. Not really."

Gary nodded. "I'm sorry. I wish I could do something."

"Thanks," said Kevin, taking a deep breath. "Not much anyone can do. Except, maybe, pray."

"That's your department, church boy," said Gary, turning back to his desk.

The connection between the two men snapped shut so suddenly that Kevin was left confused and upset. Why had the Spirit prompted him to share something so sensitive when this was the result? Kevin was glad when it was time for an appointment with a patient at the hospital. He left the office without saying goodbye.

# CHAPTER ELEVEN

A few clouds hovered high above the earth, wispy bits of white amid the vast ocean of blue. No rain would fall this Tuesday morning, nor would any cool breezes move off the Sound to comfort James Island. Even the birds' song was subdued.

Hyrum was up and out soon after telling John what the work for the day was, though it would just be a continuation from the day before. John had not yet repaired the plumbing under the house to Hyrum's satisfaction.

As Hyrum settled in his van, he threw a quick glance over his shoulder and saw John leave the barn and head toward the house. Letting someone inside his house while he was gone wasn't something Hyrum had ever done before. The plumbing still needed fixing though and Hyrum needed to go see Melinda, so he shook off his unanswered questions about John and drove off.

* * *

Two hours later, John crawled out from under the house. As he brushed dirt off his clothes, he inwardly shivered with relief that he didn't have to go back into that spider haven anymore. Just as John picked up the toolbox and started walking back to the barn with it, Hyrum drove back into the yard. Rolling down his window, Hyrum barked, "Did you just get done? I thought you said it was almost finished yesterday."

John bit his lip, smiling. "Just finished, Mr. Patches. It turned out to be a bigger job than I figured on. What would you like me to do now?"

Hyrum didn't answer right away. "I . . . I'll tell you in a little while."

John watched thoughtfully as Hyrum drove over by the house and began getting himself out of the van. *There's someone he's worried about, someone he lets himself care very much for,* thought John, as he stacked the toolbox in its place on the shelf. *I wonder who?*

In a few minutes, John knocked on the back door of the house.

"What?" demanded Hyrum, his face flushed, as he opened the door.

"What now?" asked John, wanting to help Hyrum but knowing it wasn't time for him to speak yet.

"Uh. . . ." Hyrum wanted only to be left alone. "I need to think about it."

John looked down at the porch, seeing where it needed a coat of sealant. "Well, maybe while you're figuring things out, I'll take some time off," he said. "I want to see about some things in town."

"Yeah, okay," grumbled Hyrum, slamming the door closed.

Walking into town, John pondered what he had seen in Hyrum's face and prayed in his heart for Hyrum. Halfway to town, John was nearly run off the road by a rusted, white van that carelessly crowded the outer edge of the road. John quickly jumped out of the way, then looked up to see the van disappear around the next bend in the road. *Some people need to be more careful,* he thought.

John could feel an evil emanating from the van, the sick, dark feeling that accompanied anyone who purposely treated their brothers and sisters here upon the earth as objects. He wondered what he needed to know about this van in particular, but trusted that the Lord would let him know when it was time.

Since Hyrum had paid John on Saturday for last week's work, John had money in his pocket. Taking his time, but making a straight course, he arrived at the ferry terminal before the ferry to San Juan Island left. In a few minutes the old vessel was churning up the water, pushing greenish-brown swirls and splashes in all directions and sending the sea birds hunting and calling to each other in the wake.

John wandered the decks of the ferry, leaning on the rails for long spells, thinking about nothing, feeling the water and the sky. Whenever he was tempted to worry about something, he quickly said a prayer about it and let it go to God, a habit which had taken many years of spiritual training. After a while everything was quiet inside him, relaxed and calm.

He found a place inside to sit in one of the padded booths and stretched out his legs comfortably. However, a few moments later, he quickly moved them when an older man sat down across from him. Without looking at John, he pulled out a copy of the newest self-help bestseller, *The Good Life,* and began reading. After considering the situation, John attempted to strike up a conversation with the old man, who kept his eyes in his book.

When a young woman with long, straight brown hair sat down in the padded booth next to them, John looked up. She smiled over the top of the booth at him. He smiled back.

"Beautiful day for being out," he said.

She nodded.

"My name is John."

"I'm Mary. Nice to meet you, John."

"John and Mary," he said, "names from the Bible. You remind me of that Mary."

Mary blushed, surprised, and the man sharing John's booth turned around to stare at her. Although she gave him a friendly smile, he didn't return it.

"He's been trying to talk to me about the Bible since we left Burns' Point," he complained, collecting his belongings. He stood up and walked away, but not before throwing a dark look at John.

"He wasn't very happy with you, was he?" Mary commented quietly.

"Some people like being miserable." John shook his head. "They get very angry when you suggest that maybe they could be happier with less effort."

Frowning in concentration, Mary thought about that. "I guess you're right. Funny, I never thought of it that way before."

John stood up, stretched and yawned. "Mind if I join you?" he asked.

Suddenly shy and cautious, Mary considered briefly. "Sure, you don't look like a pickpocket, or a mugger. But then, even if you were, there are a lot of people around. I guess I'm safe."

As John took the seat across from Mary, he smiled. "I'm very harmless, believe me. Except for talking about the Bible, I'm without offense."

Mary was both charmed and curious about John's smooth gracefulness. A very pretty woman, with more intelligence than most men gave her credit for, she had heard plenty of opening lines over the years. Even when given a "nonline" line, she could catch it. This man John, if he was trying to hustle her, was doing something altogether new from what she had ever seen before.

But unlike other men she had known, John had no ulterior motives. He simply gazed out the widow, at ease, at the passing islands, water, and sky, and soon Mary relaxed. A peace usually reserved for longtime friends and companions passed between and around them.

"Are you—" they both said simultaneously, then stopped surprised and burst into laughter. Their eyes sparkled, and the warm smile on each face spoke of finding a kindred spirit. John motioned Mary to go ahead.

"Are you from around here?" she asked.

"No, but I've visited many times. I like the spirit here. There is a feeling that . . . refreshes me. And you?"

"I came back here from San Diego when my father became ill and stayed on to look after him."

"How is he now?"

Mary lowered her eyes. "He died three months ago."

"I'm sorry."

Looking up, she said, "He was happier than most people, and he said he was dying with no regrets. I hope I can say the same when my time comes."

The ferry was coming into Freelan Island, one of the stops on the way to San Juan. Feeling the urge to walk, John stood up. "I think I'll stretch my legs. Maybe I'll see you again later."

"Maybe," she answered, smiling.

Making his way outside, John watched the people and cars leaving the ferry. Unexpectedly, the same rusted, white van that had almost run John over outside of Burns' Point came out of the vehicle space within the ferry. As it drove down the ramp onto the pier and sped off down the road, John once again had a brief but intense feeling of evil. This time, however, he knew he would see the van again. He also knew that it would have something to do with Kevin Taylor.

\* \* \*

Hyrum hung up the phone after speaking with Melinda's doctor and sat motionless for several minutes. There would be no reprieve, no last-minute miracle cures. Melinda was going to die. Nothing he did, or wanted, would make any difference against the certain outcome.

He slowly wheeled his chair around to face the picture window in the living room, remembering his wife's death and feeling again the old powerlessness, the inability to change things.

The coma his wife had lain in for ten days after the accident, before her death, had felt like an eternity to him. Having recovered from his own injuries, Hyrum had insisted on staying in her hospital room with her and the staff had finally set up a bed for him nearby. Hour after hour he had talked to her, prayed for her, trusting God would not take the one he needed most of all.

She had died anyway, slipping away one night after he had fallen asleep from sheer exhaustion. The staff was afraid to tell him when he awoke, for fear of his fierce temper, but his shock had left him without the energy to say anything at all.

At the funeral, surounded by his children, he could barely keep his anger under control as the bishop of the ward in Seattle gave a brief eulogy. Later, as the casket was lowered into the grave, he had vented his fury on the bishop.

"But Brother Patches," implored the bishop, "just because the Lord didn't—"

"Don't give me any more of that 'Lord' garbage anymore, and don't call me 'Brother'!" Hyrum had glared up at the bishop from his wheelchair. "If ever I needed proof there wasn't any God, this is it. If your so-called God would take someone like her, then none of it makes any sense."

As the memory faded, Hyrum realized that he was back at his house, alone. The intense, constant emptiness he felt about him and in him had been his constant companion since his wife's death. If Hyrum was to keep his promise to his friend, then he had to be with Melinda to the end. With Melinda's mother, Hyrum had been able to keep his emotions behind a carefully constructed wall. But that was something he hadn't been able to do with little Melinda. Even worse, her dying had brought up all the old grief from his wife's death—all the pain of loss and unfinished mourning, which kept back the healing he needed and which grew more insistent each day.

Hyrum worried what would happen when he could no longer hold his grief back.

# CHAPTER TWELVE

Warm sunlight shone brightly upon the passengers who disembarked from the ferry in San Juan Harbor and straggled across the dock, either alone or in small groups. Some wore backpacks and pushed bicycles for touring about the island; a young couple pushed a stroller with a sleeping baby. It was too early yet for the main tourist crush, but a few wise souls sought the quiet peacefulness of morning in the islands of North Puget Sound.

John ambled along, enjoying the luxury of not being in a hurry to get anywhere. Children from a family behind him ran past, eager to be about and explore this new place. He smiled at them.

Eventually his steps took him to the small bookstore, where he browsed through the latest bestsellers and photographic collections of island sights. Actually, John read very little, only those words he felt had something significant to offer. He agreed absolutely with what Joseph Smith had once said: "The best way to obtain truth and wisdom is not to ask it from books, but to go to God in prayer, and obtain divine teachings." Occasionally something came along that put a different light on an eternal truth, as when a person could grasp and set down in writing a sliver of the divine light that was available to all who would receive it.

In a book of quotes upon one shelf, John read, "The wind blows where it wills, and you hear the sound of it, but you do not know from where it comes or where it goes; so it is with everyone who is born of the Spirit."

Although he found that the wording was a bit different from the way his original words were translated according to the King

James English in the Bible, the meaning was the same. John remembered well the evening when Nicodemus, a member of the Sanhedrin and a secret follower of Jesus, came searching for the Master.

John and the other apostles had been resting among the trees on the hill overlooking Jerusalem, talking lightly among themselves. Jesus had been standing off by himself, as he often did, when Nicodemus came. John had drifted over that way, and heard what Jesus had told the older man about the Holy Ghost and the need to be born again.

From that moment on, John had determined that those words must never be lost. They had to be remembered and declared unto all the world, so that each person, each child of God on earth, could know what life was really about. That John's recollection of the Savior's teachings were preserved as scripture was a great joy to him. *If only the world would accept more of Jesus' teachings, there are so many more to be heard,* he thought sadly.

John left the store and was almost to the street when a pickup truck screeched to a halt next to him.

"Hey there, John," said the older man inside, "want a ride?"

John recognized Bill Gibson, owner of the hardware store in Burns' Point, and smiling, hopped in the truck. "Don't mind if I do. Where're you headed?"

Bill ground around, looking for the right gear in the old truck. It lurched a moment, then sped off. "I'm making some deliveries. I come out here every other Tuesday."

"Isn't there a hardware store out here?"

Bill grinned. "The old ladies I deliver to like me better. Can you blame them? They even think I'm worth paying a bit more for."

John chuckled, shaking his head.

Bill was full of stories, mostly true, about his years at the veterans hospital. John enjoyed the company and the scenery as they drove about the island.

After a while, John spoke up. "You were going to tell me more about Hyrum Patches."

"I was?" Bill waggled his head around. "Yeah, maybe I was. Okay, what do you want to know?"

"You were in the hospital together, right?"

"Yeah," said Bill, taking the old truck around a sharp bend in the road. "All four of us were there. My wife and I had been in a traffic accident a few weeks before they were."

"What happened to Hyrum?"

Bill was quiet, thinking, before he answered. "The man gave up on everything. When his wife died, he pulled into himself and hasn't come out since."

"Did you know him before your accidents?"

"A little. He used to come to the VA hospital for some treatments on his back. I met him one day when his car radio was acting up, and I was walking through the parking lot. You could have heard him cussing about it for miles. I fixed it—wasn't much really—and after that he talked to me whenever he came by. He used to look all over the hospital until he found me. I think he even gave me a ham that first Christmas we knew each other."

"And now he treats you like a stranger?"

"Worse, like I'd done something bad to him."

John sensed the sadness in the words and thought of the emptiness that filled Hyrum's life. "It's not you. He blames himself for his wife's death."

Bill grimaced. "I know, but . . ."

John patted his shoulder. "God is working on it. Don't worry."

"That's the funny thing," Bill said. "Before our accidents, Hyrum used to talk to me about God and us all being children of God. He was a pretty good Christian, except for that mouth of his when he got upset. He brought me a Book of Mormon to read, and I did. It made a lot of sense to me. About the time I wanted to ask him some questions, he just dropped out of the world. I wondered why someone who knew so much about why life is the way it is would give up like that."

John made a mental note to tell Kevin Taylor about Bill Gibson being a potential investigator of the Church, then said, "Things are moving along. It isn't over with Hyrum, not by a long shot."

At the ferry to Burns' Point, John and Bill parted ways. John wasn't ready to go back to Hyrum's just yet. He walked along the sidewalk enjoying the shop windows, then stopped in front of McGuffy's. Although it was new to him, it obviously had been in business for some time. As he waited to be seated in the busy place, he watched people eat and chatter until he spied a familiar face at one of the tables. He made his way to the back of the restaurant and tapped the woman on the shoulder. "We have to stop meeting this way," he teased.

Mary turned, surprised. "Why?" she said smiling.

"Want some company?" he asked, just as she motioned for him to sit.

Waving for the waitress, she asked him, "Will you trust me to order for you?"

After she gave the waitress the order, she looked at John. "Well, Mr. John, the mystery man, who just happens to show up almost everywhere I go, what have you been up to, since last we met?"

"Just driving around the island with a friend. How about you?"

"I went home," she said, "and cleaned my house. The house feels empty these days, so I come here to be around people." Despite her smile, John thought her eyes held a touch of sadness.

"I take it you don't have to work for a living," he said.

Mary played with a salt shaker on the table. "My father left me an inheritance that will last for quite a while. So . . . money isn't a problem."

He hesitated only a second. "So what is?"

She looked up and stared intently into his eyes. "You are unusual. Most people kindly leave me be and don't pry. They mean well. But you— Okay, John, you want the truth? The truth is, I didn't have much of a life before my father died, and now I feel like I have less."

"Why?"

"That's a good question. I'm not sure. I had a good job with an insurance company in San Diego, and I'm sure I could get my place back." She looked out the restaurant window. "I just can't find any reason to do much of anything. I guess it has something to do with my father dying, but then again, it doesn't completely."

Mary paused, looked around the room, then continued, "I always knew he would be there for me. My mother died when I was born and he never remarried. He raised me to be like he was, but I'm not."

"What was he like?"

"He was a writer. Actually, more a philosopher. He taught for many years at the university in Seattle, in the English department. A small publisher in the East published several of his books of poetry. I learned from him to love books."

"Sounds like a good man."

"Oh, he was. He was much better at being kind and understanding than I am, but he was very sad all those years, too. We only talked about it a few times, but I always knew it was there, even when I was little."

"I thought you said he died happy."

Her eyes grew moist and a tear crept over her bottom eyelash, then made a slow path down her cheek. John reached over and tenderly brushed the tear onto his finger. Mary closed her eyes and swallowed, before pulling a tissue out of her purse and wiping her face.

"I'm sorry," she said quietly.

"I'm not," John answered.

Mary bit her lip. "It's just . . . he taught me to keep hoping, no matter what. He was the most hopeful, trusting person I ever knew. I depended on him that way, you know, to be hopeful. Now . . . it's just—I feel like he taught me two conflicting things. I learned from him to hope for something better, and yet, to be sad. All the time I knew him, there was his sadness underneath the hope. His hoping kept most of the sadness at bay. Now that he's gone, I don't know what to hope for. And being sad seems so much easier. I don't know how to reconcile the two."

"What might you be hoping for?" John asked gently. "I know I'm almost a stranger, but I think you need to say what it is you're holding back."

Mary considered John, weighing him, calculating her hurt against his compassion. "Not here, okay? Later."

In a moment the waitress returned with their order, two plates heaped high with sandwiches and chips, and two glasses of grape juice. They were both hungry, and soon finished off what they had, then asked the waitress for apple pie.

Mary looked at John shyly. "Have you ever trusted someone right from the first moment you met?" she asked.

John smiled but didn't speak.

"That's how I feel about you. Crazy, huh?"

"Not really," he kidded. "I'm quite a decent person. At least that's what people tell me."

"One question, then, before I invite you to my house. Have you ever been married?"

John pictured his wife, long since passed on through the veil to the other side, her long brown hair much like Mary's. They each had similar sparkling eyes, yet also knew sorrow. "Yes."

"Are you divorced now?"

"She died."

"Can I ask how? I know this seems very forward, but I've learned you can tell the absolute truth about someone by asking them to talk about something that is still painful for them."

"It's all right, I understand." John sighed. "She was killed."

"Oh, I'm sorry."

"We lived in the Middle East then, and she was killed by soldiers who mistook her for someone else. My daughter died with her."

Mary watched him for a few moments, before reaching across the table to take his hand. "Why don't I treat this time? In exchange, you can come to my house and cut up some firewood for my stove."

She didn't live very far from the restaurant and since neither of them felt inclined to talk, both were quiet as Mary drove.

At her house, she handed John an ax and he spent the next hour splitting a huge pile of firewood that lay in a haphazard pile near the back door of her modest home. From time to time he stopped and considered the Madrona trees that were thick about the yard, their smooth surface so different from the rough bark of other trees.

As he worked, John thought of his wife, Rebecca, wondering how he could miss her so much when he knew all he did about eternity. She wasn't very far away. She was still sealed to him, along with their daughter. Mortality, even when it was like his and spanned centuries, was a mere blip compared to eternity. So why should he feel so empty at times without her?

*Love is forever,* he thought, as he only partially split a particularly knot-filled piece of wood. *Love* . . . he swung down harder this time . . . *is beyond space and time. So why—*

He stopped suddenly. *Face it,* he thought, *you're lonely. Sure, you're an apostle of Jesus Christ and you have an unshakable testimony of the truth, but you're still mortal. You still have your struggles to work through.*

Resting the ax on top of the resistant wood, John leaned on the handle. Out loud, he said, "That's why you don't get absolute, immediate answers to every prayer, that's why you don't get inspirations on everything, and that's why . . . that's why you are attracted to Mary."

"Some people like to talk to themselves," said Mary from the porch. Turning to find her standing there with a glass of lemonade in her hand, he blushed.

"My father said that people who talk to themselves are either very strange or very spiritual." She smiled. "I would bet on spiritual for you."

As she handed him the glass of lemonade, he wondered how much of his conversation with himself she had overheard. He sipped at the cool liquid, quenching his parched throat, then rubbed the cold glass across his forehead and throat. "Bless you," he said gratefully.

Mary watched John, remembering how her father had done the same thing with a cold glass of lemonade when he worked hard.

"I could use some more blessings," she said. Looking at the output of his efforts around him, she said, "Very impressive. You are a man of many gifts."

"I'm a man with a tired back," he noted, with some discomfort.

"Let me try something," she commented, beginning to rub the small of his back.

He closed his eyes, feeling her strong fingers find places in his muscles that were tight. He leaned into her touch, which at first brought greater pain, and then an easing. The absence of touch between friends and family was something he often missed, and he let himself enjoy the human contact.

After only a few moments he felt much better and breathed a sigh of relief. Mary stepped back, embarrassed. "That should do it," she said. Her face revealed her awkwardness at her apparent forwardness. "My father taught me how to do that. I thought it might help."

John smiled at her. "It did, thank you. Now please don't be shy. You helped me heal and that's how I took it. I can imagine the Lord doing it the same way."

At least John thought he said, "imagine," but what he genuinely said was "remember."

Mary looked at him curiously. "By Lord, you mean Jesus, don't you?"

John nodded.

"My father used to take me to church when I was little. My favorite part was the stories about Jesus." Mary smiled. "I used to wish I could have been one of the little children that he took on his knee. He sounded so kind and loving."

"He was," said John, "and is. Jesus *is* the Christ. He was resurrected and lives even now."

"I wish I knew that for sure," she said earnestly. "My father used to sing me this song when I was little about Jesus loving everyone, and taking all our fears and pains away . . . I could really use that now." Mary studied John's face, then she bit her lip. "I've keep having this dream . . . about Him. At least, I think it's Him, but I don't know. Have you ever seen Him?"

John was so completely at ease with her that he naturally spoke without restraint. "Many times," he answered, not thinking what her reaction to his words might be. John reached down to pick up the ax and resume his work. He swung and the wood split apart with a loud crackling noise.

Mary held her breath, waiting to see what John would do next. She had encountered self-serving, self-righteous promoters of false religiousness, though John did not have the slick facade of so many self-appointed "preachers" of God. She wasn't sure what to make of him now.

John sensed what Mary was thinking. Reaching down for another piece of wood, he studied the wood in his hand for a moment before saying, "Anyone who is willing to open themselves up can see Him all about them. His spirit touches everything that is good. The birds and animals of the forests see Him often." He nodded toward the rest of the wood. "I'll just finish these last pieces."

Mary nodded and went back into the house without saying anything. Inside the door, she turned around and watched John work, studying him from this new angle. Was this the man she had met in her dreams, the one who told her about Christ's teachings? Almost every night since her father died, she had had the same dream. In her dream, a man appeared and when he spoke to her, she would begin to feel at peace as she listened to what he told her. Then she would awaken. She had wondered if the personage in her dream was Christ Himself, but now, after getting to know John better, she thought perhaps the loving, compassionate being of her dream might actually be John.

John, too, was full of thoughts. He had started to tell Mary about the gospel of Christ, then stopped, feeling the unmistakable impression that she wasn't long for this world.

# CHAPTER THIRTEEN

Lacey was washing dishes when it happened. She waited a moment, thinking this might be another false alarm like before, in the rose bed, but she knew it wasn't as the dim light in front of her gradually faded away until everything was black. Her first thought was to call Kevin home, but, instead, she forced herself to finish the last of the dishes. It was no great strain to complete the task, since she had come to wash them without thinking, years ago. Doing the dishes without seeing them wasn't much of a change.

"It's time," she said aloud, her voice trembling. "It's time we had that talk, isn't it, Lord?"

Wiping her hands dry on the towel that hung from the oven handle, she went into the living room. She paused to listen for little Davey playing in the bedroom, and when she was sure he was okay, she knelt beside the couch.

"Dear God, I'm sorry I've waited so long to do this. I know it would have been easier if I had humbled myself before now, but here I am. As Thou knowest, it's happened. I'm completely blind." She paused, letting her words sink deeply into her soul.

"The blessing Thou gavest me through Kevin a while back, that I would be able to see in ways that don't require my eyes, I need that gift now. Please forgive me my pride and selfishness. My family needs me to be there for them, and I'm willing now to believe I can do it. I'm ashamed I took so long.

"If that means I have to get a guide dog, so I'm able to take care of my family, then that's what I'll do. I'll even use the stupid white cane in the closet. Just, please, Lord," she began to cry, "help me not to become totally helpless. I just can't be a burden to my family. I can't."

Davey silently came up behind her and slipped his arms around her neck. Lacey turned and melted in his arms, before pulling him into hers. "I love you, Davey."

"I love you, too, Mommy."

\* \* \*

While moving Mrs. Humphrey's leg in circles, Kevin felt an impression to leave the hospital and go home. He didn't have any sense than anyone was seriously injured or that the house was on fire; still, the impression stayed square in the middle of his mind and wouldn't leave.

"I think that should do it for today," he told her.

Having lived alone as a widow for the past eighteen years, the elderly woman enjoyed the attention and the touch. Her visits to the hospital for physical therapy following a fall and broken leg last winter were high points in her life.

"It still hurts," she said hopefully.

"Probably because you aren't doing anything during the week. You promised," he reminded her, making a note in her file, "that you would do some walking on your own each week. You haven't, so you aren't getting better as rapidly as you could."

She pouted, realizing her session was definitely over for the day. "I was waiting for the rain to stop."

Kevin laughed. "This is the Northwest. It rains practically every day here so that won't do for an excuse unless you move to Arizona. I'll see you again Friday. Now, remember, *go for a walk.*"

Pulling into his driveway a few minutes later, Kevin forced himself to walk calmly into the house even though he was acutely aware of how different things felt. What was going on?

"Lacey?"

"In here," she called softly from their bedroom.

He found her reclining on the bed, Davey's head in her lap, his soft snores occasionally punctuating the quiet.

"You okay?" he asked.

She nodded. "I am now. Please come over and sit by me."

He sat on the bed near her, and she reached over and carefully felt his face, exploring every contour, every angle, as if she had never touched him before.

"What's the matter?" Kevin said.

She put her hands down in her lap. "I'm blind," she said.

"So what else is new," he joked, hoping to lighten the mood. "That's been going on for months now."

"No, Kevin, I mean, completely."

Kevin's throat tightened. He passed his hand closely in front of her face and saw no response, not even a tiny one, from her eyes.

"Your hand is sweaty," she said, "and . . . you saw Mrs. Humphrey today."

"How do you know?"

"I can smell her perfume, the one she wears just for you."

"She does not," he muttered, feeling irrationally angry.

"Yes, she does, my love. She likes the attention you give her, even if it's related to her injury. She's very lonely."

He stood and walked over to the window, gazing out at the small part of the Sound they could see from their room. "Now, how could you know that, seeing as how the two of you have never met?"

"There are other ways to see," Lacey told him and realized that the gift of sight without her eyes had already begun. Tears of gratitude for her Father in Heaven's kindness slipped down her cheeks.

Kevin noticed her quiet tears and came back over to hold her. "Honey, it's all right. We'll work it out."

"I know," she said. "I've made up my mind to use the cane, and even a dog, if that's what it takes."

"Wow, you've been busy today."

"The Lord's been busy. I've just been growing up at last, instead of being a big baby about things. Remember how I read that one thought, about life being . . . oh, what was it? It was. . . ."

Kevin forced himself to say nothing, despite the almost overwhelming desire to say something, anything.

"'Our lives are not hard. They are but life,'" she quoted,

remembering. "'It is our resistance to the truth that gives us pain. Happiness is a measure of our acceptance of what must be.'"

He was glad those words gave her comfort, but they did nothing for him. Kevin had been carrying a secret fear since they had learned of her impending blindness. Even now, Kevin suppressed the butterflies in his stomach.

*What am I going to do?* he thought. *How can she realistically look after our children, and how can I look after her? Will I have to be released from my calling as elders quorum president or can I still do my job?*

\* \* \*

Once again Martin paced off the dimensions of the addition to the ward building. Stopping on the chapel lawn, he shook his head in disbelief. *That seems a lot bigger than we need,* he thought. *This thing is going to be* huge.

A seagull walked behind him, stopping when he did and continuing when he did. Martin noticed the bird and studied it for a moment. "What are you, a guardian bird?" he asked.

The grey and white bird tilted its head to one side, eyeing him intently, before raising its wings as if to fly away. Instead, it simply held itself that way, almost like a statue.

"You are a weird bird." Martin grinned, his mood definitely lighter now.

Lowering its wings, the bird followed Martin around the corner of the building. When Martin came to his car, seeing that the gull was still with him, he reached onto the front seat and took out a bit of leftover sandwich from his bag lunch. "Here, fella, for your company."

The bird eyed the bit of food tossed to it, then picked it up, and slowly brought it back to Martin, dropping it by his shoe.

"Stranger and stranger," Martin remarked. "I've never known a seagull to pass up a free meal. Most of you guys would eat a brick, I think, if you could digest it."

Martin retrieved the bit of sandwich and dropped it into his paper bag, then slid into the car seat. He was so busy rereading his daughter's letter that he didn't see the bird fly away.

*Dear Mom and Daddy,*

*I'm sorry it has been so long since you heard from me. I've meant to write so many times, but something always gets in the way. Maybe I don't want to put down on paper what is really going on. I know, Daddy, you said I could call collect anytime but I don't want to depend on you. I know your money doesn't go very far these days.*

*Randy is filing for divorce, at least that's what he's said. I tried to talk to him last night when he came over to see the kids, but his mind was made up. A sister in the ward told me she saw Randy a couple nights ago at the movies with a woman. The sister said they were "very friendly." I wouldn't let her tell me any more than that. It hurts too much.*

*I've cried enough tears now. It still hurts inside, but I know I have to pick myself up and make another life.*

*Randy says he'll make it hard for me to get any child support or alimony if I let you two see the kids, and as much as I hate to go along with it, I don't see what choice I have right now. He's been giving me some money, but even that isn't enough. My bishop here says he will help with food orders from the storehouse if we get strapped, but I can tell he doesn't want to give me any more than that, especially when I told him we can't attend regularly and I can't hold any callings or Randy will withhold our support then, too, or so he says. I'm so confused. My attorney says Randy can't legally do that, but I know that Randy isn't concerned about "what's legal"—he just wants control. It's so weird. Why does he care if he's leaving? But he does!*

*Oh, well. The bishop did find me a part-time job, working for a man in the ward who owns his own company. I think I have someone lined up to watch Tony during the day while I'm working, and Audrey is in school. I wish you two lived closer, then maybe Mom could watch Tony, although that doesn't make sense with what I just said about Randy, does it?*

*I'm sorry, these days my mind is a mess. Some mornings I lay in bed, hoping Randy will step out of the shower, with a big smile on his face, and I'll know this was all a bad dream. But it won't happen that way, will it?*

*Daddy, don't get mad, at least not so much that you get an ulcer again like you had before. Please don't doubt that I love you two. When I can, I'll call. Be patient. You'll see your grandchildren again.*

*Love,*
*Julie*

Martin carefully folded the letter and reinserted it into the envelope. A sad, forlorn expression formed on his face, his eyes looking out through the car windshield but not seeing anything.

\* \* \*

Jan had not been supportive of Martin's sudden trip to Seattle, but Randy's threats to gain custody of the children had now taken on a legal form. Martin wondered what kind of man would try to take a mother's children away.

Martin gripped the steering wheel so hard his fingers might have been embedded in the plastic. How dare Randy claim their daughter, Julie, was an unfit mother? Of all the unmitigated gall, when it was Randy who had run out on the family. It was Randy who went back on his promises, and Randy's drinking problems that Julie had been cautious of before they were married. So, was all that going to start again, too?

*I'll tell that character what he can do with his "unfit mother" garbage,* thought Martin.

Half an hour into the trip, Martin pulled his car over into a rest stop. While he watched people moving in and out of the public rest rooms, he mulled over his intentions for confronting Randy.

*What do you expect to accomplish?* Martin asked himself. *You know Randy. Do you really expect him to see things your way? What are you going to do if he doesn't? Beat him up?*

The thought had some appeal, but not enough for Martin. He drummed his fingers on the car seat beside him for half an hour more, considering several different ways to handle Randy. In the end, he decided to make sure his daughter had the best lawyer he could afford. The rest, Martin would leave in the Lord's hands.

*Patience,* Martin thought, *takes a lot more guts than most people think.*

# CHAPTER FOURTEEN

Saturday, John sat on a rock along the western edge of James Island, looking out over the Sound toward San Juan Island, his thoughts of Mary dancing off across the water in search of her. Four days ago they had sat talking for hours, finding bits and pieces of each other's hearts that sang as their own. The harmony and quiet togetherness between them had gently eased the tensions within him. He missed her company.

"Mortal man," he said to himself, "caught between the hopes of this life and the glory yet to come. Breathe in your peace from God above. For in this world of sorrow and strife, you will not find your true happiness."

Often, through the many years, John had contemplated his brother in the Spirit, Moroni, the last of the Nephite prophets. As Moroni had wandered for many years alone, John had spoken to him when required by circumstances for spiritual correlation and coordination. Moroni had told John how hard it had been for him to be alone after his family, friends, and father were killed, and the Nephite nations destroyed. Those were long years, particularly when he enjoyed the company of humanity so much.

"If someone had been around all the time, I could not have learned as much as I did about depending on the Spirit," Moroni had told him. "However, it was not a pleasant way for me to learn, only an efficient one."

John nodded, remembering the conversation, seeing his own life in the same way. Even when one was sure and knowledgeable in eternal matters, life could still feel heavy. One could still feel weary and need rest. Even Jesus had napped, taken time to wander in the hills, and stared into campfires to still his heart and "restring his bow" after busy times.

The love within John's heart for everyone brought him close to God, in ways most people would never know. Yet it did not insulate him against his own need for family and friends. To be sure, he made friends easily and his family was sealed to him in bonds that were unbreakable now. Still, the need for a personal, physical presence to touch, love, and share with was also something inborn in him, as it is in everyone.

Rebecca and John had been married shortly before Jesus called him to be a disciple. Her name meant *beautiful,* and she was, with her long dark hair flowing to her waist. Her eyes sparkled with the light of her goodness and tender heart, and John had loved her from the time they were children. Their daughter had been born during the time that John had followed Jesus through Galilee and to Jerusalem. Remembering the beautiful blessing Jesus had given Rebecca, his hands upon her head, John missed her even more.

Despite the almost two thousand years since her death, no one had touched his heart in the same way. No one, that is, until this young woman, Mary. Places in his heart, long set aside in focusing upon his ministry, now stirred. As much as he enjoyed feeling this way again, he also wondered about it.

How much could he let himself feel this way for Mary? Was it fair to her? He knew she was attracted to him, but he was not like other men in this world. How long could he remain with her?

He wondered, too, about his impression that she was not long for this world. What of that?

These and other questions troubled him. Prayer brought him some peace, but no clear answers, for now.

* * *

Kevin jogged easily out the front gate of the refinery, taking his time as he waited for Mr. Howks to catch up with him. This whole idea of running together as part of Howks' physical therapy still felt weird to Kevin, but if Howks thought it was worth it, then so be it. Kevin thought the roll around his middle was already beginning to diminish since the two men had begun exercising.

Howks had arranged that Kevin would meet him at Lincoln Park to run three times a week; on alternating days, Howks would run by himself along the long stretch of road that ran between the refinery and Burns' Point. When Howks had had to cancel Friday's run due to urgent refinery business, he had asked Kevin, in his usual peremptory way, to come out to the refinery to run with him on Saturday.

Howks' receptionist, however, had coldly informed Kevin that Mr. Howks was still tied up in meetings and then she had ungraciously thrust a folded piece of paper at him. Kevin quickly scanned Howks' bold, scrawling handwriting. *Start without me,* he had written. *I'll catch up as long as you don't get all the way into Burns' Point.*

Decked out in the red and gold running outfit Howks had bought for him, Kevin moved along at a comfortable pace. He expected Howks to drive up any moment and leave his car to be picked up later. So he wasn't unduly alarmed at the sound of a car engine behind him.

Kevin gradually came to a halt and turned, expecting to see Howks. He was startled to see a white van instead of Howks' Mercedes. Two young men, one with a scraggly beard and the other wearing an earring, jumped out of the van and grabbed him.

"Hey, wait, what are you—"

The man with the earring slapped a cloth with some kind of chemical on it over Kevin's mouth and nose. The men dragged him toward the van as Kevin fought to get free, choking against the fumes that were filling his lungs, his head starting to swim. Needle-like jolts of pain shot up into his shoulder as the two men twisted his arms behind him, making resistance impossible. Kevin could feel the wrenching in his shoulder and knew it could be easily dislocated with just a little more pressure. He wished briefly that he had taken up the offer from the karate instructor's wife a few years ago, when she offered him lessons in exchange for physical therapy treatment.

"Be a good boy, Howks," said one as he pulled him into the open side door of the van. "Go to sleep and nothing will happen to you."

"Except you'll be a lot poorer pretty soon," joked the other one.

*They think I'm Howks!* Kevin realized and tried to explain. But the ether-drenched cloth held over his face was doing the intended job, and in moments Kevin was beyond resisting.

Throwing Kevin none too gently on a mattress in the back of the van, Hobie complained, "For an old guy, he's pretty strong."

His companion, Mort, studied Kevin's face. "He don't look like he's around fifty. Must be all the money he's got . . . which he won't have pretty soon, will he?"

Mort came around the van and climbed into his seat, accidentally bumping the two-way radio on the dash. It slid out of the van window onto the road and landed with a crash.

"Now look what you did!" Hobie jumped out of the van and grabbed at the radio. "This is Pick up and Delivery. Are you there, Look Out?"

No answer.

"Look Out, are you there?"

"Maybe it's broke?"

"Man, if we get in trouble you're—"

"Don't worry. We got the old man so pretty soon we'll have the money. We can call Vincent from the marina."

The two hopped back in the van and drove off to where a boat was waiting.

\* \* \*

Howks drove his Mercedes slowly along the same road, looking for Kevin. When he had nearly reached town, with no sign of Kevin, he picked up his car phone and called the gate guard at the refinery. When the guard confirmed Kevin's exit, Howks asked the guard to find out Kevin's home address from the phone book.

At the Taylor home, Lacey answered the door.

"I'm Randolph Howks, general manager of the oil refinery," he introduced himself. "Your husband had an appointment for physical therapy with me this morning."

"Oh right, he left some time ago for that."

"I know. He met me out there, and then we were going out for a run together. I got a call, so I sent him on ahead."

Lacey wondered what the man was getting to.

"The gate guard said Kevin went out, but I couldn't find him anywhere on the road, and his car is still at the refinery. Do you have any idea where he might be?"

A sudden jolt of fear, laced with an intuitive knowledge of danger, shot through Lacey like a chill. "I don't know. Kevin is always so good about keeping in touch with me. He doesn't go off like this."

Howks looked around the yard, then back at Lacey. "I suppose we better alert the police. I can do it on my car phone. He probably . . . It's probably nothing, but we ought to let someone know. I'll run back to the refinery and check around, just in case he slipped back there and the guard missed him."

Lacey's face betrayed her growing dread. Howks knew of her blindness, having kept up on the Taylor family through his friendship with Martin Davis. Kevin had become very special to Howks, and in a manner that Kevin would not see as a handout, Howks was doing what he could to help his young friend.

Howks reached out and touched her arm gently. "I'm sure everything will be okay," he said. "I'll call you from the refinery."

"Thank you," she said, closing the door. Alone now, her tears broke forth.

* * *

When Kevin came to, he realized he had been blindfolded and bound. The rocking motion and the slapping of waves told him he was somewhere on a boat.

"Errr," was the only sound he could manage because of the duct tape that covered his mouth. No one answered.

The ropes on his wrists were too tight and the circulation inadequate to keep his hands from feeling numb. Those on his feet were better, but still would not allow much movement. Struggling to sit up, he banged his head on something; sharp slivers of pain and bright dancing stars filling the back of his eyes.

*Now what do I do?* he thought. *I can't believe this is happening to me. This only happens in the movies and to important people.*

He remembered it was Howks who had been the target. As much as he liked the man and didn't want him harmed either, Kevin almost wished their places were reversed.

*I have to convince these people that I am not Howks.*

A door opened nearby. "He's awake now." Kevin heard a loud male voice, with a heavy accent; the man was possibly from the East coast. A bang, and Kevin knew he was alone again, wherever that was.

"Errr!" he exclaimed futilely against the tape.

Engine sounds close by started up, a deep, rumbling sound growing so loud Kevin wished he could cover his ears. The noise subsided as the rolling motion stopped and the change in movement told him the vessel was moving.

Powerless to protect himself from what might come, Kevin felt his fear grow within him. *When they find out I'm not Howks, what will happen to me?*

\* \* \*

Vincent checked his watch for the tenth time in the last ten minutes and wondered where Mort and Hobie were. He had emphasized how important it was for them to be at the refinery when Howks left the administration building for his daily run. Only a few places on the refinery road were secluded enough to abduct someone without being observed, and there was little enough time to do it, even on Saturday. Things like that took split-second timing.

Vincent had learned from Howks' secretary, who liked to talk to her secretarial friends at lunch, that the general manager of the refinery had begun running with his physical therapist three times a week. Tuesdays, Thursdays, and Saturdays, Howks ran alone. Unfortunately, Vincent hadn't learned that Howks had invited Kevin to run with him today, nor that Howks had sent Kevin on ahead of him.

Vincent swore at the sight of the general manager stepping into his car and driving out the refinery gate. "What the—Why isn't he running?" he asked, as he tried to get through to Mort and Hobie on his radio. There was no answer.

Angry and perplexed, Vincent watched Howks drive into town, his Mercedes disappearing between the buildings. A few minutes later, Vincent drove out the refinery gate himself, pushing his old VW bug as fast as it could go toward the marina. Something wasn't right.

At the marina, he pulled up beside the van. "What are you two doing here?" he yelled.

The two inside stared dumbly at him before saying at the same time, "The radio is busted."

"This idiot here pushed the radio out the door. That's why we couldn't call in."

"It was an accident—"

Vincent cut them both off impatiently. "You were supposed to get Howks but he—"

"We did get him," Hobie protested. "He's on the boat now."

"I saw him drive into town," Vincent snarled. "I don't know who you got, but it wasn't Howks."

"He had red and gold running stuff on."

"Yeah, well, I watched Howks drive into town." He frowned, thinking. "Hell, you must have got the other guy."

"What other guy?"

"Never mind, let me think. I better tell Harli and Skink to hold onto the guy until I can figure this out."

# CHAPTER FIFTEEN

The rhythmic pounding of the boat through the heavy waves was making Kevin seasick. The kidnappers' boat struggled northward up the Sound toward Canadian waters, fighting the strong wind that had come up over the Olympic Peninsula and down toward Seattle. The cold Arctic wind hammered the thirty-foot launch, throwing foam-capped swells at it, so that at times the craft rose and slammed down with a bone-rattling shudder. Time and again, the launch crashed with a groan, shaking everything and everyone aboard. Kevin held onto a slim hope for escape, even as he wedged himself up against the boat wall to keep from being thrown around. Now and then he caught sounds of the engine missing.

Harli, her long black hair flying in the wind, came up from below, wearing a deep frown. Kicking the cabin door shut, she winced from her hangover and swore. Her nightly drinking episodes were beginning to wear on her. *Someday*, she told herself, *I've got to quit these nightly dives.* But even as she thought it, she craved another drink.

"Those half-wits snatched the wrong man," she shouted over the wind at her partner.

"What?" Skink yelled, wrestling to keep the boat on course for the destined island.

"I said, we got the wrong man down there."

"How'd that happen?"

"How would I know?" she threw back. "That's what Vincent said on the radio."

Skink disliked women intensely, a dislike that was amply fueled from his time shared with Harli. Skink had an uncanny knack for getting attached to women who would use and abuse him. He had learned to see the problem as that of women in general, and not his own poor judgement. Harli's self-centered, aggressive nature easily fit Skink's expectation of abuse. Given half a chance, Skink would have liked to show Harli who was boss, the way he had the last woman who had used him.

"So let's head back and dump the guy somewhere," Skink yelled over the noise of the boat, wind, and waves.

Harli shook her head. "Vincent said to keep going and take this guy, whoever he is, to the island and wait there 'til we get word what to do next."

Skink offered the wheel to Harli, who took it, while it was his turn to complain.

"So, we're just supposed to sit on our hands until Vincent decides what's next?" he fumed. "Who made him supreme commander? Man, I'm getting tired of him bossing everyone around all the time. I say we dump this bum over the side and head back in. This weather isn't going to get any better, and it's still a long way to the island."

The boat engine missed once, twice, as he spoke.

Harli shouted, "You better go below and see what's wrong."

"I'm not a boat mechanic. What am I supposed to do?"

She handed him back the wheel and went to check the engine herself, thinking dark thoughts about Skink and men overall. Harli threw open an old toolbox, and just then the boat lurched to one side, dumping her and the toolbox contents onto the floor. A large wrench caught her broadside on the temple. Swearing louder than usual, she blamed Skink, as usual, for everything.

"Idiot men," Harli grumbled, pulling herself up. She continued to swear as she inspected the engine. The last guy she had lived with would have recognized the tone of her words, and he would probably still be rubbing the sore place on his jaw where she had hit him with an iron skillet.

Harli and Skink were a real pair.

Fifteen minutes later, Harli reappeared topside.

"I don't think this tub is going to make it all the way. The fuel line is leaking. I patched it with some gunk I found, but that's only going to slow the leak down. The bilge pump wires—"

"What?" Skink looked at her blankly.

Irritated, Harli raised her voice. "I said, the bilge pump wires look like something out of a horror movie, and I'll bet they're causing a short that keeps screwing up the carburetor."

"So?"

"I'd just yank the wires out," she continued, shooting daggers at him with her eyes, "but I'm afraid this tub would sink without the pump. Besides, the fuel line is leaking. Maybe we better head back."

"With him down there? No way. I'm not showing up back at Burns' Point with someone the police are probably looking for right now."

"I thought you said you wanted to take him back?"

"That was before . . ." Skink strained to keep the boat straight on course as the wind pushed it toward the mainland.

"I knew you were gutless," she sneered.

"So, put the anchor on him, and over he goes," Skink suggested cruelly.

"Shut up!" she snarled, then thought about Skink's words. "Okay, there's a place," she said as she looked off to the starboard side of the boat, "on one of these islands. Someone started to build a house there. I used to go there years ago when I was a kid, so maybe it's still there."

Harli squinted, searching through her mind for the one island she wanted. "No one except me ever went on the island because it was too hard to get past the rocks. I had to anchor off and swim in. With these waves though, if we timed it right, we could leave him there for now."

"Fine. Just find the place," muttered Skink.

About forty minutes later, both of them were exhausted and drenched to the bone from fighting to get close enough to the small, rock-encircled island. When they managed to land, they pulled Kevin from the skiff and dragged him along between them until they reached their destination.

"This is it," said Harli, pushing Kevin to the ground in front of the old house. She stepped inside and looked around, considering how to secure their prisoner there while they returned to Burns' Point. Tomorrow they could return and take him to the group's true hideaway in Canadian waters.

"We can chain him to this pillar over here," she told Skink, grabbing Kevin by the collar and jerking him up. "Get up!"

"What chain?" asked Skink. His face clouded up, suspecting more work was coming. He didn't like it one bit.

"The one back in the boat cabin. Remember we took it off the boat at the pier? Go back and get it. It should be laying on the floor with a padlock on it."

"Why me?" he protested, tired of everyone ordering him around.

"Because I told you to," she said flatly. "Or do you want to tell Vincent why you didn't take this guy where he said?"

Skink, for all his loud complaints and blustering, was afraid of Vincent, whom he secretly called a "nutcase" but wouldn't stand up to. He was also afraid of Harli, though he was much larger and could have knocked her out with one punch. Face-to-face confrontation with someone who stood up to him was not his style. Skink preferred an element of surprise. With a dirty look, he stomped off back to the boat cabin.

Harli hauled a seasick and stumbling Kevin into the old building, pushing him down against a thick pillar in the center of what was intended to be a living room. She scanned the place, noting all the rotting vegetation that had either blown in or grown up through cracks in the floors since she had been there as a kid. The house seemed smaller than it had then, but it was still solid enough to be fixed up if someone had wanted to put in the time and money. While waiting for Skink, she tested the railing of the stairs leading upstairs. Satisfied that things were still fairly solid, she slowly went up the stairs to look around, at the same time keeping a close eye on Kevin.

While Kevin was genuinely sick, he was not as far gone as he wanted his captors to think. They had removed the rope that bound his feet on the boat so he could walk on the island though his hands were still tied behind him. A blindfold covered his eyes, and the irritating duct tape over his mouth made talking impossible and breathing difficult.

Satisfied that her captive was too far gone to be much of a threat, Harli was still making her way up the stairs when Kevin jumped up and made a break for the doorway.

Unable to see his way around, he was forced to move slowly as he struggled to remember where the doorway had been. He bounced twice against the wall, rubbing the blindfold off against the door jamb, before he found the opening. Stumbling into the open, he ran across the stone porch and fell headlong onto the ground. Although he was up and running by the time Harli raced out the doorway, she caught him quickly.

Kevin had never fought with a woman before. He was trying to be gentle, but then Harli punched him in the stomach, hard, nearly knocking out all his wind. She grabbed his hair as he doubled over in pain, intending to pull him back toward the house, but Kevin instinctively brought his head up sharply and caught her right under the chin. Harli bit right through her lip, drawing blood, and fell back onto the ground, dazed.

Kevin stumbled off into the thick brush, crashing into trees and bushes. With his vision clear at last, he could see where he was going although his hands, still tied behind his back, could not protect him from the brush that slapped and caught at him. Even though he had no idea how to get off the island, it was enough for the moment just to be free.

\* \* \*

Martin looked over his list of names to be considered for ward callings, sipping a cup of herbal tea his wife had set on the desk before him along with some oatmeal cookies. She had gone into Burns' Point to do some shopping, leaving Martin alone at their home in Glen Cove for a few hours. As Martin stared at the different names, he realized that he needed Kevin's opinion on some people before formally calling ward members to certain positions. He absentmindedly dialed the Taylor number, wondering if he would ever get used to the constant reshuffling of callings within the ward.

When Lacey answered, Martin spoke quickly, "Hi, Lacey, this is Bishop Davis. Kevin said he would be back by now from his appointment, so could I please talk with him for a few moments? I promise not to tie up his Saturday time with your family. I know how precious that is when the kids are little."

Lacey hesitated before saying, "I'm sorry, Bishop, he's not here yet."

Martin was slightly disconcerted. "Oh, all right. Could you have him call me when he comes in?"

Another pause. "Bishop, I don't know where he is. Nobody does."

Martin didn't know what to make of Lacey's words. "Lacey, I don't understand," he said slowly.

"He went to his appointment at the refinery, but . . ." She began to cry.

Troubled, Martin asked, "Lacey, what's happening?"

Lacey took a deep breath. "The last anyone saw him was when he jogged out the refinery gate. Mr. Howks was going to catch up with him, but Kevin just disappeared. Bishop, his car is still at the refinery. I don't know what happened to him."

"So you called the police?" Martin asked, trying to think, to do something that might help.

"Mr. Howks did, but that was hours ago. Bishop, I'm scared something awful has happened to Kevin. I tried to call a while ago, but you weren't there."

"I'm sorry. I was out in my backyard trying to turn that miserable patch of ground into a garden. Lacey, why don't I come over for a while?"

He could hear the gratitude in her voice. "I know there isn't much you can do, but I'm so scared. I haven't even told the kids anything."

"I'll be there in a jiff," he said. "Have faith. Kevin wouldn't just wander off. There has to be an explanation. See you soon. Bye."

Martin thought for a moment, then dialed the Relief Society president's number and asked her to meet him at the Taylor home. Next he dialed the number of the Burns' Point police department, trying to remember the name of the chief he had met at a Lions Club lunch not long ago. He knew that at some point he would need to talk to Randolph Howks and find out what he knew.

\* \* \*

Hyrum wheeled out onto the front porch and watched John build a new fence at the end of the drive. Feeling uneasy, but unable to pinpoint the reason, Hyrum had fidgeted and puttered around all morning, unable to find any peace. Driven by forces he barely recognized, Hyrum at last called John over to him and engaged his hired man in a conversation.

"So, had enough working for me?" he asked, secretly hoping John would not say yes. Hyrum had come to like John, in spite of himself, and would have sorely missed him if John took off now.

"Naw, I like working for you," replied John easily, laying his toolbox down on the porch steps. "You're tough, but fair. You're an honest man, Hyrum Patches, at least as far as working goes."

John sat down on the porch steps, tilting his head back, letting the sun warm his face. Thick clouds overhead shifted briefly to allow the sunlight to filter down upon the soggy land below. A cool breeze was starting to blow down from the north. John sensed that events were moving faster now; the reasons he was here were accelerating. The congested mass that always preceded change and opportunities for growth was about to unravel. The time for dancing around Hyrum was coming to a quick end. What the old man needed now was the truth, no matter how hard that would be to accept.

"But it's the things like love and caring that hang you up." John continued, gazing steadily at Hyrum.

Hyrum's jaw tightened and an impulse to fire John shot through him. How dare he talk this way? Who did he think he was?

"For the past four days," John said, "you've been unable to relax. I know, I can feel it all the way out in the barn. It's obvious you're worried about someone."

Involuntarily Hyrum pictured little Melinda, wasting away more each day. The image made a sharp ache in his heart and tears welled up in his eyes. He wheeled sharply away from John to hide his face.

"I also know you haven't let yourself care about anyone since your wife died," John called after him, "but this is one person you don't want to close off on. So why are you, Hyrum?"

Hyrum didn't want to talk about his feelings with John. At the same time, he felt drawn to open up to him, he *needed* to open up. But something held him back.

"God has been calling to you for a long time, Hyrum. Jesus has wanted to put his hands upon you and heal your heart, but you shut the door on him. Why not let it end now?"

"I . . ." Hyrum suddenly felt small, like a little child. Something about John had been creeping into him, something that his heart welcomed, but that his head could not quite accept.

"You were saying?" John prompted.

"Well, since you're a Mormon—"

"Your name is on the Church rolls, too," John said quietly.

Hyrum ignored him. "You tell me how a little child's death could be part of God's plan for the world? Why does someone old like me keep hanging on, and someone innocent has to die?"

It wasn't often he thought of it these days, but John could remember his own great loss. He knew a great deal about clinging to hope in Christ to help shoulder the pain of losing someone.

"I told you I was married once," John said, "but I didn't tell you about my daughter. She was killed when my wife was. My daughter wasn't even five years old when she was murdered."

Hyrum had seen his share of death. The death of children, the senseless snuffing out of such innocence, was the hardest to accept. John's still tender recollections of his own personal tragedy and loss reached into Hyrum in a way that a sermon never would.

John continued, "I wasn't there when it happened, so I've had to glean understanding of what happened from the accounts told to me. I do know my daughter and she would have felt right at home when she passed through the veil. She's that kind of spirit."

"I'm sorry," said Hyrum, genuinely.

"Using logic," continued John, "it makes no sense that they killed my wife and daughter. The men who did it thought they were someone else. From what the Spirit has told me, the men who did it didn't even know who they were aiming at, until it was too late." John saw the Roman soldier's faces, the ones who had killed his family, on the day he had finally found them.

The two Roman soldiers had been transferred out of scorching Palestine, their garrison now called to defend Rome's interest in the cold forests of Gaul. The two men had thought their troubles with the Jews were behind them, but when they were told who John was and why he had searched so long to find them, their eyes grew hard and defensive.

Confused that a Jew would be allowed to confront them over the death of an unimportant woman and child, they both looked over at their centurion questioningly. They couldn't even remember the incident. So it was a mistake; mistakes happened. Death happened in war, for that's what it had been in Palestine—war between the Roman army and the Jewish zealots.

The centurion had watched the scene with amusement as he fingered the gold pieces in his pouch, John's price for the meeting. What could a lone Jew do against two battle-hardened Roman soldiers anyway? The centurion figured he would permit the one-sided fight to go on, then dispose of the Jew's body later. Fondling his new gold pieces, he had thought it a good day's pay and some badly needed entertainment for those abandoned to the wilderness of Gaul.

"I know the two of you killed my wife and daughter," John said, speaking their language. The two soldiers' faces were like stone. "It has taken me a long time to find you, and I have thought for a long time about what I would do when this moment came."

The larger of the two soldiers squinted, sizing up their opponent. The smaller soldier fingered his short sword in its scabbard.

"I know you didn't plan on killing them," John continued softly. "They were just in the wrong place, at the wrong time. They were innocent of any wrongdoing. Yet, there has to be payment for what happened. There must be justice."

The soldiers tensed, expecting an attack.

John came slowly forward, his hands raised to show that they were empty.

The smaller soldier started to pull his sword from its scabbard.

Swiftly John gave each of them a kiss on the cheek. The men were too stunned to move, only their eyes betraying their confusion.

"I forgive you for what happened, my brothers. *Your* hearts need healing now; those who have died have found their peace. May you now find peace in the only true God. Jesus Christ has already paid for your crimes, but you won't find any peace with it, until you come unto him. I urge you to do that."

The smaller of the two soldiers eventually joined the church and became a Christian, touched by the unconditional love John had extended to him. The other threw himself more deeply into his denial, and at last came to a miserable end, run through by a lance in an unnamed, forgotten battle on the frontier of Britain.

Shifting back to the present, John sighed. "Hyrum, the child will die soon. You would do better to enjoy the moments left between the two of you, rather than hide from her suffering. It isn't her suffering you're hiding from, but your own. You hurt, because you won't give the hurt to God and receive His healing in return."

Hyrum started to protest, but John cut him off. "Don't waste the time left arguing with me. Go be with her. She has only hours now."

Hyrum considered his words as John rose and carried the toolbox toward the barn. After a few moments, Hyrum locked his house and drove off, without a word to John.

# CHAPTER SIXTEEN

Kevin could hear Harli running through the brush after him, her heavy footfalls coming closer. Knowing he could not outrun her with his hands tied behind his back, he crouched down in the middle of a thick stand of small trees and peered out as she ran by. His ragged breath seemed so loud to him that he thought it must certainly echo off the trees. He feared she would hear him, but soon her sounds faded away, and he knew for now, he was free.

*Now what do I do?*

He forced himself to breath in slowly and deeply, pausing to hold his breath as long as he could to help slow his breathing and his heart. Then he closed his eyes and exhaled. Thoughts of Lacey and his children filtered into his consciousness. Caressing the visual images tenderly for a moment, Kevin put them carefully aside and began to form some kind of plan to get off the island.

*Father in Heaven, please help me get home to my family.*

\* \* \*

"Harli!" Skink called from where he stood in front of the house. Nervously he rattled the chain he held in his hands. "Harli, where'd you go?"

Skink didn't like this, not one bit. *Something is major wrong here,* he thought. No one was inside and he couldn't get any answer from Harli. What had happened while he was gone?

He took a deep breath and began to shout, "Har—"

"Stop yelling," she said unexpectedly behind him, causing him to jump.

Angrily, Skink turned on her. "Where've you been? Where's the guy?"

"He ran off," she said sullenly.

Skink's jaw dropped open. "He ran off?"

"That's what I said," she shouted at him, not wanting to be questioned. "He about busted my jaw," she muttered, rubbing her chin and licking her lip where she bit through it.

Skink snorted. "I knew you couldn't handle him without me here."

Harli glared at him. "Yeah right, big tough guy. I saw you the last time we were in that bar in Seattle. Remember the little guy who made you get out of 'his' booth? You put your tail between your legs and ran so fast—"

"No way! I did not—"

"It doesn't matter!" Harli said coldly. "What's important is that we find this guy. Listen, if Vincent finds out about this, you're going to get it just like me."

Skink mulled that one over, his eyes darting around the thick forest that surrounded them. "Where are we going to find this guy in all these trees?" During the past few minutes a cold rain had begun falling, which drifted sideways into his face, making him squint to see her.

"We leave him," she said flatly, walking off toward the boat.

"Leave him?" Skink hopped along behind her, dragging the chain on the ground. "Don't we have to tie him up at least?"

"We can't tie up what we can't find. Besides, he has no boat, his hands are tied, and there's a storm coming in. Nobody—but *nobody*—is going to come around and rescue this guy. I say we leave him here for tonight and pick him up tomorrow. Even if he could find something dry to burn, he doesn't have any matches. He'll be so cold by tomorrow, he'll come running to see us."

Skink followed Harli along the barely visible path to the boat, thinking over her advice. At last, just as they came up on the boat, he said, "Okay, I've decided. We'll leave him here for tonight. Vincent don't need to know he's running loose on the island. Tomorrow we'll bring Hobie's dog to find this character."

Harli smiled at Skink. "For once, you make some sense. I guess you're not as stupid as you look."

If Skink had not been so ticked at Harli for that comment, he might have done a better job pushing the launch over the rocks toward the open Sound. And if Skink had been doing his share, Harli wouldn't have had to concentrate so hard that she slipped, plunging into a sinkhole in the rock outcropping underwater around the island. Completely submerged in the icy water, she had come up sputtering and swearing, and because she was drenched and shivering when she climbed into the boat, checking the engine wasn't a foremost priority for her. Nor was it for Skink, who disliked getting his hands dirty and had no intention of doing so. After they had drifted away from the island, they started the boat and turned it around for Burns' Point.

Down below in the engine compartment, fuel had been leaking steadily while they were on the island. Nearby, the bilge pump, set for automatic bail when water rose to a certain level, mistook the fuel for water, and kicked in again. Sparks flew from the disintegrating electrical connections on the old piece of machinery.

Two hundred yards out, disaster struck the boat.

* * *

Kevin watched his two kidnappers struggle to push the launch over the rock. He saw the woman go under, but felt no sympathy for her after the vicious punch to his stomach she had given him earlier. He knew he would be sore for days. As the rain flowed down his face, dripping off the trees overhead, he considered his predicament. The other islands were miles away, and he had no matches to build a fire to signal someone.

The boat moved off in the direction of Burns' Point, and Kevin began another prayer for help, one of the many he had said silently during the past hours. Abruptly a flash of light, followed by a boom, interrupted his plea for help. Ragged pieces of the craft shot high into the air as a cloud of white and yellow smoke erupted upward in the now driving rain.

He strained to see if either of the two had survived the blast but could see no movement where the boat had been. Stunned by the traumatic events of the past few hours, Kevin stood up from his kneeling position, staring at the empty place where the boat had been before the explosion. Did anyone else know where he was? Were those two his last link with rescue?

Behind his back, his rope-bound wrists were swollen and sore. The duct tape over his mouth had finally come loose from the rain and the sweat produced by his frantic flight through the forest. He could speak now, but he wondered what difference it made. Who would hear his cries for help?

Kevin looked around him. What should he do?

*Get your hands free,* he thought. *Get your hands free.*

\* \* \*

"Are you sure you don't need me to stay here tonight?" Gayle asked Lacey. "I can be very comfortable on your couch." Bishop Davis had left some time earlier, hoping that his Relief Society president could find the words to comfort Lacey when he could not.

"We've already talked about this," Lacey said, squeezing her friend's arm affectionately. "I'll be fine. I may be blind, but I'm not helpless. You're just a phone call away. Don't worry."

After Gayle left, Lacey wandered back to the kitchen and stood beside the phone, placing her hand on it, hoping, wishing, Kevin would call. She longed for his disappearance to be nothing more than a silly miscommunication. The rain flicked lightly against the window, and she suddenly felt cold, as if she were standing outside in the rain, alone.

She had the impression of a forest, or maybe thick trees beside the Sound, like . . . like an island. The alone feeling intensified. *What is this?* she wondered.

She sensed that more than a passing thought or feeling, it was a message of some kind. As she strained to receive more of it, her thoughts were interrupted by the two older girls, who wanted to know what was going to happen to their daddy.

She held them close to her and tried to find words.

\* \* \*

Hyrum drove directly to Melinda's home. The old grandmother welcomed him and described the dying girl's condition as he listened stoically. Wheeling into Melinda's room, seeing how pale she had become, he swallowed hard. He felt the atmosphere of death hovering over her.

Hyrum squared his shoulders, prepared to battle his fears and face the hopelessness that tried to invade his heart. He willed his love for Melinda to prevail. Something John had said to him had hit home. "It isn't *her* suffering you're hiding from," he had said, "but your own. You hurt, because you won't give the hurt to God and receive His healing in return."

Running from suffering made Hyrum a coward, and he despised cowards. *This is one time you aren't walking away from someone you love, just because you can't do anything about the hurting,* he thought, as he watched the child sleep. *Not this time.*

\* \* \*

As John rode the ferry out toward San Juan Island, he saw that the vessel held fewer people than the time before. The cold rain and rough water had discouraged most of the tourist types. All day long John had been getting the impression he needed to see Mary again, and all day long he had been trying to decide if it was inspiration, or merely his personal inclination. Just before the ferry touched the pier to let him off, he decided it was a bit of both.

Mary opened her front door to find a very wet John, the water running off him in a flood. First surprised, then delighted, she said, "What in the world? Well, come in, before you drown out there."

He shook himself on her porch before coming inside the house, grinning shyly. "Surprise."

"Not that much," she told him. "All day I kept feeling you were at my door, but I stopped looking out the window a while ago, deciding it was just my imagination. Now, here you are."

"If I told you I kept feeling I needed to be here, would you think I was crazy?" he asked, knowing the kind of spirit she was, but wanting to ask anyway.

She shook her head. "Nope. I believe in that kind of thing. So, you want something hot to drink—maybe some cider and cookies? I made a bunch of them—had to do something with all my nervous energy while I waited for you to show." She laughed self-consciously. "Anyone would think I really like you, or something."

John smiled warmly at her while he took off his soaked jacket. When Mary looked into his eyes, she fell in love at that moment, although she would not know it for a while. She took his coat out into the kitchen to hang on a hook

"Why don't you make a fire?" she said from the kitchen.

Moving stiffly over to the wood stove, John found the matches and kindling he needed, and started wadding up some old newspapers from a nearby pile. "Good idea to have the coldest person make the fire," he called to her. "They always get the fire going the quickest."

It wasn't long before the white ceramic stove was radiating a delicious heat into the room. John sat closest to it, holding a mug of steaming hot cider in his hands. On the couch beside him, Mary drank her own cider and munched a cookie, basking in his presence. Everything was quiet but for the occasional pop from the burning wood in the stove.

"I have a question for you," she said slowly. "What do you do if you know someone likes you, but they're too shy to let you know? They want to be your friend, but they don't say much about it. Do you make it really easy for them and let them know that you know?"

John leaned back into the couch, stretching his legs out full, his heart and senses reaching out to touch her spirit. "So, this person doesn't know the other person likes them back?" he asked.

"Oh, let's say they do. And . . . both of them know, but neither of them is saying anything about it."

"Are they in any hurry? Or can this thing take its time?" he asked.

Mary suddenly felt sad, as if the mention of time changed everything between them.

"You changed," he said tenderly, looking over her face. The beauty in her soul gripped him tightly, so tightly that his next words were difficult to speak. "Did I say something wrong?"

She shook her head, set the mug down on the coffee table in front of them, and left the room. John listened to the rain on the roof.

After a moment, Mary returned and took her seat beside him. Turning to him, she lifted her hand and caressed his face, delighting in the feel of his skin under her hand. It had been so long since she had touched anyone with love. He returned her touch with his eyes, feeling the barrier of the long years alone.

"I love you, John," Mary said softly.

He started to speak, but she kissed him before he could say anything. After the kiss, she became shy and lay her head upon his still damp chest, wanting to hold onto the feeling between them. John set his mug down on the floor and held her, enjoying the closeness, loving her back.

*Yes, I'm an apostle, but I'm also a man,* he thought. *I still love my wife, but I can also love Mary.*

They stayed as they were for a few minutes, neither of them moving.

*Would you take her with you, if you could, when it's time to leave?*

The last thought pained him. The truth, the awful truth of it was inescapable. He had a calling from his Lord, Jesus Christ, to minister to the world, until the end. How could he allow himself to become involved with Mary? How could he love her as he wanted to, as she needed him to, when the day would come that he would have to leave?

And, too, John knew her time was short.

Already knowing the answer to his dilemma, John simply held her closer, their hearts beating almost as one.

# CHAPTER SEVENTEEN

Martin had done everything he could think of to help Lacey Taylor. He had even called the Burns' Point Chief of Police three times, but it made no difference. Kevin had not been missing for twenty-four hours. No matter how much everyone who knew Kevin insisted something terrible must have happened to make him disappear, the police held to their procedure. They would not begin a formal investigation until twenty-four hours had passed. Actually, as a favor to Martin, the chief had discreetly done some checking on his own, but with no results.

The chief told Martin to expect a ransom note within the first few hours if it truly was a kidnapping and if it played out as expected. Of course, if a ransom note showed up, then the police could jump into high gear and call in the FBI.

It was now ten-thirty in the evening, with still no word.

*  *  *

Darkness had settled over the small island hours ago. Kevin was shivering so hard he could barely hold onto the sharp piece of metal he found in the unfinished house. The metal was slowly cutting through the rope, but the strain of working behind his back was exhausting.

Stopping to rest, Kevin prayed aloud. "Lord, please comfort Lacey and the children. I know they'll be worried and scared. Whatever pain I'm feeling now, it doesn't matter compared to theirs. Please let them know I'm all right."

He contemplated what might be going on at home if he were there now, and he could see how often he had failed to appreciate his family. How frequently selfishness and hurry had hustled him past the hearts of his family members. When he got back, he promised himself and God, things would be different.

Ending his prayer, Kevin resumed sawing on the rope as hard as he could. Moments later, the rope fell from his wrists, and he eased his arms forward, stretching and rubbing his wrists. Then he bowed his head, partly in gratitude to God for His help, and partly to rest. Since early this morning, more than twelve hours ago, the stress and strain of this ordeal had been pounding on him.

He found that rubbing his wrists didn't relieve the pain much, and he knew it would be quite a while until his hands felt right again. Meanwhile, he needed to find a way to keep warm without a fire. After several trips in and out of the semi-constructed building, he managed to build a pile of leaves and pine boughs in the corner of the building, the best he could do for the moment. Crawling under them, Kevin resolved to make some kind of floating device tomorrow and begin swimming away. At least out in the Sound someone might see him.

Despite the discomfort, he quickly slid down into an exhausted, dreamless sleep.

* * *

Lacey, on the other hand, was finding sleep impossible. Every time she began to relax, impressions about Kevin filled her mind. She could almost see him tied up and shivering. *Almost*, that is. Because even though Lacey believed in spiritual visions, this was the first time she had ever experienced one, and the experience was still too new for her to be fully confident of it.

She climbed out of bed and wandered down the hall, pausing to listen to the children's breathing. The rhythmic sounds of their innocent sleep were comforting, when everything else in her world felt out of kilter. Another quote she had committed to heart came to her, that

God made sleep so parents would fall in love again with their children each night. She smiled at the thought.

Now, if only Kevin were home, gently snoring alongside her, the picture would be complete.

Lacey swallowed back her sorrow and continued into the kitchen, flicking on the light out of habit, before remembering she didn't need it.

*I took him for granted so much,* she thought. *If he would only walk in the door right now, I—*

The phone next to her rang unexpectedly in the still house, jolting her violently.

"He . . . Hello?" she said.

"Mrs. Taylor?"

"Yes?"

"Mrs. Taylor, this is . . . Sergeant . . . Brown, with the Burns' Point Police Department. Sorry to disturb you at this hour."

"That's all right. I couldn't sleep anyway. Do you have some word about Kevin?"

"Well, not exactly, that's what I called you about. There are a few questions I'd like to ask you. Do you have a moment now?"

"Yes, that's fine. I'll do whatever I can do to help you find my husband."

"Okay, do you have any, let's see, do you have any idea where your husband might go to . . . get away from things?"

"I don't understand," she said, confused by the question. "What do you mean, get away from things?'"

"I don't mean to alarm you, but if he wanted to just disappear, for some quiet time, would he go out to the islands somewhere? Does he have access to a boat?"

Lacey searched her memory for anything that might match up with these questions, but found nothing. "Kevin's not like that."

On the other end of the connection, Vincent tensed, drumming on the table in front of him. Two of his people had disappeared into thin air, along with Kevin Taylor. Vincent knew that if his people were alive and in charge, they would have radioed by now. Had this Taylor somehow overpowered his people, taken over . . . ? Vincent frowned. That didn't make much sense. Still, maybe Taylor's wife could tell him something.

Vincent tried again. "Does he know how to use a large boat, say something thirty feet or more, and does he know how to navigate around the islands up north?"

"No, he doesn't. I don't see what this has to do with—"

"Thank you, Mrs. Taylor, you've been very helpful. Sorry to disturb you this late. Good night."

Lacey set the phone down slowly, confused and more worried than before. What were the police getting at? Did they think Kevin had taken some boat and wandered off by himself? That was ridiculous.

* * *

Vincent set the phone down none too gently. His conversation with Lacey Taylor had not given him any answers about what had happened to Harli and Skink, Kevin Taylor, or the launch. Vincent should have had some word hours ago. Something was very wrong.

In the barn rented from an old farmer, just outside the small town of Woolsey, Vincent paced as he waited for the other members of the group to rejoin him. He had sent them out hours ago to look discreetly around. He knew the police had not started any formal investigation, and the launch had never docked at the marina in Victoria, according to the plan.

*What am I going to do about Howks now?* Vincent asked himself. Snatching him wasn't going to be as easy as before. The man's routine was upset now and it would probably be a long time before it got back to normal. Maybe it was time to use the backup plan. Vincent looked over toward the corner of the barn, where the explosives had been buried three feet underground, beneath a stack of hay bales.

Harli and Skink's boat was probably just having radio problems, and it was taking longer to get to the hideaway with the rough weather. Vincent kicked an empty gas can and watched it ricochet off the barn wall, before falling noisily against some old farm equipment.

*That better be all it is,* he thought angrily, *or I'll have their hides.*

The tightness in Vincent's neck brought on the throbbing

headache behind his eyes that he had awakened with that morning. Each day, for the past week, Vincent had dreamed of his sister, Emily.

Emily had been eight when she died, and Vincent fifteen. When she died of leukemia, she had begged him to promise to pray everyday. "So we can be in heaven together," she said to him the night she died.

Obviously, Vincent wasn't keeping the promise he made to his dying sister. Flipping a couple of headache pills into his mouth, he swigged a can of soda, hoping the dreams would stop.

# CHAPTER EIGHTEEN

Sunday, the day after the kidnapping, rain continued to fall intermittently. Kevin had awakened feeling sore and itchy, and was now struggling to construct some manner of raft by wrapping supple young tree branches around some thicker logs he had found washed up against the rock. He suffered from more bruises and aches than he could count, but he had to keep working if he was ever going to get off the island. Only out in the open Sound did he hope that someone might see and help him.

Never had he remembered his bed at home with such fondness. If . . . *No! When* he got back home, he vowed never again to take the simple joys of home life for granted.

"Ouch!"

The sharp point of a branch, broken off to construct the raft, rammed painfully into his hand. Kevin paused momentarily under a wave of helplessness. He felt dizzy and nauseous seeing the blood run across his hand. It would have been so easy to give into hopelessness and despair, much easier than fighting to live. A vision of his family swept briefly through him, their love for him and his for them helping him find a fresh reserve of determination. After a quick prayer for strength, and a few more seconds to set his head again, he was back to working on the raft.

*Lacey, don't worry,* he vowed silently. *I'm going to get back. I will.*

\* \* \*

From the front porch steps of Mary's home, John stared out over the Sound, aware that someone was in trouble out there and that he would

need a boat to find them. So intently focused was he that he didn't notice
the cool morning breeze brush over his face as it moved past Mary's front
porch. Mary had fallen asleep on the couch in the front room.

John had accepted and made peace with his situation. Mary was
someone he could love in much the same way that his heart cherished
his wife, but this was not the place or the time. His apostolic calling
made that impossible; his higher responsibilities came first.

John would soon move on, and Mary could not go with him.

They had talked until the late hours, sharing laughter and joys,
memories, hopes, and expectations, as neither had for a long time. The
moments they had spent through those sweet hours had been precious
jewels of time, beyond price, as those are when spirit touches spirit.
Some time after midnight, exhausted and secure, Mary had eventually
fallen asleep in John's arms. Reluctant to let the moment go, John had
held her gently for some time, enjoying the moment, before carefully
laying her on the sofa and pulling a nearby afghan over her. With a last
look at Mary's peaceful face, he had slipped out the door, locking it
behind him. More than sleep, he needed to walk, to sort things through.

\* \* \*

Only an hour ago he had returned, and for a time had watched
her through the front window as she slept on the couch. Now and
then he rubbed his neck, trying to work out the crick in his shoulders. The cold night air and drizzling rain had settled in his bones
while he walked the roads through the night. As he moved his head
around in slow circles to ease the pain, the front door opened behind
him, and gentle hands began massaging his neck.

"Thank you," he said, turning toward her. She slipped her arms
around him and hugged him, her head on his chest.

"No, thank *you*," she whispered. "You are the best man I have
never known."

As John held her, he searched his thoughts, looking for the right
words. Mary looked up at him, reading his troubled face, sensing
what he meant to say more powerfully than any words could have
told her.

*I understand now,* she thought, pulling back. *You can't stay and you can't take me with you. Watching you through the window, when I woke up a few minutes ago, something told me.*

As John looked down at Mary, reading in her eyes what she couldn't yet bring herself to say, a rush of love for her nearly overwhelmed him. As he came to know her better, every aspect of this woman impressed him. How could he help but love this noble, selfless spirit? He loved her even more with each passing revelation of her strength and goodness. So much so that his decision to leave her behind became more intensely painful with every moment they were together.

The raucous call of a crow from behind the house broke the spell that lay across them.

"I was just thinking out here. God means more to me than anything else," John tried to explain. "Anything good in me comes from my faith in Him. Without my faith, I would have no love in my heart for anyone. At times that means I must trust *His* timetable and direction, when my own judgement would lead me elsewhere." John smiled at her, and she tried to smile back.

"No love we gain in this life is ever lost, you know," he went on. "Sometimes it's just saved for another, better time. Besides, affection given through the heart, and in the right spirit, always means more than anything physical."

"So, you don't find me physically attractive?" she teased, purposefully stepping around the pain of the moment.

"Hardly," John said with a chuckle. "It would be so much easier if that were only true!"

"So, I'm bearable, huh?"

"You're going to make this really difficult, aren't you?" he asked, and Mary nodded, grinning. He looked at her, admiring her eyes, then said, "You are one of the most beautiful women I have ever met, inside and out. Now, are you happy with that?"

Mary pouted teasingly, her eyes sparkling at him, then she sobered. "In some ways I feel like I know you so well, and yet, you're still a stranger in so many ways. I don't understand how God could want to keep us apart. Who *are* you, John, that it has to be this way? I can feel, I *know* that what you're saying is true, but I don't like it. I want you here, with me. Or I want to go with you, wherever that means." She stopped and looking up at him with eyes full of unshed tears, she asked, "You'll come back, won't you?"

John looked deeply into her eyes. "Mary, I'll never really be away from you again. No matter what, no matter where, you'll be part of me forever."

It wasn't enough but Mary could feel it was all he could say. Not wanting to ruin whatever time they had left, she determined to put aside her hurt and turn to face the new day, and the present moment, with John.

Swallowing hard, she asked, "You want some breakfast?"

John surprised her. "Can you get a boat somewhere?" he asked.

"You want to eat a boat for breakfast?" she teased.

He ignored her poke. "Someone is in trouble out there." He looked past her, out into the Sound. "And things are about to get worse."

Mary could sense how serious he was. "Well, there's an elderly man down the road who has a good-sized boat. He lets me take it out sometimes. I could call him and ask. Do you think we'll have to go a long way?"

John closed his eyes, weighing the impression. "No, it's not that far. We just have to hurry."

Mary studied him only a moment more, and satisfied with what she saw—with what she had come to *know* about John—asked no further questions before going inside to make the call.

* * *

Long before his first meeting was scheduled, as was his habit each Sabbath day, Martin slid his key to the ward building into the lock. He was glad to see that no one had left the door unlocked as he sometimes found it. With so many keys floating around in the hands of a volunteer organization, it was bound to happen but it shouldn't. He flipped the lights on in the hallway and followed his custom of looking over the classrooms and chapel before going into his office.

Crayle Eskra, the ward custodian, had done his job to perfection. Everything in the building sparkled.

Sitting down at his desk, Martin felt the weight of his worry for Kevin Taylor and his family. There was still no word. The police department would wait before officially announcing that foul play was involved. Martin was sure now that there must be. Checking his watch first, he called the Taylor home.

"Lacey, this is Bishop Davis. How are you this morning?"

Neither had any new insights and, having nothing of any real consequence to share, they soon finished their conversation. Lacey asked if her children could come to church and sit with his wife, Jan, in sacrament meeting. Lacey didn't feel up to coming. Martin readily agreed. Hanging up, he thought of how many people he couldn't seem to help these days.

* * *

The child's breath was barely noticeable now; Hyrum's bedside vigil would soon end. Through the night, Melinda gradually continued her passage from this world into the next, her physical image seeming to diminish by the hour. The AIDS virus that destroyed her body's ability to fight off infection would soon kill its host. Within a short time the child would be beyond mortal cares. Hyrum leaned over Melinda and gently brushed a silky strand of hair off her forehead. She seemed so frail as to be almost invisible. His heart wrenched at the innocent sweetness of her. The depth of love he felt for this child surprised and amazed him. For so long he had felt he was past love, for anyone.

"Mr. Patches, can I get you something to eat?" Melissa's grandmother, her face pale and her eyes wet, slipped quietly into the room behind Hyrum.

He shook his head, but smiled a little at her. After looking at her granddaughter for a moment, she left the room.

Hyrum's back ached from sitting so many hours in the same position, but with a savage determination he ignored it, almost relishing the pain. At least he could suffer and share little Melinda's death that way. He could feel the sting of tears behind his eyes, pent up behind his eyelids and threatening to break through, but he would not give in to them. Not now, not yet.

"Melinda," he said softly, "I haven't been a very good man. Your father was much better than I am. I haven't lived as . . . God would have had me do. Still, I want you to know there *is* a God, and he loves you very much." The child gave no sign she was aware of him.

"Very soon you will be with God . . ." The visual image of his wife and Melinda's mother and father welcoming the little girl through the veil appeared in his mind, and a lump in his throat made it hard to talk. He persevered.

"When you get there . . ."

What was he going to tell her, that heaven was wonderful and beautiful? That there wouldn't be any more misery or pain, and that her parents would again be with her? How could he say that when so much doubt still filled his own heart? And yet, how could he not?

Melinda's grandmother was a good woman, but she had no religious background, nothing to share with Melinda. If Hyrum didn't provide it, who would?

While he was debating with himself, Melinda's eyes fluttered open. She looked past him, smiling, then looked back to him. "Mr. Patches," she said slowly, "Mommy and Daddy . . . came. They were standing right behind you."

Hyrum nodded, mostly to be polite. How he wished it could be true.

"Daddy said to tell you—" Melinda coughed, a deep, retching complaint that tore at Hyrum's heart. When she could talk again, she said, "Daddy said to tell you thank you. He said, you're a good man." Melinda closed her eyes again.

Hyrum's throat closed up, Melinda's words hurting more than the pain in his back. He wanted to accept the vision, believe the words, but he felt so unworthy.

"Daddy said also that John and Mr. Taylor will need your help."

Hyrum gasped. What was she talking about? How did she know John?

"Melinda, honey," he said gently, "I don't know any Mr.

Taylor." Then, he remembered Kevin Taylor, the elders quorum president from the LDS ward in Burns' Point. But Melinda surely couldn't know him. Hyrum started to speak, but he saw that Melinda was asleep again.

\* \* \*

Slowly Kevin paddled away from the island, his legs already shaking from the icy water. Since the raft could not take all his weight without starting to sink to one side, he held himself precariously half on and half off. Looking ahead to another island, some miles away, he set his mind intently on his objective and did his best to ignore the cold.

A seagull flew overhead, circled him twice, then continued on. Kevin wished he could fly himself home that easily.

A swell moved past his legs, the rush of water making the crude raft even more unsteady. Kevin stopped kicking his legs, suddenly afraid, but unsure why. When the tall black and white fin of a killer whale rose barely forty feet in front of him, he knew why.

*They don't kill people,* he told himself, shivering from something more than just the cold water. *Their real name is Orca . . . I'm okay.*

As the whale slowly circled Kevin, the minutes felt like hours. Kevin knew he couldn't wait forever. Whatever was going to happen, he had to keep moving. Praying desperately, he began to kick again, the little wake behind him an insignificant ripple in the immense area of the open water of Puget Sound.

\* \* \*

Lacey rose from praying beside the living room couch. Although she was relieved to have the peace of the empty house, she felt guilty about being home alone. The girls had taken Davey and walked over to the chapel by themselves, Lacey promising to catch up with them, perhaps, at sacrament meeting. At the moment, the last thing she wanted to do was face a lot of well-meaning questions and comments from people asking about Kevin. The Burns' Point Police Department had called to say they were starting an official investigation into her husband's disappearance, but they weren't ready to call it a kidnapping without a ransom demand.

Lacey thought about listening to an audio tape of the Book of Mormon but decided against it. Learning Braille needed to become a priority now. Yes, it was time to take Brother Julio up on his offer to teach her. Brother Julio had been born blind and had more than once offered to teach her to read Braille, but Lacey had resisted. Resistance was foolish now. Especially if Kevin never came back, and Lacey had to . . . what? The thought was unimaginable.

The thought of never seeing Kevin alive in this life brought new tears. Lacey bowed her head to pray again, seeking more reassurance from the Spirit to tell her things would be all right, when she heard the sound.

At the back of the house, in the family room, was a sliding door. Most people would never have heard anything, but losing her vision had sharpened her other senses. Lacey heard the slightest grating sound of the door opening, and then stealthy footsteps moving slowly down the hallway. At first she thought it might be Kevin, but the cadence of the steps was wrong. Nor was it one of her children. Anyone who would come in the back way was there without permission. Silently she hurried into the kitchen and took a large knife from the holder by the stove. Holding it behind her back, she waited.

The steps ended just at the doorway of the kitchen.

"Where is your husband, Mrs. Taylor?" the voice of a stranger asked.

"Who are you?" Lacey demanded to know, trying to sound strong instead of terrified.

"That doesn't matter. Where is your husband?"

"I don't know." She had a sudden flash of inspiration. "You do, don't you? You're the one who took him away."

Vincent was caught off balance by Lacey's comment and he wondered how she could know. He could see in the window behind her the reflection of a large knife in her hands. He had not come planning to harm her and he didn't want any trouble, but he didn't know where else to look for Harli and Skink. Or for Kevin Taylor. Lacey was the only one who might know something.

"It might look like that, but I promise you, I never laid a hand on your husband. I know who took him but they're missing, too. That's why I came here to talk with you. I thought maybe you might have some idea where they might be."

Lacey would have laughed if she not been so frightened. It was ludicrous to think that her husband could be somewhere away from his family and able to return, but hadn't. Or that he might have turned on his captors and was holding them captive instead.

"Get out of my house," she ordered. "Get out now, or I'll call—"

"I wouldn't try to call the police, Mrs. Taylor," Vincent warned, his thin veneer of civility wearing off to reveal the cold hardness underneath. "I'm in no mood to put up with any smart moves. Tell me where your husband is, now."

"Get out," she yelled, pulling the knife out from behind her.

Vincent scowled at her. His plans were being messed up by incompetent associates and ignorant bystanders. And he could imagine the reaction of his benefactors in the Middle East. Vincent rushed forward, angrier than he had been for some time, determined to brush aside this silly woman's threats. Instead, he caught the edge of the knife along his left hand.

"Damn you," he complained, surprised and infuriated as the blood flowed down his hand. Lacey raised the knife to swing at him again, more for effect than to inflict any mortal damage, but her action prompted a powerful backhand from Vincent with his good hand.

The blow caught her square on the jaw. She went down, bouncing off the counter behind her, and then against the refrigerator. Still clutching the knife, it caught her leg as she fell, the blade slashing through her robe, nightgown, and garments to find an artery in her leg.

At that moment there was a loud knocking on the front door. "Lacey, it's Bishop Davis. Lacey?"

Lacey lay dazed on the floor, her head still spinning.

The front door opened. "Sister Taylor, are you there?"

Vincent sprinted down the hallway into the bedroom at the end of the hall. Pushing the screen out of the window, he climbed through it, leaving a streak of blood on the sill. The grate creaked loudly as he shoved it open and sprinted across the open field behind the house.

Martin, meanwhile, slowly inspected the house, until Lacey's moans drew him to the kitchen.

"Oh, my . . . what happened?" Martin exclaimed. Sizing up the situation, he grabbed a dish towel and pressed it against the wound. Lacey's head began to clear enough that she could form some words.

"Someone—a man—came into the house. He wanted to— What's the matter with my leg?"

"Looks like a nasty cut." Martin took the knife from her hand and put it in the sink. "Let's get you to the hospital right now. Do you think you can walk?"

Lacey tried to get up from where she sat up against the counter, but everything hurt too much. "I don't think I can . . . right now."

Martin made a tourniquet of sorts by tying a larger dish towel around her leg. Then he dialed the number for the emergency room—a number that had been committed to memory early on in his duties as bishop. "This is Martin Davis," he spoke quickly. "I'm bringing a woman in who has been stabbed in the leg. I think she cut an artery. We should be there in just a few minutes . . . good. Bye."

Although he wanted to ask Lacey about the intruder in her home, Martin was more concerned about getting Lacey to the hospital and taking care of the leg wound. There would be time later for questions.

# CHAPTER NINETEEN

Kevin's raft was breaking up. The tree saplings he had used to bind his raft together were swelling with sea water and losing their grip around the larger pieces of wood. He tried to hold the raft together himself, but couldn't keep himself up high enough out of the water to hold the pieces securely together. His legs were exhausted and numb from kicking so long in the cold water, and his back felt as if hot knives were cutting into the muscle. His teeth chattered incessantly.

The Orca kept him company, disappearing occasionally only to reappear a few moments later. Once Kevin caught sight of a huge eye regarding him as the whale rolled to one side, studying the solitary human. If he got out of this alive, he was going to have one "whale of a tale" to tell back home, he thought humorously.

"A whale of a tale"—that was from the Disney's movie *Twenty Thousand Leagues under the Sea*, wasn't it? Bits of the movie sloshed around in his mind, and he found himself humming for a while until the pain in his back brought him back to a grim reality.

\* \* \*

Mary competently guided the old forty-foot-long fishing boat through the Sound as John searched ahead with binoculars, one leg braced to keep him upright as the vessel jumped through the swells.

"Any sign yet?" Mary asked.

John lowered the glasses and shook his head. "No. I think we ought to head over that way, on your left."

"You mean toward Snook's Island? Gee, anyone by that place would be in trouble. There are all kinds of hidden rock ledges just under the surface. More than one boat has had its bottom torn by them."

John continued his vigil as she brought the boat around. "You know a lot about this place," he commented.

"My father taught me most of it," she answered. "He loved collecting local bits of history and folklore. I wish I had listened more . . . when there was time." A surge of sorrow caught in Mary's throat, before she swallowed it back down.

Some time later John said, "There's something over that way," as he lowered the binoculars and pointed. Mary immediately turned the boat where he pointed.

* * *

The slice in Lacey's leg took twenty stitches in two layers to close. Beads of sweat ran down the ER doctor's face before the operation was finished, but even she was pleased with the results at the end. Lacey was still pale and shaken from being attacked in her own home. Shock from the incident compounded the stress of her husband's mysterious disappearance.

Bishop Davis stood nearby for support. "How's it looking?" he asked the tired doctor.

The woman, still new at her profession, managed a slight smile. "You got her here in time. The blood loss was kept to a minimum. Still, that's going to be one sore leg. If I were you," she told Lacey, "I'd stay off it for a few days."

Lacey eased down off the gurney and laughed through her pain. "I wonder how I'll do that with three kids? Ouch, that smarts!"

"We can take care of that," Martin said, glad that there was something in his power to do for Lacey. Getting the Relief Society to help would be the one thing he could do right now for the Taylor family.

"So this was an accident with a knife?" the doctor asked. "Would you say your recent loss of vision was part of the problem?" She had looked skeptical when Martin had told her the wound had been an accident.

To Lacey's relief, Martin redirected the doctor's attention. "Working on Sundays must be hard. You'd probably rather be in church."

The doctor's eyebrows shot up, but she only said, "Ah, no. I'm not much of a church goer."

"Things go better when we let God be in charge," Martin offered.

"That's what my mother always tells me," answered the doctor as she led them out of the emergency room area.

On the way home, Lacey, unable to keep her courage up any longer, began to cry and Martin almost stopped the car. Instead he took her hand and squeezed it, glad when she squeezed back. Now, if only they could find Kevin.

* * *

The makeshift raft disintegrated without a sound, dumping Kevin into Puget Sound, the logs bobbing away with the waves. He thrashed around for a few minutes, trying to hold onto something to keep his head above water, his panic growing with every passing second.

*So, this is the way it ends,* he thought, choking on a mouthful of salt water. *After everything, I drown and no one will ever know.*

Rage against his life ending in such a way gave him a surge of strength to stay afloat. How dare those people ruin his life? He had plans, hopes for the future. He had his kids to watch grow up, and a wife who now, more than ever, needed him. But after a few minutes, the cold water took the last of his strength, and his anger faded into desperation as he felt himself go under. His last thoughts were of Lacey and their children, before darkness took him.

* * *

Through the binoculars John watched Kevin go under as the boat sped toward him, but it would be too late by the time they arrived. Closing his eyes, he sought the same miracle Kevin had prayed for just seconds before.

A long two minutes later the boat slowed near the spot Kevin went down. Mary and John searched the area, afraid of what they might find. "Where is he?" she asked.

"There," pointed John, toward a spot some sixty feet from the boat.

Mary's eyes widened, not sure if she was actually seeing what it was. It looked like a man was being pushed gently through the water by the large snout of an Orca. As the strange procession gradually neared the boat, she asked, "Is that what I think it is?"

John nodded. "Behold, a miracle," he said with a smile that was both knowing and relieved.

John was able to grab Kevin without getting any more than his feet wet on the diving platform at the back of the boat as the Orca approached the craft. When Kevin was safely in, John waved at the whale, who rose up, apparently taking a last look at its human errand before gliding away and disappearing.

"No one will ever believe this," said Mary, shaking her head, as she lay a blanket over Kevin. "No one."

"That's all right. We know," said John, "and God knows."

* * *

Martin and Lacey waited in Martin's car, the two of them hoping their mutual impression to come to the marina made some sense. Lacey could tell that a boat was coming in, and she listened intently for a few minutes, before painfully climbing out of the car. As Martin hurried to her side and took her arm, she limped down the pier, ignoring the burning pain in her leg.

She knew there was no logical reason for her to believe they should go to the marina. If Martin had not felt a similar prompting, Lacey would probably not have insisted. Yet the pull to be here, to wait for Kevin, was clear and unmistakable. This had to be him coming in, it had to be. She could feel it with all her heart.

As the craft came to a stop beside the pier, the loud diesel engine made speech impossible.

Lacey held her hands tightly, waiting. At last she heard a voice she recognized. It was John.

"Lacey, I've got someone here you'll want to give a hug to."

"Lacey," Kevin called, and Lacey felt his arms around her.

"Oh Lord, thank you" she cried out, her legs almost giving out from under her. Together they held each other and wept. John's and Martin's eyes were also moist. Mary wept unashamedly, watching from the deck of the boat, not wanting to intrude on this sacred moment of reunion.

Martin was the first to speak. "I wonder if we better get you to the hospital, too, Kevin," he said, the Spirit having given him some idea of the trauma Kevin had experienced.

After helping Kevin and Lacey into the car, John stayed behind with Mary as Martin sped off toward the hospital. Turning to Mary and taking both her hands in his, John whispered, "God is very pleased with you, sweet Mary."

Mary wiped her tears away with her shirtsleeve, trying to swallow back the lump in her throat. "When will I see you again?" she asked.

"Soon," John said. "There are some things here I need to take care of first, but then I'll be out your way."

She nodded silently, wanting to say more, but finding no words. She quickly kissed John on the cheek, then hurried over to cast off the bowline. John tossed over the sternline and waved as she started the boat engine and skillfully eased the craft away from the floating dock.

He was still watching her when she looked back near the end of the marina. Why couldn't he stay with her? Or why couldn't she come with him? He was tired of being so alone.

* * *

A contact at the hospital told Vincent of Kevin Taylor's arrival there. The same staff source also overheard the account of the abduction and the explosion that had killed the two kidnappers. With the mystery solved about what happened to his people, Vincent shifted into the alternative plan, determined to realize the extortion money originally planned on. He also wanted revenge. Kevin Taylor had killed two of his people and Vincent wasn't going to let him get away with it.

# CHAPTER TWENTY

The hospice nurse left around 1:00 A.M. early Monday morning. Melinda's grandmother was asleep on the living room couch while Hyrum dozed uneasily in his wheelchair, slipping into and out of wakefulness, clouds of guilt and concern descending upon him whenever he awoke.

As he was dreaming about angels taking Melinda to heaven with them, Hyrum opened his eyes to find her watching him. The only part with any life left now were her eyes, and they were wide and bright.

"I have to go now," she whispered to him.

Hyrum had not been there when his wife had died. After countless hours of watching, he'd fallen into an exhausted sleep sitting near her bedside. Ever since then, his guilt at "abandoning" her had haunted him. As he watched the gradual disintegration of the bonds that kept Melinda's spirit captive to her frail body, he realized how wrong his perspective had been. Life and death were only parts of something larger. To deny one, was to only partially live the other.

Melinda closed her eyes and smiled before arching her back in pain. When the painful spasm passed, she sank down into the bed. Hyrum reached over to touch her face with his big hand, and so felt her spirit pass from life into eternity.

Warm tears spilled down his face as Hyrum cried as if he had never cried before. Perhaps the tears were less for Melinda, who was now beyond this world of sorrows, than for himself, because he wasn't. Or perhaps the tears were for his wife, whom he had never completely let himself love and whose love he had never been completely able to accept.

Perhaps, too, he cried in relief. For in the moment Melinda died, and Hyrum wept for her, the Savior took away the old wounds, Hyrum's heart at last open enough to let it happen.

John was on the porch, the van headlights illuminating him, as Hyrum pulled up at the house around four in the morning.

"How come you're not sleeping?" Hyrum asked, leaning out the van window, trying unsuccessfully to sound gruff.

"I thought you might need some company, now that Melinda's gone," John said.

"How did you . . . ?"

"It's logical," John said, smiling gently.

Worn out from his long bedside vigil, Hyrum let John wheel him up the ramp to the back door. Inside, John said, "I'd like to give you a blessing, my brother. There are things your God would enjoy doing for you."

Hyrum's accumulated weariness, long held behind a mask, would no longer be denied. Too tired to resist, thinking his image as a tough cop was certainly crumbling, he could only shrug.

"Brother Hyrum," John began, his hands firmly upon Hyrum's head, "in the authority of the Holy Melchizedek priesthood, I lay my hands upon you, that the blessings of God might more fully descend upon your spirit. Know this, Brother Hyrum, God is pleased with you. He has seen your love for little Melinda, and He wants you to know she is now with Him in His kingdom, where her parents are rejoicing in her arrival. There is no pain for her, neither hurt, nor fear. Only joy and love surround that precious spirit now."

Hearing this, Hyrum felt the tears begin afresh.

"Your love for Melinda has freed you, Hyrum. The Lord knows it was hard for you to watch her die. He sent angels to be there as you waited for her time to end on this earth. When you felt that peace in your heart, even as sorrow welled up, the angels reached out and touched you. Heavenly Father is pleased you did not push them away, as you did when your wife was dying.

"The angels tried also to bring you even closer to God, but you hesitated. I bless you now with an increased awareness of the Holy Spirit moving through your life. Embrace it, Hyrum. Life is short, so very short. Never do we have much time, no matter how much time we are given.

"Yet, there still remains a work for you to do here on earth. Someone not far from here needs your love and care. It is what is in your heart they need, not what is in your head.

"Make prayer part of your life again, my brother. Open your heart and take all things to our Father above. Believe Jesus Christ died for you, and that He has seen all of your life in the Garden of Gethsemane, where he took your sin and pain upon Himself."

Hyrum made his way to his room, his face stained with tears, and John let himself quietly out the door.

\* \* \*

4:45 A.M. Randolph Howks was working in his office at the refinery. He often came early to work, enjoying the solitude and silence before anyone showed up for work. Only moments before he had called the hospital, checking on Kevin Taylor's condition. In fact, the phone on the desk was still warm from his ear when the office door opened and a man walked in.

Howks was surprised to see anyone else in the building at this hour. When he saw that it was just a maintenance man, he said, "If you need to work on something in here, check with my secretary later to see when I'll be out."

To his surprise, Vincent sat down in a comfortable chair across the desk from Howks and said, "You and I are going to have a good talk, bossman."

Howks felt a flash of indignation. "I don't know who you think you are, but—"

Pulling a semi-automatic pistol out of his coveralls, Vincent pointed it at Howks. "I'm the guy who has the gun, that's who I am."

Howks made himself stay calm, drawing on years of executive training. "So, now what? You didn't get a raise you deserved, or is this a robbery? Mr . . . ?"

"You can call me Vincent."

Howks nonchalantly took a pencil off the top of the desk, and started to open his desk drawer as if intending to put the pencil away.

"It's not there." Vincent casually indicated the desk with his gun.

"What's not?" Howks asked, the pencil still in his hand.

"Your gun's not there anymore. I took it out."

Howks' face was blank as he pulled the drawer out and set the pencil in. Moving a sheet of paper to one side, he saw his gun was indeed gone.

"When?"

"Last night."

"Okay, how much?"

Vincent smiled, then chuckled. "Keep your money, Howks. Your own pile anyway. What we're after is bigger than that. I know you're well off, but what we have in mind is much bigger."

"We?"

"Sure, you don't think holding the whole refinery hostage is a one-man operation, do you?"

"How much do you want?" Howks asked, trying to gauge if this guy was just a crackpot, or someone violently capable.

With his other hand, Vincent pulled a cell phone out of another pocket and punched up a number. "Do it now," he said.

A few seconds later, the lights blinked twice, went out, then came back on.

"Try your desk phone," Vincent directed.

Howks picked up the receiver and listened for a dial tone. "Phone lines are out," he said, flatly.

"Now the cellular you always carry on you," Vincent said.

Howks checked the cell phone in his sports jacket pocket. That one was inoperative as well.

Vincent punched up the number again. "We're set. Make the call."

"Good trick," Howks commented. "How come your phone still works?"

"Selective jamming," Vincent said, looking bored with the conversation. "The regular phone lines were just cut. Cell phones take a little more."

"Like what?"

"Don't push it, Howks. You won't learn enough to make any difference, and you might get your nose into something that I'll have to make you pay for. I don't like you or any of your kind. Far as I'm concerned, fat cats like you should all be shot. And don't give me the 'I-worked-hard-for-what-I-got' garbage. I've heard it all before. It doesn't change the truth."

"Which is what?" Howks asked.

"That no one should have so much more than anyone else. People shouldn't have to worry where their next meal is coming from or how they're going to keep warm."

Howks smiled cynically. "I doubt very much you care about the poor."

Vincent glared at Howks for daring to question his motives. "Shut up!" he snapped. He was about to say more, but his cell phone chirped.

"What? Okay, patch them through. Hello, Chief, glad you called." Vincent's lips curled as he looked at Howks. "Looks like the Burns' Point police finally have something important to worry about." Vincent paused, listening. "What do we want? The Free Earth Revolutionary Army demands fifty million dollars or we detonate charges that will destroy the refinery and the town. What? That's your problem. Just do it!" Vincent rolled his eyes. "Stupid pig!" he muttered. "Listen, I got Randolph Howks here. You want to talk to him?"

Vincent motioned for Howks to pick up his own cell phone, which began to ring.

Howks spoke briefly. "You know my voice, Chief. This is real. I don't know if he can do all he says he can, but I don't know he can't." Then his line went dead.

Picking up his own cell phone, Vincent resumed his conversation with the Chief of Police. "In one hour, approximately 6:00 A.M." he continued, checking his watch, "either you will have started arranging for the money, or we will blow up something in town. Something you don't want to lose. You won't know where until it happens but you'll sure know afterwards." He switched off his phone and got up to walk around the office. Stopping at a large picture window that overlooked the refinery and the bay, his back purposely to Howks, Vincent said, "Now we'll see how stupid these hick cops are."

* * *

6:00 A.M. Martin Davis sped over the bridge that linked James Island with the mainland. Checking his watch, he noted the time. He wondered if the hospital staff would mind him showing up so early to visit Kevin Taylor. It was too early for much traffic, and the off and on ramps that veered off toward the small refinery island were empty.

Besides this bridge, there was only one other bridge off the island. It was at the south end of the island and served to connect James Island to Kibey Island. Except for the ferry, these bridges were the only land access to the island.

Not three seconds after Martin drove off the bridge, a huge explosion behind him sent shock waves through the pavement under the car and threw it off the road into the ditch. Martin's head slammed against the window next to him, and his shoulder was wrenched under the shoulder harness of his seat belt.

Martin groaned and opened the door. Climbing painfully out of his car, which was tilted at an angle that brought it close to tipping over into the marsh below, he staggered up to the road and looked back. The bridge had been completely destroyed by the force of the explosion.

Small remnants remained at each end, but everything else along the long span was now in pieces in the marsh, as thick dust filled the air. The magnitude of the destruction stunned Martin. What had happened?

* * *

Vincent lowered his binoculars. "That was the bridge into Mount Placer," he announced to the Burns' Point police chief through the cell phone. "Maybe now you'll know we aren't kidding. Listen to this." The sound of distant rumblings, like a far off thunder storm, could be heard. "That was the bridge to Kibey Island. This . . . ," more rumblings followed, "was the ferry mooring. That's it for all the main ways off the island. So, you have the oil people call me within an hour or something worse will happen." Smiling with satisfaction, Vincent disconnected the call.

Also feeling the explosions in the bay was a submerged mini-sub waiting just off the shore of James Island. In a pinch it could hold twenty-five people. Bought and paid for by the same Middle East leader who represented terrorists groups there, it was standing by to evacuate Vincent's group when he called for a pickup.

# CHAPTER TWENTY-ONE

Standing on the bridge that linked James Island southward to Kibey Island, one could look out over the quarter-mile span between the high cliffs of both islands. Known as Deception Pass, the drop to the water below was several hundred feet. It was a scene frequently featured in tourist photographs of the area. The south end of James Island was mostly uninhabited as it was part of the state forest system. Unless there was vehicular travel, it was usually deserted.

When Vincent's group set off the explosive charges, miraculously no one was on the bridge. However, two tour buses, filled with tourists from Japan, were scarcely two hundred feet from the bridge, heading toward it, when the first explosion went off at the far end. Fortunately the first bus driver braked quickly, but the second driver wasn't as alert. Plowing into the first, the two buses careened forward as a second blast, from the near end of the bridge, threw the buses off their wheels and onto their sides. Grinding metal and shooting sparks in all directions, the two buses slid along, barely grinding to a halt as the first bus stopped with half its length hanging out over nothing.

Those passengers in the first bus who had not been knocked unconscious by the crash quickly became aware of how close to dying they still were. Many had been sleeping at that early hour, and were jolted awake by the explosions and crash. Screams of fear and pain, cries for help, weeping, and prayer filled the bus, as twisted pieces of the destroyed bridge crashed down on the rocks and water far below.

Two cars, driving far too fast for the winding switchback road, came up on the buses, couldn't stop in time and one after the other slammed into the pile, edging the first bus a bit further forward. As the bus rocked back and forth over the chasm, the wailing inside increased.

* * *

When the first explosion was set off, John, only four miles away, was instantly awake. Dropping to his knees in prayer, he knew immediately what the need was, and pulling his clothes on, sprinted for the house.

"Hyrum," John called, banging on the back door. "Hyrum, wake up!"

With no answer from inside, and unwilling to waste valuable time, John touched the lock in the door with his finger and the locked door sprung open. Inside, John hurried into Hyrum's bedroom and firmly roused the old man.

"Hyrum, people are hurt. We need to go."

"What?" Hyrum gurgled, struggling to make his eyes focus straight ahead.

"Let's go," John insisted, pulling Hyrum up and out of bed.

Moments later, Hyrum drove the two of them toward Deception Pass, still shaking his head to clear away the cobwebs. Two hours sleep wasn't getting him very far. He was too old for running around like this anymore.

"Did you hear this on the radio or something?" Hyrum asked.

"Nope, a higher source. Besides, you would have heard it too, if you didn't snore like a train," John said, intent on the road ahead.

"I don't . . ." Hyrum felt a twinge in his conscience, so he modified his defense to "I don't snore *that* loud."

John chuckled. "How would you know? You're asleep. I can hear you clear out in the barn."

The banter between the two men, so informal compared to just a few short weeks ago, reflected the change in Hyrum's heart. A lot of healing work still remained to be done, but the important beginning was going nicely. Hyrum himself would not be aware of it, until later, but John knew, and he intended to make the most of the little time he had left with this brother.

John was also making sure Hyrum was relaxed and ready for whatever came, before they got to the accident, because then they would have no time for anything but work.

Coming around the last bend in the winding two-lane road, Hyrum expected to see the Deception Pass bridge, but only open air faced them, except for a tangled mass of cars and buses in front of the pass. He slowed the van and stopped. As John hopped out, Hyrum switched on his CB radio and called for help. The police dispatcher told him someone else at the accident scene had already called it in. Hyrum began using the lift in the van to lower himself outside on the road although what an old, fat man in a wheelchair could do, he wasn't sure.

\* \* \*

6:10 A.M. Just about the time that John and Hyrum were arriving at Deception Pass, Martin was able to thumb a ride with a UPS delivery driver just coming out of Burns' Point on his way to the mainland and Mount Placer. The driver stopped his truck next to Martin's car, and after observing the damage to the bridge, he shrugged and prepared to head back to Burns' Point.

"I heard the blast," said the driver, "but guessed it was construction, or something. Guess I better call my boss and tell him I won't be able to finish my route today, because there's a little problem with the bridge."

Martin smiled weakly, rubbing his shoulder where it had slammed up against the car door when he went into the ditch. Two police cars sped past the van, going toward the bridge, sirens blaring. A fire truck wasn't far behind. Martin shook his head, knowing he had been the only person near the bridge when it went up. "I have a feeling," he told the driver, "things are only going to get worse today."

"Worse than somebody blowing up the bridge? How much worse could it get?" the driver asked.

"The other explosions I heard are probably part of the 'worse,'" Martin said wryly.

\* \* \*

6:12 A.M. Mary, John's friend from San Juan Island, was bringing her friend's boat to the Burns' Point marina when she heard the explosions. Seeing the clouds of smoke from the demolition of the Deception Pass bridge and the ferry pier, her first thought was to make sure John was all right.

A little voice in her heart had awakened her early that morning, and kept up a steady stream of chatter all the way to James Island. Something terrible was happening, and John was in the thick of it. Whatever it was, she would rather be by his side, danger or not.

She maneuvered the vessel into a berth and tied it up quickly, then called Hyrum's place, where there was no answer. Determined not to be put off, Mary ran several blocks to a friend's home and borrowed a car.

"I heard on my police scanner something about both bridges being blown up," her friend said. "What in the world is going on?"

Mary had no answers for her friend nor the people who were standing around outside by the street. Heading out for Deception Pass, Mary made for the place she felt John would be. While she fought back the fear and wiped her tears away, she prayed for his safety.

\* \* \*

6:32 A.M. John eased into the bus through a broken side window, noting how easily it could slide off the cliff, taking everyone inside to their deaths. Four men and one woman had managed to crawl out one window, but the remaining twenty-three passengers were either too injured or frightened to try. The interior of the bus was a tangled mess of mangled seats and overhead luggage compartments that had come loose. Several of the passengers were holding handkerchiefs to head and facial wounds, and the bus was filled with the sounds of terror and pain. John spoke soothingly in Japanese to the passengers, touching cheeks, squeezing hands, urging them to be calm and patient, until help arrived.

"There's a lady stuck back there," said the driver, indicating the far end of the bus that hung precariously over the pass. "We'll need a cutting torch to get her out."

John nodded, knowing a torch was nowhere handy. Patting the driver on the shoulder, he suggested he look after the other passengers. Cautiously moving forward, John surveyed the situation to see what could be done for the trapped woman.

She seemed to be unconscious, which was good. Fear and pain might cause her to rock the bus. John could see that the woman was pinned against the side of the bus that had caved in when the vehicle turned over. Although John moved around carefully, the bus shifted dangerously toward the pass below.

John paused, weighing the consequences of getting everyone out of the bus at the other end. Evacuating everyone but the woman would make rescuing her that much harder. Without the other passengers' weight to keep things steady, the balance point of the bus would shift out over open air. Nothing after that could keep the bus from plummeting down to the rocks below. And yet, rescuing the woman before evacuating the other passengers would put them at risk.

John made a decision. "Let's get you out of here first," John told the driver. "You can help your passengers down on the outside."

Knowing that a few passengers leaving would not yet upset the hanging bus, John began helping people out of the bus. As he worked, he prayed silently that no fires from the crashed buses and cars would begin. The Spirit reassured him it would not happen, and he breathed a little easier. But not much.

Hyrum, meanwhile, was directing the two drivers of the cars on how to look after the bus survivors. Miraculously, neither of them had been hurt much.

"Give that woman your coat," he told the one local man. "She's in shock. You don't need it." Hyrum's voice was gruff but caring. He could not do much with his body, but his years on the police force counted for a lot in the emergency. He had been at countless accidents, natural disasters, and bungled bank robberies, and knew a great deal about first aid. Directing others right then was what the situation called for.

He was in the thick of things when a young woman appeared next to him.

"Has anyone seen a man named John?" she asked, her voice trembling.

"He's in the first bus," Hyrum told her, with barely a glance.

As she sprinted off, Hyrum shouted. "Hey! You can't go in there. Come back!"

At the bus, Mary helped a passenger climb out a window before she leaned inside and called, "John?" She could feel the bus shudder under her hand.

"Mary?"

"John, are you okay?"

"Get back away from the bus. It's not safe. I don't know how long—"

The wailing siren of an arriving police car drowned out John's last words. With barely a pause, Mary started climbing in the window. A police officer saw her and called, "Hey, you can't go in there," but she ignored him.

Inside the bus, she quickly found John. "What can I do to help?" she asked.

"That was not a smart move," he said, shaking his head but smiling slightly.

She kissed him lightly on the cheek. "Too bad, I'm here now."

John eyed her a moment before giving in. "Keep these people moving out. Especially keep them from going toward the other end of the bus. Things aren't balanced so well right now. We don't need anyone trying to be a hero."

"You mean like you?" she said, grinning at him, even as she began helping an old woman out the window.

"Hero?" he muttered to himself. "Incompetent rescuer is more like it." The bus shifted again with a grinding noise, sliding another foot toward the pass, bringing forth more cries from victims and rescuers alike. John uttered another silent prayer that he would have enough time left to get to the trapped woman in the front.

# CHAPTER TWENTY-TWO

6:50 A.M. Howks paced back and forth in front of the large windows in his office, watching members of the terrorist crew moving about his refinery. The largest member of Vincent's group sat in the secretary's office next door, making sure the hostage didn't try to escape. The night before, Vincent had sent one of his crew to seal the rear door to the executive office shut. Howks learned that the door had been sealed when he tried unsuccessfully to open it.

Meanwhile, a Coast Guard cutter steamed slowly back and forth out by the tanker mooring. Perhaps theirs was only a routine check on the area, but more likely, Howks surmised, they were making sure the terrorists didn't try to escape by boat. He also figured that the head office of Maxwell Oil had been notified of the situation by now and was looking into payment of the ransom demand. At least, he hoped they were looking into it.

Vincent entered the office and sat again in the chair across from the desk. "Looks like your bosses think you and this ecological nightmare are worth the money. My contact in New York tells me they talked to our Brazilian bank about arranging the deposit."

Howks stared at Vincent. "You don't really think anyone is going to let you waltz out of the country with fifty million dollars, especially after you destroyed a good share of this island, do you?" Howks' voice came out harsher than he'd planned but no differently from how he felt. "If it were up to me, the Air Force could level this place, and me with it, if it meant you and your slimy pals were dust."

"Touchy, touchy." Vincent was glad to see the pressure was

getting to his hostage. "Don't forget you're supposed to be the big-time, powerful executive. The kind nothing gets to and who is always in control."

"Little boy," Howks shot back, "I could beat your kind of kindergarten head games before you were even born. Go back to your fantasies about taking over the world."

Howks had struck Vincent in a tender place. Suppressing an urge to shoot Howks, or least have some of the guys rough him up some, he came up with a better payback.

"Since you like to dish it out, big man, let's see how well you take it," Vincent growled as he punched in the number for the Burns' Point police. "Get me your chief," he ordered, "and get him now!"

Vincent smiled at Howks as he waited, but when the chief answered, Vincent let him know that he didn't appreciate the wait. "Mr. Howks here likes to play games, so we're going to play a game. Here's how it works. Under your streets are a maze of gas pipelines. The pipelines go into a lot of the homes and businesses in your town. Now, what would happen if we detonated some of those pipelines?"

Apparently Vincent didn't like what the police chief said. "Don't mess with me, man!" he said coldly. "This one's going to be for you. You and Howks here. You're both full of it."

Vincent pushed a button on his cell phone as a signal, and moments later the sound of an explosion coming from the town rumbled across the bay to the refinery. "How's that, Chief? Know what that was? Try the warehouse district by the wharf, on the west side. By now, it's toast. It could just as well have been any number of homes, churches, or even the schools. Now, you get that Coast Guard ship out of my sight, and that money coming, or Burns' Point is going to live up to its name. I mean, it is going to *burn*, man! And listen, if you try to turn off the gas in the town, we'll know before you try, and it won't be pretty."

As the door to the office closed behind Vincent, Howks slammed his fist down on the desk. "Damn!" He felt unbearably powerless to stop the violence.

\* \* \*

Sliding uncomfortably into the black and yellow taxi, the only one in town, Kevin Taylor could hear the protests of his nurse at the hospital. "You can't go home yet," she kept saying, even as she kept looking nervously out the window near the main nursing station. "What on earth is going *on* out there?"

Kevin shrugged but kept walking down the hallway and out the front door. No matter what was going on around the island, he was on his way home. Lacey hadn't fought his coming home when he talked to her on the phone before leaving, but he had to admit, she hadn't seemed all that happy about it either.

The cab was climbing the hill away from the hospital when an explosion down by the wharf warehouses shook the town. The cab driver pulled over and jumped out of the car, exclaiming, "Man, will you look at that! Now it's down there."

Kevin turned, peering out the back of the cab, wondering what was going on, as the cabbie got back in.

"I called home a while ago and my wife told me somebody's blowing up things all over the island." The driver kept looking in his rearview mirror back down the hill at the fire as he talked. "I thought she was mixing her medications again, you know."

Kevin was too worn out to care. He just felt tired and empty. There had to be some sort of logical explanation for the noise, whatever the cabbie thought.

Silence reigned in the cab until Kevin arrived at his home. The cabbie waved off taking a fare. "Forget it. I'm out of here. I don't like none of this stuff. This is a day to stay home and keep everybody safe." The cab was gone in a flash.

Kevin came up the driveway as Lacey opened the front door. "Welcome home, bad boy," she said. "You should be in the hospital. But with things so strange around here, I'm glad you're home."

He hugged her. "Hospitals are for sick people. I'm just tired and sore. What's for breakfast? Let's see what the radio says about the big bangs all over."

Lacey let him go and hurried to turn on the gas stove so she could make her sweetheart some bacon and eggs. Holding her hand about a foot over the burner, she confirmed, along with her hearing and smell, that the burner had come on.

"I hope things are going to settle down now," Kevin said, fiddling with the radio. "I've had enough excitement to last a lifetime."

\* \* \*

6:58 A.M. Almost an hour after the bridge went down, more people were at the crash site, including a fire truck, a sheriff's deputy who lived on the island, and several paramedics from the hospital. Emergency crews were scattered all over the island trying to set up detours and blockades to prevent problems where explosions had gone off, and working to help those who were injured by explosions.

The Japanese tourists were being treated for facial and scalp lacerations, dislocated limbs and fingers, fractures, and one concussion. Shock had numbed all of the bus passengers. A few people who lived on that end of the island came around to gawk, but most of them were now trying to help where they could.

After helping the next to the last passenger out of the bus, John and Mary began to argue about her leaving.

"I said, I'm not going."

"You have to," John said firmly. "There's nothing you can do here."

"So how are you going to get that poor woman out by yourself?"

"I don't know, but you can't stay. This bus won't stay put like this for very long; it shouldn't have held for this long. Do I have to bodily throw you out?"

Hands on her hips, she narrowed her eyes as she looked at him. "You can try. I'm a lot stronger than you think and more trouble than I look."

"No," he grinned tiredly, shaking his head, "you're just as much trouble as you look. Fine, stay. Just . . . be careful, and do what I say. Okay?"

Mary grinned back, triumphantly, and nodded her assent.

Someone outside began scrambling up on the roof of the overturned bus to get in. Grinding like fingernails on a blackboard, the bus shifted forward further down toward the pass, the landward end of it rising a foot off the ground.

"No, don't!" John called a warning to whoever was out there as he grasped Mary's arm tightly to steady her. "You can't help by coming in. We have one more passenger, but she's trapped in the end out over the pass. Don't try to come in here."

The sheriff's deputy jumped down off the bus. "We're going to try and winch the bus back away from the edge," he yelled, keeping one hand on the bus, to alert himself in case it suddenly shifted around.

John shook his head. *It's not going to work*, he thought. He turned and considered how best to move the injured and unconscious woman. The fallen seats were preventing much movement of the wall, so John decided first to remove the seats from the pile. Carefully, he pulled them off one by one, and set them to the side.

"I wish you would be a good girl and leave," he said to Mary as she tried to help.

Ignoring him, she asked, "How is she?"

"It's a good thing she's unconscious or she'd been in terrible pain."

When he could finally reach her, John lay his hands upon the injured woman's head, blessing her with a petition that God would help her recover completely. Watching from where she stood, Mary fell in love with John all over again and wished even more that he could stay with her.

Both looked up at the loud banging on the side of the bus. "We're going to start winching the bus," the deputy called.

"Tell him to give me ten more minutes," John said, and Mary crept along the bus to relay the message to the deputy.

"Ten minutes," agreed the deputy, "then tell him we crank up the winch, and you two come out."

Mary eased her way back to John, who nodded at her message. Breathing slowly and deeply, John prayed silently before taking hold of the bus wall. With the greatest care and precision, he stood and pulled the metal up off the woman, the groaning steel seeming to pull the whole bus up with it. Mary could see his muscles straining, yet sensed there was something more than John's physical strength at work here. The recognition almost took her breath away, and she knew that no matter how strong the metal might be, a far greater power was working through John.

As the metal rose high enough that they could pull the woman free, the landward end of the bus creaked upward as the bus shifted several inches down toward the pass.

Awakening enough to moan in Japanese, the woman grimaced in pain as John and Mary worked together to lift her up and carry her toward the other end of the bus where the deputy and paramedics waited just outside. When they had eased the woman through the window, John reached for Mary to help her out.

At that moment, the tow truck winch at the end of a thick cable came to life, taking up the slack where the cable was secured to the bus undercarriage. Even as the cable began to pull against gravity, to move the bus away from the pass, the undercarriage gave way with a screech of tearing metal, and the bus hesitated, trembled, and slid away.

"Go!" John yelled, pushing Mary up with all his strength. Faster than John could move, the bus lurched further over the cliff, knocking him off his feet. Mary fell back, hitting her head against a jagged piece of metal.

Unaware of Mary's injury, John reached out for something to pull himself up as the bus grated and ground closer to the abyss. Just as he found his feet, he caught sight of Mary's face and the trickle of blood on her forehead.

"Mary!" he cried, his heart in his throat, as the bus reached the edge of the cliff, and fell.

There was a horrible silence for some seconds after the bus disappeared, followed by a monumental crash as it fell against the jagged rocks below.

# CHAPTER TWENTY-THREE

7:21 A.M. Without much success, Hyrum had been struggling to use the bits and pieces of what little Japanese he knew to console one of the injured passengers. As the bus went over the edge, the sound of the scraping and grinding jerked his attention away toward the pass. He knew John was still in the bus and realized instantly what the sound meant.

No one moved.

Finally, Hyrum wheeled slowly over to where the bus had been, stopping between the deep-cut gouges in the road the bus had made going into the pass. Three of the Japanese tourists came up behind him, and two Burns' Point police officers peered over the unstable edge where the bus had slid out of sight to fall on the treacherous rocks in the bottom of the pass, to be sucked into the fast moving whirlpools in the deep, cold waters. It was impossible to believe anyone could survive that fall and no way for anyone at the top of the cliff to do anything about it.

Shocked into silence, no one spoke. There was nothing to say.

When everyone else had at last backed away from the edge and gone back about the business of caring for the wounded, Hyrum remained alone. Moving closer, he hefted himself up on the arms of his chair and peered down, staring at the mangled bus where it lay almost fully submerged in the water, far below. Only the mangled tail of the bus was visible as the water washed over and poured into the broken rear window. Later, grief would fill his heart, but for the moment, shock blocked everything.

*  *  *

7:22 A.M. Despite one delay after another, Martin at last arrived at the hospital, only to find that Kevin Taylor had gone home already. When he tried to call his wife, the phone lines weren't working.

Trudging up the hill away from the hospital, he stopped to catch his breath several times, watching the fire at the wharf warehouses behind him. From the higher viewpoint, he sadly observed the tall flames and the crowds watching the fire crews fight it. He shook his head, wishing whatever, or whoever, was doing all this, would stop. What kind of world was this becoming?

Moving again back up the hill, Martin decided to check on the chapel since it was so near the Taylors' home. Maybe he could find someone with a cellular phone he could borrow and call his wife. Those couldn't be out, too, could they?

*  *  *

Even as Martin hiked up the hill, the local police chief's call for help had begun bringing together an army of law enforcement officers. Gathering on the mainland side of the marshy area where the bridge to Mount Placer had been destroyed, they were busy making sure all their equipment was ready. Plans had already been laid, and all had been smoothly coordinated in an amazingly short period of time. These men were professionals.

From their vantage point, they could view the east side of James Island and the refinery. Concealed under the trees and behind the thick brush, they kept hidden, waiting until the word came for them to move in with an amphibious strike. Waiting was the hardest part.

Almost two and a half hours after the terrorists had sent out their demand, a helicopter carrying an oil company representative from the regional Seattle office was hurrying to Burns' Point. The local commander of the Army National Guard was doing an on-site evaluation to give the governor information to decide if mobilizing the reservists was needed.

Things in Burns' Point were going from bad to worse.

* * *

Falling several hundred feet to the jagged rocks below, the bus crumbled into a mangled pile of steel. After a small bounce, it split in half, and the front end of the wreckage fell into the steep drop-off, filling with salty water from the Sound.

As the bus had fallen off the ledge, John had clutched Mary in his arms, praying fervently for a miracle not so unlike many he had been part of for thousands of years. God could protect Mary, as he always had John. God *could.*

Even before he finished his plea, John had known that was not the plan. Mary's life would end with her sacrifice. Her days on this earth would go no further. Although John had no doubts about the Atonement and Resurrection, his heart was still torn at the loss of her from this life, from *his* life, for now.

A fraction of a second after the bus fell off the cliff, Mary's eyes had fluttered open and she had smiled up at John as he prayed. A moment later, the impact tore her out of John's arms and smashed her body against the bus roof. She died instantly.

John's tears fell like rain upon Mary's face. Holding her in his lap, he wept and gently wiped the blood from her face with his shirt, as the mortal, physical part of him struggled to accept her death.

"She's such a wonderful spirit, Lord," he whispered through his sobs. "But then, Thou knowest her better than I do. I thank Thee for the time we had together. Give her a hug for me, please."

As John wept, the stresses and strains of being afloat in time broke loose within him. Even as his spirit was anchored in timelessness and his loved ones eternally connected to him, he was also alone and apart in mortality. Through the endless march of days, the thousands of marks on the calendar he had seen had taken their toll. He knew all things were truly one, as in a circle, but he was not yet immortal and needed to weep with sorrow in his mourning for Mary.

As if by a huge, gentle hand, a faint sphere of protective golden light formed around him.

After a time, the eternal spirit inside his mortal body gave a deep sigh, and gave everything to his God. His tears now changed from sorrow, to marking his joy for the gifts of the Atonement, of salvation and eternal life for her.

John tenderly pushed the loose hair away from Mary's eyes, as the light around him faded and left. Sighing heavily, he laid Mary's body carefully to rest and kissed her cheek before leaving.

Rescuers would be down to check on the wreck. They would find Mary's body but not John's and would suppose he was in the part of bus that went into the water. Efforts to find him there would also be unsuccessful. He would be listed as missing and it would be assumed that his body had washed through the tangled metal into the turbulent waters of the pass. After all, no one could have been in that bus and survived.

# CHAPTER TWENTY-FOUR

Hyrum's mind automatically answered the deputy's questions about John and Mary while his heart wondered how he would get along without his "hired man." John had become so much more to him than just an employee. Unable to swallow back the lump in his throat, Hyrum realized John had become his friend.

"I don't know very much about him," Hyrum said wearily. "He's only worked for me a few weeks, and before that, your guess is as good as mine." He knew more about John, but nothing you could fit into an accident report.

Behind Hyrum, a Burns' Point police officer radioed for Coast Guard support. "One of the buses went over the edge," reported the officer. "You guys can get down there and get the bodies a whole lot easier than we can."

As ambulances from the hospital pulled up to transport the injured away, Hyrum visualized John's and Mary's bodies in the fallen bus at the bottom of the pass and his eyes teared up.

"I . . . I don't know anything else," he stammered. The deputy, seeing signs of shock, thoughtfully put away his official procedure and got a blanket to put over Hyrum. Moving out of the ambulance's way, Hyrum sat alone by the side of the road, looking at but not noticing the scene before him.

\* \* \*

8:31 A.M. "You okay here?" gasped an exhausted Martin, still recovering from his trek uphill from the hospital.

"Come in, Bishop," Lacey invited. "I didn't hear your car."

Martin took several deep breaths before answering. "I walked from the hospital. Whew! Man, am I ever out of shape. That hill on Freeman Street is a killer."

Shutting the door behind him, Lacey answered, "That's why all the kids like to ride their bikes down it. So where's your car?"

"Lost it when the bridge to Mount Placer went down. I went into the ditch. It wouldn't surprise me if my axle was busted."

"Oh, no," Lacey sympathized. "We heard on the radio something about an explosion. Kevin said it must have been done on purpose."

"I'd believe that. Bridges don't explode on their own."

"I wonder why there wasn't any mention of the other explosions?" Lacey mused.

Lacey led Martin into the living room where Kevin was resting in a recliner, his one concession to Lacey's concerns over him. "Hey, Bishop. Be a buddy and tell her I'm fine. I'm tired but not sick."

"Kidnapping and almost drowning appeal to you, do they?" Martin kidded.

"So what's your theory about the explosions?" Kevin asked.

Martin started to answer, then stopped, sniffing. "What's that smell?"

Lacey figured it out first. "Gas. The stove must be leaking again."

Martin nodded. "I had a furnace that did that off and on when we lived back East. Never did it consistently, and the gas company guys couldn't find where it was coming from. Hope your stove works better than that."

* * *

High above the bus, John looked down from a small rock outcropping some hundred yards away from where the bus had landed on the jagged rocks below. A Coast Guard helicopter carefully lowered a man on a hoist down next to the bus, the long line swaying in the wind. Coming out of the bus, the man looked around on the rocks and in the shallow water near the shoreline. John's body, of course, was nowhere to be found.

Face raised skyward, John closed his eyes, mourning for Mary. Now was not the time though; there were things only he could do and dangers still to be faced. Concentrating intensely, he put himself in order and then set off through the thick forest. The Savior would take care of Mary now, as He had before and as He always would.

* * *

8:59 A.M. Rising up from the ground, a deep, slow rumble ran through Burns' Point. An old man scanned the sky, expecting to see clouds to go with the "thunder," although the sky was clear that Washington coast morning. The cabbie who'd given Martin a ride earlier ran out the front door of his house, checking to see if something else was on fire in town, and was both disappointed and relieved to find no new disaster.

It was unclear to anyone what was going on; the news reports on the radio and television were minimal and so worded to avoid panic. Since most people on the two islands commuted over the bridges or on ferries to the mainland to work, the same people gathered now at the ferry landing and bridges, surveying the damage, trying to figure out what they were going to do.

Law enforcement and fire crews kept sirens and obvious signs of trouble at a minimum, wanting to avoid alarming anyone. The last thing they needed was public hysteria. Despite the precautions, though, people were frightened. Bits and pieces of the truth moved quickly through the island, and everyone wondered, and worried, what was going on. Without phone service, people were showing up at the police station, demanding to know what was going on. The official answers pleased no one. A large group of men stood a block from the police station, complaining about the lack of available information.

Another rumble moved through town, and this time a crack appeared in the White Gull Hotel and Restaurant, near the center of town. Scheduled for completion soon, the brand new building boasted of the latest construction materials and techniques with twice as many earthquake beams installed as required by law.

The crack ran along the foundation and then up the inside of a vertical wall, right next to where a retired couple from California were standing. Despite the explosions, a white-haired man and woman in the nearby cafe were toasting their good fortune with glasses of orange juice. Used to living in earthquake country, they paid little attention to what sounded like distant rumblings.

Deep underground, beneath James Island and the bay toward the refinery, gas leakage had begun to ignite spontaneously, weakening the bedrock foundations under the homes of unsuspecting people far above.

* * *

Vincent and his group of terrorists were beginning to realize the events they had set in motion were changing into something they could not control.

"I want to know which of the explosives that was, and who gave the order to set it off," Vincent yelled into his cell phone. "Somebody—" Angrily he turned the phone off and stomped out of the administration building, over to the maintenance shed. Inside, Holtz was working at the computer terminal that coordinated the microwave signals that detonated the explosives at the refinery and around the island.

"Holtz, you idiot, who gave you the order to set off more charges in town?" Vincent screamed as he charged through the doorway of the shed.

Holtz looked over his computer, frowning. "I . . . I don't know *what* that was."

Vincent's eyes bulged with fury. "You're supposed—"

"Shut up and listen, for a minute," Holtz yelled over Vincent's words. "All our instruments say we didn't set anything off. I don't know what that was."

As Holtz's message finally got through, Vincent turned to look out the open doorway across the bay to Burns' Point. "Could those be spin-off blasts?" he muttered to himself, wondering about the warehouses they destroyed earlier. *Accidental explosions*, he pondered. Would they provide extra advantage, or not?

* * *

Ray Penzatta, senior FBI agent assigned to dealing with the refinery takeover, conferred with the county sheriff and the National Guard commander. The Burns' Point police chief, trapped in town, was included in the meeting by radio.

Penzatta's body was that of an aging Olympic wrestler. Six feet tall, with a shock of steel grey hair, his eyes still burned with the same intensity as during his years representing the U.S.A. in international wrestling matches. However, his body could no longer fight the inevitable decline of time. A roll was developing around his middle, and his joints ached most of the time.

"We have to assume for the time being," Penzatta was saying, "that the refinery is the focus point. It was the terrorists' initial point of attack, and it's the easiest for them to hold while they keep tabs on the area. That would make it the detonation control center for these explosive charges."

"Why don't we just get the gas company to shut off the gas flow to the island? That seems the simplest way to stop all this," the police chief said.

"Sounds easy," countered Penzatta, glaring at the speaker phone as if the chief were standing there, "which means it wouldn't be. The terrorists have proved they can pick and choose their targets. They also said they have the technology to know if we try and shut off the gas. Maybe they do and maybe they don't. For the time being, I don't think it's wise to push the issue."

Shaking his head, he continued, "No. We position ourselves first and then take the gas out when it suits us. We'll do it when we know the likelihood of catching them off guard is the greatest."

The chief mulled that over a moment. "Well, we've got some real problems over here. What are we supposed to do, sit and twiddle our thumbs while you guys take your time over there? When am I going to get some help?"

"Chief, we'll come when the time is right," Penzatta snapped. "You just take care of things over there."

"Well, we can expect the refinery money to show up, can't we?" the sheriff asked.

Penzatta shook his head. "Maybe the money is coming, and maybe it isn't. The refinery representative was rather cagey about it, and the oil company says they want to do their own negotiating. So I wouldn't count on anything at this point. One thing I've learned in this business is, don't depend on civilians to do what they said they would. That's the best way to get people hurt. When we're ready, we do what we have to."

Penzatta ended the meeting and left the hastily thrown-up tent where the main communications equipment was stationed. Walking far beyond the amphibious trucks and clusters of men, Ray sought a quiet place in the brush where he could be alone.

Ray's nerves felt like they were on fire. He needed a vacation, and he needed one now. His wife had been after him for the past year to take some time off and sneak away with her to a place in Mexico she had found. But it always seemed there was one more thing that needed taking care of before they could go.

Truth was, Ray hated vacations. He didn't know how to relax and enjoy himself. Driven to achieve all his life, to be the best, he had become a legend in the FBI, while turning his heart and guts into a doctor's prescription drug jungle. Just in the last month, he had doubled over in pain three times, his insides twisting and turning. Ray told his doctor it felt like "an alligator with an elephant in its mouth."

In fact, Ray had finally made up his mind to call up his boss in the bureau and tell him he was going off to Mexico with his wife, and he had no idea when he'd be coming back. But then this business with the refinery had come up, and, well, after that things went like they always did.

For some time now the crack had been widening in Ray's determination to die the best agent the FBI ever had. "So, what will I have on my gravestone?" he asked aloud, talking to nobody but the bushes. "Here lies Ray Penzatta, best agent the FBI ever had." He broke off a branch of a nearby bush. "And who'll care? Not my family, not anyone who has any sense."

He tossed the branch away, feeling a strange rumble from under his feet. What were they getting now, an earthquake? Clenching his fists, he started walking, then broke into a run, back toward the communication tent.

# CHAPTER TWENTY-FIVE

9:47 A.M. Another rumble ran under the island, as if Atlas had shivered and the whole world trembled on his shoulders. John stopped running through the woods, bending his knees to ride out the moving ground, like a surfer on an ocean wave. As it ended, he dropped down on one knee, praying silently.

Assured that his prayer had been heard and answered, John took off again. He moved through the forest with a specific destination in mind—one that would mean a great deal to the people of Burns' Point. Meanwhile, Vincent would find it harder to blow up anything else on the island.

\* \* \*

"It's almost ten, Chief—" Vincent heard a call waiting tone and hung up on the police chief. Switching calls, he snapped, "What?"

It was the oil company executive, who explained that they were arranging the ransom money, but it would still take a bit longer.

Vincent was livid. "Fifty million is chicken feed to you thieves!" he screamed. "The next part of this town that goes up is on your head. How's your conscience, smart guy?" Ending the call, Vincent shouted to Holtz, "Trip the next one!"

Holtz worked busily over a computer console, mumbling to himself, sweat forming on his brow.

"Do it!" Vincent insisted.

Holtz threw up his hands helplessly. "I did! I sent the

command, and nothing happened."

"So where's your backup?"

"I tried that, too," Holtz defended himself, his fingers flying over the computer keyboard. "It should have worked."

"Re-route for another line," Vincent ordered.

Holtz nodded and tapped the keys hurriedly, then bit his lip. "Nothing's going. Man, this can't be. Try your cell phone."

Vincent called the Burns' Point police but disconnected as someone there answered. "It works. So what?"

"If your phone is working, then our signals should be getting through."

"I don't want to hear 'should.' I want *answers.*"

"Then you sit here and tell me what's wrong," Holtz retorted.

Vincent, no computer whiz himself, glared at his electronics expert. "You idiot—"

Just then the ground beneath their feet moved up three inches, dropped, then rose again, before dropping to rest. Cracks appeared in the concrete floor as the steel girders supporting the roof groaned. Everyone rushed for the door, scrambling to get out. Vincent was the last person through before the ground shook again, and the building collapsed into a pile of rubble.

Holtz whistled softly. "That was close. What a weird earthquake!"

Vincent grabbed his shoulder. "What are you going to do about the charges in town?"

Holtz shook Vincent off. "Nothing, man. They're history. My computer is junk, so your bombs might as well not exist, for all the control we have over them." Smiling cynically, he asked, "So, smart guy, what's the backup plan?"

Vincent narrowed his eyes, rapidly calculating other options. After a moment, he walked off behind another building and pulled out his cell phone. Punching in a number that only one other member of the Free Earth group knew, he waited for an answer.

"Yeah."

"Jenny, it's me. You still able to get the chopper?"

"No problem. I was at the National Guard airstrip yesterday, and the security around the aircraft is so thin my grandmother could steal the thing."

"Good, because I don't like the way this thing is going down. If our friends don't show when they said they would, we've had it."

"I'll be ready. Let me know."

"You just make sure you can get it."

"Look, I said I could. Lighten up, man."

As Vincent hung up, Jenny jammed her cell phone in her pocket. *Why did I ever agree to have anything to do with Vincent?* she asked herself. If things went as planned, she was going to make sure a good chunk of that fifty million dollars of ransom money ended up in her own pocket. She'd take the chopper and hightail it north to Canada and from there catch a boat to the Orient. That way Vincent would have a harder time trying to trace her.

It was time for life to be a whole lot better. Her time in the army should have turned out better than it did. If those jerks in her helicopter squadron hadn't turned her in, it would have. She'd only run a small operation, not even worth noticing compared to so many bigger drug operations in the military. She thought the dishonorable discharge had been a gross overreaction, though it had kept her out of prison.

Jenny slipped her old car in gear and turned around from her lookout on the hill above the airbase. Heading for her boyfriend's place, she laughed to herself. *What a chump Vincent is,* she thought. *He has no idea he's being used.*

\* \* \*

Although Vincent's Free Earth Revolutionary Army group was forced to change plans, they had already set certain events in motion. Far below the surface of the ground, the foundations of the island started to shift, huge sections of rock grating across each other. Gas from the town's ruptured pipelines continued to pour into the underground fissures, igniting into firestorms. A huge slab of bedrock under the refinery moved more than a foot from its companion pieces.

Main Street in Burns' Point quivered, before a half-mile piece dropped ten feet, effectively closing off traffic and dumping more than fifty cars into the hole. Miraculously, no one was seriously injured, though several got cuts and bruises.

In the Taylor neighborhood, the gas line was leaking freely now. A man who lived several houses down from Kevin and Lacey stomped out of his house in the middle of a very loud argument with his wife. Muttering angrily to himself, he plugged in the cord to his electric lawnmower. Turning from the outlet on the side of his house, he saw a plume of flame shooting up from beneath the mower. The small pocket of gas in the rock underneath his lawn was all it took to burn his machine to a crisp.

"Louise!" he yelled, his eyes wide, "Call the fire department!" Yanking the cord out of the outlet, he ran back into the house.

* * *

9:52 A.M. Kevin was in his bathroom, shaving, when he wondered if the sewer lines had backed up. "Phew!" he complained, in midstroke. "Lacey?" he called, "do you smell that?"

Lacey met him in the hallway. "Kevin, we need to get out of here."

"What?"

Lacey was already gathering the kids, even as Kevin remained dumbstruck in the hallway, still holding his razor. Small bits of shaving foam dropped off onto the carpet. "Honey, why?"

Going out the front door with the kids, she called, "Kevin, we've got to go right *now*. Girls, we're going on a hike, over to the church. *Hurry*, Davey."

Kevin trailed after them, flipping his razor onto his bed and shutting the door after him with a puzzled look on his face. As he stepped off the low porch onto the driveway, a shudder ran under his feet. The same Spirit that prompted Lacey to leave the house now whispered to Kevin to grab his family and run.

Running up the cul-de-sac they lived on, the Taylors met many of their neighbors leaving their own homes. Something frightening was about to happen, and a kindly heaven had given anyone who would listen a warning.

Where the cul-de-sac connected to the main road, the crowd came to wait. It didn't take long.

It started at the house where the skeleton of the lawnmower still sat, wisps of smoke still trailing upwards. Slowly, the house began to slide into a sinkhole beneath it, and it was soon followed by two more homes. Three on the other side of the street sank as well, more quickly than the previous ones, and then the Taylors' house began to drop. Next, the main road began breaking up, forcing the people to move south, toward the LDS chapel building.

"Our home," whispered Lacey. "It's gone, isn't it?"

"Yes, honey," Kevin answered with a heavy heart. "It's gone."

Lacey wanted to cry, but she was too stubborn. "What are we going to do?"

Kevin forced himself to sound both confident and calm. "The house is insured, but we'll just have to figure all that out later. Right now we need to find some place to be."

* * *

Hearing a loud knocking on his office door, Martin responded quickly. It was John. At first his warning about the earthquake-like events about to happen had seemed too farfetched to believe, but standing outside the building, Martin both heard and felt the strange rumblings. His heart took a sharp spiritual jab, and he believed. He urged the crowd into the chapel, hoping the Lord would spare the dedicated and holy place as a refuge for those who had lost their homes.

John moved among the suffering, comforting where he could; he prayed with some, occasionally holding a hand or a child, trying to impart the hope and faith they all needed. Martin and Kevin conferred about the ward members, then Kevin gathered together the brethren who lived near him. They would carry out a specific family-by-family check on the ward members, though it would be difficult without the phones working. It didn't help that the ward population was spread over the whole island. Over ninety-nine percent of the island was not LDS, so the Saints needed to offer help and refuge to the island population at large, wherever they could.

\* \* \*

10:51 A.M. An hour after the Taylors lost their home, Vincent prepared to set off the explosives that would destroy part of the refinery. Out of the refinery would fly a cloud of contaminants that would infect the surrounding area for years. So intent was Vincent on finding some way to carry out his plans, it hardly crossed his mind that the water of Puget Sound would suffer an even worse pollution from the unrefined petroleum pouring into it.

It was the sight of the law enforcement army across the bay that made up his mind. Even if the ransom money never worked out, the refinery was dead. He would show everyone that his group was for real, and at last he would get the respect he deserved.

\* \* \*

Even as the destruction was being set to continue, Ray Penzatta finished getting clearance from his superiors for an assault on the refinery. Handing the scrambled secure cell phone to his assistants, he rubbed his hands together, glad at last to do something.

"We have the go-ahead," he announced.

"About time," complained the National Guard commander. "Conditions on the island are getting worse. We have a report that the earthquake destroyed a lot of the downtown area, and several homes in the residential section have disappeared down sinkholes. I need to get my people in there to help."

Penzatta nodded, appreciating how the natural disaster needs were dovetailing perfectly with his assault against the terrorists. "Chief?" The police chief signaled he was still there on the speaker phone. "Make sure your people are in place. When the signal comes, there won't be any room for mistakes."

\* \* \*

People kept showing up at the LDS chapel, some were members but most were just lost and frightened souls, unsure what they should do. Tremors on the island were increasing in frequency and strength, destroying more homes. The White Gull Inn was a pile of rubble, but it had disintegrated slowly enough that no one had been injured by its demise.

Earthquake experts at nearby Seattle University were monitoring the activity on James Island, but were mystified at the containment of the earth movement. Their instruments showed something similar to previous seismic activity and yet it was different. Normally an earthquake of such intensity affected a wider radius of area and could be picked up on monitors for hundreds of miles. The one on James Island appeared to affect only the island itself.

In his prayer John had asked the Lord to rest his hand upon the island, keeping the earthquake within the small area, but as with all inspired prayers, his words had only expressed what the Lord intended all along.

# CHAPTER TWENTY-SIX

12:05 P.M. Since the first earth tremors had cut off power to the island, it was impossible to tell the time, save by the position of the sun nearly overhead, a personal watch, or battery-operated clock. Law enforcement authorities were unwilling to risk injury or death to yet more people due to further possible explosions, so help from other islands and the mainland was being held back.

The terrorists had been strangely quiet for over two hours now. Calls to them on the cellular phone had gone unanswered. Ray Penzatta would have preferred constant communication with the group at the refinery, since silence usually meant surprises.

The LDS chapel wasn't the only place people were gathering to, but it was one of the largest groups. Members of the Church whose homes had not been lost generously shared their food and water storage with their neighbors.

\* \* \*

"I understand your concern, Brother Tilden," Martin said, suppressing his irritation, "but if we look at it correctly, the food isn't even ours. It belongs to the Lord, so it's His to decide who gets it, not ours."

Brother Sam Tilden shook his head. "We could be like this for quite a while. My family comes first—everybody else has to come second."

"Don't you think a two-years' supply is more than you will need, even if this emergency goes on for a week?" Bishop Davis asked, hoping to find some kind of rational response in this brother.

"Well, Bishop, some of the ward members I'll share with. But only those who have listened to the prophet, not people who live like there's no God."

The bishop glanced around him, at the children and women who were lying on mattresses and blankets, hauled over from homes that had not yet been completely destroyed. All he saw was innocent suffering among Heavenly Father's children.

"I'm sorry you see it that way," he said. "God loves all his children, not just those who see themselves as such. Who among us is without sin?"

Tilden shook his head and walked off. Bishop Davis had suspected earlier that a hefty streak of judgmental anger ran through the man, but hoped he had been wrong. Now was not the time for people to hold onto their food storage like it was a life raft. No, it was more like a ladder that would help everyone climb up out of a dark pit, both those who borrowed the ladder and those who shared it.

"I got through!" Crayle Eskra ran up to the bishop, holding a cell phone in his hand. "The man I know in Mount Placer used his CB to talk to your neighbor. Your wife, Jan, is on the phone here, Bishop."

Gratefully Bishop Davis took the phone and spoke quietly with his wife. Assured that she was safe and unhurt by the recent earthquake, he promised to call her later. The knowledge that neighbors were looking after her helped him return to his duties on the island, even if it would be awhile before he could get home.

As the bishop ended his call, Lacey and Gayle passed out paper cups of water among the crowd. Watching them, Martin marveled at how smoothly Lacey managed to get about, despite her blindness and the still tender stitches in her leg.

Kevin Taylor came through a doorway of the multipurpose room and stopped to talk with his wife for a moment before approaching the bishop.

"Word is, buildings are down all over the island. Water lines are broken, and as you already know, the power is out. If we don't all pull together through this, we're sunk." Kevin rubbed his back, still sore from the kidnapping. "Things are going ahead. I got at least four guys to go out and start a check on the members. Some of the brethren are real jewels. Some of the others. . . ." The rest of the thought was left hanging but was understood.

"I know," Bishop Davis agreed. "I've had my own disappointments here. Looks like some of the flock don't understand what it means to be Christian. Then again, some of them . . ." tears formed in his eyes. "Times like this bring out what's deepest in people, good *or* bad."

Kevin nodded in agreement and gave Martin's shoulder a reassuring squeeze. "Maybe we need to stock up on some barbecue grills and get cooking," he noted.

"That's what the Relief Society told me ten minutes ago."

Kevin laughed tiredly. "Bless the sisters. What would the guys do without them?"

It wasn't long before food was being prepared, and the barriers between the LDS Church members and their neighbors were dissolving. At least for the moment, the designation of member or nonmember was mostly unimportant. Only brothers and sisters in the family of God, coming together to help each other.

\* \* \*

Hyrum pulled up at the LDS chapel, not exactly sure why he was there. Searching, looking for someplace to be, he was simply following a tug on his heart that would not go away. Ever since he'd watched the tour bus go over the cliff with John and Mary in it, Hyrum could not find his old self. It was almost as if the bus had taken part of him along with the two trapped inside. Lost and off balance, he wandered about, looking for some sure handhold.

Hyrum looked out the van window at the chapel, watching some men cook over half oil-drum grills. Smoke from the greasy drippings of the cooking meat swirled up around their heads, and the delectable smell reached out to the parking lot where the van rested. It looked like an ordinary ward get-together.

People were gradually coming out of the building, and several lay under the trees on the grass and talked quietly. A man walked out of the chapel. Something about him was familiar to Hyrum, but the box he carried before him obscured his face. When the man put the box down next to the grills, his back turned toward Hyrum, the hair on Hyrum's neck stood on end. As if feeling Hyrum's gaze, the man turned to look in Hyrum's direction, then smiled and waved before going back inside.

Hyrum felt as if his heart had forgotten to beat. That man, it was— no, it *couldn't* be. But it *looked* just like him. Hyrum shook his head, trying to clear the fog in his mind.

It wasn't possible. Yet, unless Hyrum was hallucinating, it had to be what he saw. John was alive!

Getting out of his van as fast as the lift would allow him, Hyrum wheeled into the chapel, looking for someone he knew. Finding Kevin at work in the kitchen, Hyrum said, "I saw John! He was here!"

Kevin barely had time to respond with a nod, before hurrying out with another box of meat to cook on the grills. With power out, and no likelihood that it would come back on soon, one couple had donated two freezers of assorted meat to feed everyone.

Hyrum wheeled about, still trying to find out about John. When Bishop Davis noticed him and came over, Hyrum asked, "Did you see John here? The man who worked for me?"

"Yeah, he's here somewhere." The bishop looked about. "I don't know where he is now, but he's been here ever since the quake took out all the houses around here."

Hyrum grabbed the bishop's shirt sleeve. "But that can't be. He's dead! I saw the bus go over the cliff myself."

Bishop Davis stared at Hyrum, wondering if this was another case of shock. He wondered if he should call the EMT or one of the two nurses who were treating people in the church building.

Hyrum caught the look and recoiled angrily. "I'm not losing it, I know what I saw. He was there."

"I'm not arguing with you," the bishop said wearily.

"He went over the cliff, out at Deception Pass where the tour buses went over. You must have heard the explosions, even from here."

"Somebody said something about the bridge going down. But—"

"John's *dead*. If he's here, he must be a ghost."

Bishop Davis was feeling his age. His supply of strength was wearing thin, and his eyelids drooped, betraying his fatigue. Interpreting his glazed look as disinterest, Hyrum angrily pushed his wheelchair off down the hall, determined to look around for himself and find John. Or whoever or whatever he had seen outside.

* * *

"Monica? Where are you, Monica?" Gary Stillman, Kevin's partner at the hospital, searched frantically through the rubble that only a short time ago had been his expensive home. Dried blood from a scalp laceration was caked to the side of his face, and under his torn clothing was a mass of cuts and bruises. His eyes were glassy as he called his wife's name again and again.

Gary's two teenage boys were staying with friends since school was out for a statewide teacher's convention. Gary and his wife had had plans to go on a trip to Europe. The trip had been planned for over a year, but now would never happen.

Gary had been in the basement, playing pool on his new $3,000 pool table while his wife listened to the radio for more news concerning the terrorists. Gary had refused to believe things were as bad as the radio announcer made it sound, and he and his wife had argued about it.

Just as he made a great bank shot, everything trembled and the pool balls rolled to one end of the table. A popping sound came next, followed by the house rising up, then tilting over on end as it collapsed. Ever since Gary had regained consciousness, he had been searching for his wife, fighting back the fear that she was already dead.

Finally, reaching what had once been the kitchen, he found her under the refrigerator. The large, double-door appliance had slid fifteen feet across the kitchen, crushing the life out of her in a heartbeat.

None of Gary's possessions mattered at that moment. All the money he had stashed away in stocks and bonds were useless now, completely unable to change what had happened.

Gone was his wife, the woman he had taken for granted and whose love he had taken for granted so many times the past years. With her suddenly dead, he realized all his money and possessions meant nothing. Alone with his grief, cut off from God behind his wall of pride, Gary cried out in agonizing pain.

* * *

2:42 P.M. Almost six hours after the refinery was taken over, the FBI lead strike force began its assault. In the front, riding in an amphibious truck, rode Ray Penzatta.

With the thick marsh brush mostly concealing them, the amphibious vehicles moved into the water. Everyone in the force was quiet, preparing for whatever was ahead as they confronted the reality of possible death or of killing another human being. From this point on, lives would hang in the balance, and each wondered if the any of the lives lost would be his own.

* * *

Pointing his Uzi at Howks, the burly man with the shaved head said, "Let's go." Vincent had called him Frank, Howks remembered vaguely. He stood and stretched, glad for the chance to move around. Another terrorist followed Howks as they exited Howks' office and made their way through the empty secretary's office and down the stairway.

At the front door of the administration building into the open, Howks paused to look around the compound. He had felt the earth tremors earlier, but other than some cracking of the walls, his office building was apparently untouched. The condition of the other buildings, however, caused him immediate concern about the stability of the plant.

The three men wound their way through the refinery complex, then stopped at the bottom of the main tower. Frank handed his gun to his partner, who remained on the ground while Frank led Howks up the ladder steps of the tallest tower. At the top Howks paused to catch his breath. After the long, hand-over-hand climb, his arms trembled from the unaccustomed effort.

"Quite a view, isn't it?" Vincent said, stepping out from behind an exhaust shaft that was used to burn off minor amounts of gas from the petroleum refinement process. Pointing his own gun at Howks, he handed a set of handcuffs to Frank. When Howks had been secured to the handrail, Vincent dismissed Frank with a careless nod of his head.

Deciding not to say anything more to Vincent, Howks looked around him and spied a glint of light on something metal off in the marsh brush. A moment later, the faint outline of something mechanical moved through the marsh before it vanished. Hoping to keep Vincent from seeing the movement in the marsh, Howks quickly turned toward the snow-covered mountain off to the east. "Ever snow ski?"

Vincent looked skeptical. "Ever seen something like this refinery go up, all at once?"

"I don't think you're stupid enough to do that," said Howks. "You'd go up with it, too, wouldn't you?"

Vincent didn't answer. He had been handwiring the explosive charges the past few hours, and he was tired. It was dangerous and nerve-wracking work. He would have ordered someone else to do it, but other than Holtz, Vincent wasn't sure any of the others could be trusted to do it right. There couldn't be any more screwups. Things had to go right from there on out.

Meanwhile, Vincent was tired of thinking about wiring. He wanted the pleasure of taunting Howks. "You want to know how I'm going to do it?" he asked. Not waiting for Howks' answer, he continued, "Our computer got mashed in one of the quakes a while ago. We needed it to operate the microwave that set off the detonations. It was gone, so I handwired the charges."

"So how do you get away before the big bang?" Howks asked.

"We have a backup plan," Vincent said calmly.

"Going to hold your breath and walk underwater?"

Vincent smiled. "Close. We're going to *float* right out of here."

Howks looked down at the ground, two hundred feet below.

Feeling sudden vertigo, he immediately took a half step back from the railing. "You expect the Coast Guard cutter out there not to notice you? Or are you going to call in a battleship to blow it up for you?"

"They can't shoot what they can't see, can they? Now, the refinery, that's something else. It's going up in a big ball of flames. And you get the best seat to watch from. From up here you can see what happens best of all. I kind of envy you, man."

"So find another set of cuffs and join me, scumbag," Howks responded.

"Feisty to the last," Vincent sneered. "No, as Frost said, 'I have miles to go before I sleep.'"

Howks winced. "Spare me your attempts at culture," he said. "You're a lowlife now and you always will be. All the poetry spouting in the world won't change that."

Vincent simply smiled cruelly, as if envisioning the last moment of life for his captive, before descending the ladder himself.

\* \* \*

John stood by the road, near the main entrance to the refinery, watching the FBI part of the assault team make its way through the marsh area. Most of what he saw came through spiritual sight, rather than physical, so it was doubtful that any of the terrorists at the refinery could see what John saw.

Turning back toward the refinery complex, John spied a lone figure up on top of the tower, radiating waves of anger and fear. Someone else was climbing down the tower. John quickly walked up to the gate booth toward the man who acted as guard.

The combination of John's sudden, silent appearance and his air of complete innocence startled the man so badly, he fell backwards off his chair. Recovering enough to holler, "What are you doing here?" he stood and aimed his gun, but John reached out quickly and touched him on the neck. The man's eyelids closed and the gun slid out of his hands. In seconds he was sound asleep.

\* \* \*

When Vincent called the gate guard and got no answer, he automatically assumed that something was wrong. Heading for the gate to check things out for himself, he came around the end of the administration building and saw John before John saw him. Ducking back, Vincent narrowed his eyes in thought. He had an idea.

# CHAPTER TWENTY-SEVEN

John made his way to the main tower where Howks was hand-cuffed, careful not to let anyone else see him. As he was about to step up on the tower, one hand gripping the step above his head, a sharp voice behind him commanded, "Stop right there."

The pistol was aimed directly at John's belly as he turned and faced Vincent, barely a yard away. "You could use some lessons in following people," John said. "I've heard you ever since we passed what used to be the maintenance building."

Vincent searched John's face. "You a cop?"

"No."

"Federal agent?"

"No."

It irritated Vincent that John didn't feel like a cop, but he couldn't place him as anything else. "Then what are you doing here? Just looking to do a good deed for the old man up there?"

Unexpectedly, John gave a deep, heartfelt yawn, which he covered with one hand. "Excuse me," he said. "And no offense, but it's already been a long day. The man you chained up on this tower, well, he needs to come down before you try blowing everything up."

Vincent frowned. "So you're just going to waltz in here and play hero, is that it?"

"No, I'm not a hero, just a man like you. Well, maybe not quite like you. I don't get any pleasure out of hurting others. Vincent—" John paused then continued softly, "once it would have mattered what your sister, Emily, thought of all this. You even made a promise to her . . ."

Vincent's face froze. No one, not even the FBI, knew about his sister Emily. As for the promise he had made to her before she died, about being good, so they could be together in heaven, that was another lifetime ago. His persistent headache returned, worse than ever. Wincing with the pain, Vincent wondered how this man knew about Emily.

John started climbing the ladder, and immediately Vincent reacted, shoving the gun barrel against John's back. John stepped back slowly and turned. "I'm not going to let you hurt Randolph. It isn't his time to die. Nor yours, unless you make that choice."

When Vincent didn't answer, John began to climb again. Vincent put the gun to John's back and pulled the trigger three times.

John paused just long enough to say, "It won't work," before continuing to climb.

Checking the chamber, Vincent found the bullets all looked okay. Perplexed, he fired at a small drum of grease that was nearby. With its usual efficiency, the gun fired cleanly and a hole appeared in the side of the drum, followed by the greenish grease oozing out. Satisfied that the gun was working as it should, Vincent aimed up at John and pulled the trigger.

Nothing happened.

Sick anxiety filled Vincent's stomach, not very different from when he was a child and knew in his heart he was doing something very wrong. His conscience had been much stronger then, but even so he usually found a reason to do what he wanted to. It was no different now.

Staring at John, Vincent angrily shoved away any emotion that might have caused him to change his mind. *If this one guy could make it inside, more could be coming,* he told himself. Time to get moving.

John climbed steadily toward Howks. Once he stopped to look about, observing the assault force moving stealthily through the marsh.

"That's not the way it's going to be," he said to himself as he continued climbing. *God has a different plan.*

From the top of the tower John could see the assault force clear the marsh. He also saw that Vincent had returned to his command center. The next events, John knew, were going to move like lightning.

"We don't have much time," he said as he slipped the handcuffs off Howks like rubber bands. Howks' eyebrows shot up.

"Who are you?" he asked, grateful to be free but suspicious of his rescuer.

"I'm a friend of Martin Davis and Kevin Taylor," John said. "Come on, we have to hurry down and get out of here. This refinery isn't going to be here much longer."

Howks looked down at the assault force, which was now beginning to climb up the rough rocks that ringed the refinery island. "I know. I've been watching that group down there. The way they're armed, I hope they're careful what they shoot at. Refineries don't take kindly to bullets."

The two men had started down the long ladder, John first, when one of Vincent's men aimed his gun and fired. The battle had begun.

* * *

"Come in *now*," Vincent ordered the minisub waiting for them out in the bay. "The Coast Guard cutter won't see you when you get up under the dock. We'll meet you there in ten minutes. Now move it."

Dropping the two-way radio, Vincent turned to Holtz and said simply, "Do it."

In two minutes, the first explosion rocked the north end of the refinery. The tower where John and Howks were still climbing down swayed back and forth. Both held on until the worst was over, then rapidly resumed their descent.

In the next moment, a second explosion sheared the main tower off at the base. After a pause, the tower leaned to one side and went down. Still well over one hundred feet above the ground, John yelled, "Jump!"

Howks couldn't process the impossible circumstances. Surviving a jump over ten stories high was not going to happen, but riding the tower down was sure suicide. Unable to decide, he froze.

Reaching up, John took hold of Howks' leg and jumped out into nothing. Howks held fast to the ladder for an instant, before he was pulled out into the void.

* * *

Ray Penzatta directed his fire along the edge of the rocky ledge, glancing over at the deputy who lay half in the water, holding his hand tightly over a bullet wound to his leg.

Penzatta swore under his breath. Mouth to the radio microphone, he barked, "Forget phase one. We don't have time. Circle around to the north side and drive inward. Coast Guard, start your push—"

First one explosion, then another, rocked the area. Everyone in the assault force paused, evaluating what it meant to their position. Penzatta snatched up his binoculars and sought out the tower just in time to see two figures jump off into nothing.

Lowering the binoculars slowly, he shook his head. "So much for those two," he said softly.

* * *

Time slows when so much happens at once. *Am I really floating,* wondered Howks, *instead of falling like a rock to the concrete below?* John had let go of his leg, and if Howks hadn't known it was impossible, he would have said that for some of the fall, John wasn't even there.

With a crash, and then blackness, the fall ended.

Ten minutes later, Howks came around, feeling like someone had twisted his shoulder around backwards. The pain said he was still alive, but how?

"Let's go, Jack in the Beanstalk," said John, pulling Howks to his feet. "We've got to get out of here. Our friends with the dynamite are going to level this place."

Howks stumbled out of the room, trying to place it in his mind, but it wasn't until he and John came out the front door of the building that he knew this was the crude oil receiving station. They must have fallen through the roof of the building when they jumped from the teetering tower. How in the world—?

"How come we aren't dead?"

John paused long enough to say, "The tower threw us out a ways, and the roof collapsed enough to break our fall."

Howks looked down at his dirty insulation- and plaster-covered clothes and then looked at John's relatively clean clothes. "So why don't you look like I do then?"

"Some people aren't as naturally neat as others, I guess," John said over his shoulder. "You're alive, that's what matters. Let's go, before things get really crazy here." John started to run.

* * *

Vincent and thirteen of his crew stood on the pier, looking nervously about for their ride, while the refinery behind them went up in pieces. Already noxious fumes were beginning to rise into a large cloud over the area. Next, raw petroleum would be sliding into Puget Sound in the worst such disaster in the lower forty-eight states.

"Base to Pickup, come in," Vincent said for the fourth time. Still, no answer. The assault force was rapidly overrunning the refinery, and Vincent's rear guard men were engaged in a fight for their lives.

The minisub had not appeared, and Vincent, eyeing the Coast Guard Cutter as it moved steadily toward the pier, felt he knew why. The cowards in the sub had probably grown a yellow streak a mile wide, and run away, leaving Vincent and his crew behind. Well, then the thirty-foot launch tied up at the pier would have to do, and they could take their chances with the Coast Guard. Staying put was not an option.

Vincent waved his crew aboard the boat. "What about Holtz?" Hobie asked.

"He's not here. That's his problem," Vincent spat back, ordering the boat to shove off, only minutes before Holtz and another man came running up the dock, waving their arms wildly. Seconds later fifteen heavily armed Sheriff deputies, FBI agents, and National Guardsman followed them up the pier.

* * *

Fingering his deadly weapon, Holtz took one last look at the departing boatload of traitorous comrades, now some fifty yards out. Knowing death was the only other option, Holtz dropped his weapon, motioning for his companion to do the same. Prison was better than bullet holes. No way was there anything here worth dying for.

At that moment everyone was thrown to the ground as the largest of the explosions thus far rocked the refinery island. Even the terrorists' boat shook in the water, as concussion waves radiated outward from the island. Immediately a gigantic ball of flame and smoke leapt upward in the air, and a wave of crude oil spilled into the salty water.

* * *

John picked Howks up from where the last explosion threw him down.

"I've got to stop this. Everything around here is going to be poisoned," Howks groaned.

John eyed the huge fireball behind them. "There's nothing anyone can do now, except God. We've got to run for the bay."

Howks took less than a second to agree, and answered by running as fast as he could for a second pier, much smaller than the one the terrorists had recently vacated.

Diving off the pier almost as one, the two men began swimming toward Burns' Point, half a mile away. Howks briefly panicked, knowing he had never, ever, swum that far before in his life. *Not that it matters,* he thought, *we'll probably die from something else before we get there.*

Earthquake tremors had been still for hours now, but after the refinery went up, they erupted again. The bedrock beneath the refinery island shifted dramatically, the plates pulling away from each other faster than a man could run.

The assault forces were mostly around the perimeters of the island, creating a squeeze maneuver. Washed over by waves from the Sound, they backed away from the gaping hole between the plates. At the same moment, the refinery sank out of sight, along with most of the crude oil that had begun to foul the water.

Struggling to tread water, Howks watched the amazing disappearance of the refinery. Now far away, the terrorists in their stolen boat, the Coast Guard cutter, and the water-treading assault force watched the event with amazement. Only John was unfazed.

Immediately the plates reversed their course, and slammed back into each other, forming a perfect seal, entombing the deadly chemicals and fumes deep in the earth. Bay water moved in to fill the gap, the twenty-foot waves crashing into each other and radiating outward in a huge circle. Smaller waves, no more than ten feet high, moved across the shallow part of the bay toward Burns' Point, not five hundred yards off. Behind them, there was no evidence that a refinery had ever existed.

Howks closed his eyes in relief. When he opened his eyes again, he was surprised to see that an abandoned rowboat, which had been used at the refinery to check on tanker moorings, had appeared out of nowhere. Still, the battle against the ten-foot waves made the next few minutes the most terrifying of his life, and getting into the rowboat was a nightmare. When John finally pulled him into the boat, Howks fell exhausted into the bottom.

"Hold on, we'll make it!" John yelled just as a huge wave caught the boat sideways, turning it almost completely over. Howks swallowed and choked up saltwater, and John had to grab him to prevent his being washed away.

As Howks lay in the boat bottom, exhausted, terrified, and hyperventilating, John picked up some oars Howks would have sworn weren't there before and began rowing toward town.

"The water gets deeper toward town," said John. "Things are going to get pretty wild over there."

The amphibious assault crew was picked up as the rest of the assault force began rescuing people from the water. Miraculously, the assault crew and the two captured terrorists who had been on the island when it went down, had all survived. Only one amphibious assault vehicle was lost.

Knocked back and forth as waves radiated out from the refinery sinking, the Coast Guard cutter was powerless to pursue the terrorists. With the cutter's radio antenna demolished as well, neither could the commander call for help.

Awakening out of their surprised stupor, Vincent and his bunch resumed their flight toward Burns' Point, just ahead of the waves that raced at them. Vincent had lost the battle, but the war was far from over.

# CHAPTER TWENTY-EIGHT

From his vantage point on the hill behind the chapel, Kevin Taylor watched the refinery drama unfold. He was still trying to comprehend how an entire island—even a small one like the refinery was on—could disappear so quickly, swallowed up as if it had never been. Twenty minutes afterward, the only sign of the event was the huge black and white cloud over the bay, which was slowly dissolving under the heavy rain that had begun falling. Over by the mainland, Kevin could make out the beginnings of a minor oil slick on the water. Along the east side of James Island, where the waves from the refinery had landed, most of the boats moored inside the marina had taken vicious hits; many were smashed or sinking.

Lacey sat next to Kevin on the log, under a big Madrona tree, holding an umbrella over their heads. "I can smell what is left of the refinery, but the smoke is breaking up, isn't it?"

"Hmmm . . ." Kevin agreed absently as he studied the group of people landing at the marina on the north side of the island. They had come from the refinery, but looked different from the law enforcement group. Kevin was surprised that the separate group had outrun the rolling waves from the refinery.

"Something about that bunch down there doesn't feel right. I don't know why, but they don't," he said thoughtfully.

"What bunch?" Lacey asked.

"The ones who came over in a launch from the refinery, just before everything went nuts there. They . . . feel dark."

After a few moments of silence, Kevin said, "Let's go back to the chapel. This rain looks like it's not going to stop for a while. Besides, we need to start planning for tonight. We have to get things set for everybody sleeping in the chapel."

Some time later Kevin took the bishop aside. "I'd like to check out something I saw earlier, while Lacey and I were up on the hill. I think the people who blew up the refinery and the bridges are here in town now."

Martin's face was troubled. "Are you sure?"

"No, but there was something about the group who landed at the North Marina. It just felt really bad to me. Maybe I'm spooked from what's happened so far, but maybe . . ."

Bishop Davis responded by pulling the cell phone out of his back pocket and punching in the police department number. "This is Martin Davis. I'm calling for the chief. He said to call him if I had anything he needed to know."

His hand over the mouthpiece, Martin said, "The chief should know if those criminals are here . . . Chief? I bet you're busy so I won't take much of your time. One of my Church members thinks the bunch that blew everything up around here made it over to town, just before the refinery went up. Have you heard anything?"

Martin shook his head twice, listening. "I know, and I appreciate your time. Sorry if I took you away from something more important. Thanks again."

Flipping the cell phone off, he said, "So much for going to the source."

"Did he say it wasn't what I thought?" Kevin asked.

"No, but it's what he didn't say that worries me. The man knows more than he's saying. I can understand not wanting to tell civilians, though. You know, panic and all. I don't know. I got the feeling the police aren't all that confident about dealing with the problem." He paused, then said, "Why don't we go have a prayer and see what the Lord wants us to do?"

* * *

It was almost seven that evening when Lacey and Kevin left the chapel. The rain continued pouring down, much heavier than the usual drizzle that the Pacific Northwest was famous for. Kevin was still unhappy about taking Lacey with him to carry out the plan.

"Don't be angry," she said, reaching out from under the waterproof poncho she wore to touch her husband's arm.

"I'm not angry," he said gruffly, pulling a bit too hard on her hand in his. The heavy cloud cover had brought night early, and all about them was dark. A few small bits of light could be seen from homes that were still standing, the brave glow of a few feeble candles and stronger kerosene camp lights.

Trying to change the subject and lessen the tension between them, Lacey offered, "The bishop said he heard we had been declared a disaster area, and supplies and help would be coming in soon."

Kevin walked along in moody silence, shining his flashlight here and there over what was left of the roadway. Lacey kept trying. "Honey, don't you think tomorrow the power company will restore some of the power on the island?"

"Nobody is going to run around here working on anything if they think they're going to run into a bunch of terrorists," he grumbled. "And I don't see how—"

"Taking a blind woman along to help you will do any good," she finished for him.

Kevin stopped so abruptly Lacey bumped into him.

"I know the Lord said to take you along with me to find out what's going on in town. I know the bishop got the same message, and so did you. But it doesn't make any sense."

Lacey squeezed his hand tighter. "Since when did everything the Lord asks of us make sense to us at the time?"

Kevin frowned, unable to argue with the logic she was presenting. "Never. I'm just—"

"Afraid I'll get hurt," she said quickly.

Kevin pushed back his poncho hood. "Isn't it bad enough that you've lost your sight? Do you have to be the one who runs around all over the island, in the dark, looking for the bad guys? Why not some of the men?"

"For one, I can see better in the dark than you can."

Kevin turned to walk off, almost letting go of her hand before remembering that he was her Seeing Eye dog.

"Look out for the—" She spoke too late.

Kevin tripped over the power pole that was lying across the road, landing with a painful clunk on the other side. His as yet unhealed aches from the recent kidnapping came storming back.

Lacey stepped over the pole and helped Kevin up. "Maybe you better let me lead," she said smiling.

"Very funny." Kevin rubbed his throbbing shin. "How did you know that was there?"

"I felt it."

"You *felt* a telephone pole?"

"Sure. Since my eyesight left, my 'polarity' has changed." Lacey laughed at her own joke, but Kevin was still feeling sorry for himself.

"Very funny. Let's go, my see-in-the-dark batwoman. And if you 'feel' anything else I'm going to trip over, please tell me sooner, okay?"

"I love you," she said.

"I love you, too," he answered, starting to walk off.

Lacey didn't budge, pulling him back to her. "I love you."

Finally understanding, Kevin kissed her. "I love you, too. Now, can we get going," he pulled his hood back up, "before we need an ark to get around in?"

\* \* \*

7:23 P.M. The storm outside showed signs of increasing into a full-fledged thunder storm, which was unusual weather for the coast. A gust of wind through a partially open window blew a stack of papers off the desk where Vincent sat.

The members of the Burns' Point Police Department—at least, the ones who were in the office when Vincent and his crew had shown up—were cooling their heels in the jail section of the building. As other members of the department checked in, they were added to the group. Martin Davis' call had been taken, first, by one of the terrorists, and the phone given to the chief, who had been extremely conscious of the submachine gun aimed at his head.

Having left Holtz behind, Vincent had assigned Jordan, a short, barrel-chested man, the role of second in command. The two men stood across the room from the others of the group. Vincent peered through a closed blind, staring out the window into the night.

"We got lucky, man," Jordan smirked. "It could have been a lot worse. Too bad about Holtz."

"Shut up about Holtz, will you? I'm trying to think," Vincent snapped. He flipped on his cell phone, and said, "Jenny, you there?"

Jenny's voice could be heard saying some very unladylike things before Vincent could cut her off. "Can it!" he yelled. "Yeah, I know things are different. Did you get the chopper? Good, then this is how we go. You meet us at the hill up behind the church . . . What? No, we can't wait until morning! Yeah, I know there's a storm out there, I'm not deaf. You wait until morning, and somebody is going to shoot us down. So we do it tonight, yeah, with night goggles."

Vincent listened a moment, then swore savagely. "That's *why* it has to be tonight—nobody else in their right mind is going to fly in this weather. So do it or so help me when I get out of here, there won't be any place you can hide."

He flipped off the phone. "Morons," he complained. To the other men who were now coming into the room, he said, "Time to go. We'll leave Phil and Mont here until we're in position. Jordan, make sure we bring those chains and locks you found here; we may need them later. I've got an idea how we can make getting out of here easier."

* * *

Vincent's group left the Burns' Point Police headquarters not more than twenty minutes before Ray Penzatta showed up. If Ray and Vincent had encountered each other in the pouring rain, a bloodbath would certainly have taken place. As it was, Penzatta had a hunch something wasn't right and set his men around the building. An hour later, they still hadn't heard from the police chief. Then one of Ray's snipers with a scope got a peek through a jail window and saw the officers locked up in their own jail.

The tear gas lobbed inside the jail would make everyone, including the Burns' Point officers, pretty sick, but ultimately it would save lives. Now, if only Penzatta didn't have the sinking feeling that all the rats weren't in the one nest.

* * *

8:01 P.M. Even before Kevin heard the sounds coming up the ravine, Lacey felt it. They had stopped to rest before continuing into town to see what was going on.

"I think—" Kevin began.

"Shhh." Lacey put her hand up to Kevin's mouth. "Someone's coming."

Kevin strained to hear anything through the rain. "I don't hear any—" Then he heard faintly the sounds of metal clinking on metal and muffled voices.

"I count nine, maybe ten people," Lacey whispered, indicating the ravine in front of them. "And they're carrying things."

In the rain-filled darkness, Lacey and Kevin were invisible as the group passed before them in the ravine below. When they were gone, Lacey whispered in Kevin's ear, "We've got to get back to the church. That's where they're going."

"What? How do you know?"

"Someone said they'd get out of the rain by breaking into the church. And someone else said something about getting 'picked up.'"

"Picked up? Where? How?"

"I don't know."

Kevin thought quickly. "If we take the road, it's faster than the ravine. But then, what if they come out of there while we're going by?"

"Let's not think about it," she suggested. "Let's just trust God and run fast."

After several terrifying minutes, with Kevin sure they were going to run into the terrorists at any moment and Lacey worried she would step wrong, fall, and break a leg, they made it back to the church.

"Bishop," Kevin said panting, "you know how you sometimes say, things are about as bad as they can get. Well, they just got worse. We're going to have company really quick, and they aren't church goers."

\* \* \*

Dry clothes were just a memory as Howks followed John, struggling to ignore the ache in his legs and arms. The swim in the bay had not killed him, though being bounced around in the shock waves from the sinking island almost did. Howks still did not understand clearly how come he was still alive.

The big ravine that ran through the hilly part of town opened up in front of them, and John nimbly ran down the side of it. Howks took a deep breath and followed him. He owed John his life, more than once, so if John needed him, then Howks would follow.

Stepping close enough to be heard over the rain, John said, "Up ahead of us is the group from the refinery. They're going to the church."

Howks clenched his fists in anger and determination. At last he could do something. Violence had practically destroyed this sleepy little place he called home. Like most capable and self-confident men, he found powerlessness intolerable.

"How do we stop them?" he asked.

"We don't," answered John, "but we are going to keep them from hurting anyone there. That much I can promise you."

\* \* \*

Vincent carefully opened the back door of the church building and walked down the darkened hallway, his machine gun in one hand and a penlight in the other. Behind him came the rest of the group, except for the two who were circling outside to the front of the building.

As if on cue, singing began in the chapel. Some of the voices were strong and sure, and others hesitating and weak. A piano accompanied the singing as the organ required electricity.

Vincent listened for a moment, peering through the gap between the double doors of the chapel. After sending two men to cover the chapel's outside exit, he opened both doors and strode confidently inside.

*"The Lord is my light; He is my joy and my song. By day and by night he leads . . ."*

The singing gradually stopped as Vincent walked to the front of the room and stepped up behind the candle-lit podium. People looked around nervously at the hard-faced men who pointed their guns at them. Bishop Davis stood from his seat behind the podium. "Are you here in peace, or to harm us?" he asked.

Not since he was a teenager had Vincent seen the inside of a church. The moral restrictions had infuriated him back then, and for the moment he was amused at what he saw as a self-righteous and pathetic religious ritual.

"That depends on how cooperative you all are going to be," he said. "We don't intend to be here long. If everyone stays right where they are and doesn't do anything stupid, then when we leave, everybody will be fine. If not . . ." He raised his machine gun.

"We have no intention of resisting you. This is a house of God, not a battlefield," Martin said, his voice measured and careful.

"So, who are you, the minister?"

"You could call me that. In our church, I'm the bishop."

"You come with me. Everyone else stays here."

Martin followed Vincent out of the chapel. As before, at the police department, two of Vincent's men stayed behind to guard the captives.

* * *

Outside Kevin peered through the window into the chapel. "The bishop left with the guy who's probably the leader," he said.

"Okay, now what do we do?" Lacey asked.

Two men jammed gun barrels into Kevin and Lacey's backs. "Lay down on the ground," said a gruff voice.

As the two of them lay on the ground, Kevin heard a grunt, then the sound of a body falling. Turning, he saw two men wrestling, before a third joined them. One man dropped quickly, eased down by the other two. In the dark the two figures looked vaguely familiar.

"Mr. Howks? John?" Kevin called out softly.

"Kevin Taylor?" Howks peered in the dark toward Kevin. As he and John approached, Kevin heard Howks ask John, "How did you do that?"

"Therapeutic touch," John quipped, helping Lacey up.

"Was that some kind of martial arts pressure point?" Howks persisted.

"Sort of," John said. "Now, shhh . . . There are two more terrorists out front, just around the corner of the building. Give me a minute or two, then follow me." He disappeared out of sight in the darkness, and when Howks and the Taylors caught up to him, they found two more men on the ground, unconscious.

"You've got to show me sometime how you do that," Howks said admiringly.

"Did you get the guns from the other two?" John asked.

"Right here," Kevin answered.

"Why don't we hide the guns in the bushes over there in the woods?" John suggested. "No sense asking for more trouble."

* * *

Jenny wiped the sweat from her face as she lifted the stolen National Guard helicopter off the ground. She was more afraid of flying in this storm than she had been ever before in her life. If she got to the pickup point, collected everyone, and got away clean, it would be a miracle. Even the wad of money she hoped to run off with hardly made it worth flying in such crazy weather.

* * *

Holtz didn't feel he owed Vincent any favors. "Hey, FBI guy," he said to Ray Penzatta not long after his capture, "I know where everybody went. You give me a break, and I can make all this easier for you. We got a deal?"

In no time at all Penzatta's strike force was on its way to the Burns' Point church building. Because of all the breaks in the roads, the men found it necessary to slog through the mud on foot. Penzatta's group included several very disgruntled local police officers. After being made fools of in their own jail, there was no way anybody, even the president of the United States, was going to keep the Burns' Point police officers out of this fight.

# CHAPTER TWENTY-NINE

9:54 P.M. Though he had searched among the people at the church for over an hour, Hyrum never found John again that Monday afternoon. Thoroughly worn out, he eventually went home. His house was far enough away from town to avoid the damage suffered by many, although the electricity was out so he listened to a battery-powered radio much of the afternoon for information about the island. James Island was big news all over the country, even internationally. The combination of earthquake, terrorist attack, and possible ecological disaster from the oil refinery had sparked the interest of a jaded public. The ever-hungry news media were exploiting the trouble all they could.

Hyrum finally turned the radio off, tiring of the same misinformation over and over. Knowing the whole story wasn't being shared with the public, he shifted uncomfortably in his wheelchair as he listened to the rain. Flickering light from two candles on the table by the window illuminated his face.

*There's going to be some serious flooding,* Hyrum thought. Storm drains everywhere had no doubt been broken open by the earthquake. Ruptured sewer lines could quickly spread disease. *Things are going to be a real mess to clean up.*

Now and then, thunder erupted in the thick clouds overhead and rolled over the house, followed by lightening strikes. After one especially loud clap of thunder, Hyrum heard a rhythmic popping noise high above. As he concentrated, his eyes narrowed to slits. He recognized the sound. It came from a large, military style helicopter, heading north, toward town.

He peered out into the darkness, weighing the severity of the storm against his knowledge about flying. He quickly came to a decision. With a quick puff on each candle, he was out of the house and headed toward the van. The wet gravel in the driveway made it difficult to get to his van, and Hyrum was sweating heavily by the time he finally made it to his van. His hunch about the helicopter kept him going.

Hyrum guessed the people most likely to be flying in such crazy weather were not those on the side of good, but on the side of evil—which meant that the terrorists might just get away. Hyrum thought his FBI friend, Ray Penzatta, would already know about the chopper coming in. Then again, maybe he didn't. Either way, Hyrum was going to check it out.

\* \* \*

Vincent's cell phone chirped at him, breaking the silence in the bishop's office. After a brief conversation, he snapped it off and said to Martin, "Our ride is almost here. Time to go."

Martin hoped that meant the innocent people in the church would be left in peace, but he doubted it. Four of Vincent's men had disappeared outside, without a trace, and the tensions inside had increased considerably. Even getting permission for anyone to use the bathroom was a matter of serious negotiation.

"I'll go with you," said Martin. "Just leave everyone else here."

Vincent stood up and pushed back his chair. "Now, isn't that kind—a voluntary hostage. You know, I'll think about it."

Jordan came over and whispered in Vincent's ear. Vincent chewed on his lip for a moment, then said, "We're going to take you up on your offer, my friend. One hostage isn't going to be enough, though. It seems we have company outside. The cops have finally found us, which is probably why four of my men seem to have disappeared."

\* \* \*

Setting up the assault on the church, Ray Penzatta was doing what he did best. A complicating factor, he knew, was the presence of hostages inside the church. Negotiations for getting the bad guys out while keeping the good people safe would be tricky, as they always were. Ray would not risk one hostage life—even for ten terrorists— unless there was no other way. Now, if he could just keep the local Burns' Point police from doing something stupid. Ever since being released from their own jail, they were looking for trouble. One foolish move could kill a lot of innocent people.

The church itself also made things harder. Ray had been a devout altar boy in his church as a child and had expected to become a priest one day. Then his father had died in a work accident. Left as the oldest boy, Ray had had to put aside his dream in order to support the family. By the time circumstances turned around for the better, his life had been forever changed. Yet his reverence for the sanctuary of a church never left him. Having to fight inside one would be hard to swallow.

Ray froze when a car with its headlights off drove up behind the line of men around the chapel. From where he crouched in the darkness, he yelled, "Get that thing out of here!"

"Hey, Penzatta, you big mouth, come here!"

Ray's eyes narrowed as he rose to a standing position and hurried over to the side of the van away from the church building. No sense giving anyone inside a full target if they had night sights.

Jerking the passenger door open, Ray exclaimed, "What kind of idiot—"

"Lighten up, Ray. It's me, Hyrum Patches. You got more trouble than you think. So shut up and listen."

Ray's past professional friendship with Hyrum had begun with a few mutually beneficial law enforcement operations. Through the years, Ray had learned to respect Hyrum's incisive mind and keen perspective in dealing with the criminal mind. He listened without a word as Hyrum told him about the chopper, then called in to the command center on the mainland after Hyrum drove off. Unfortunately, with all the interference from the storm, radar could not confirm or deny the existence of the helicopter. Whoever was piloting it was coming in so low the trees were masking the signal.

Ray stared up into the night. Did a chopper coming in mean reinforcements for the bunch inside the church, or was it their escape route?

* * *

The small group led by John hid in the bushes between the church and Penzatta's law enforcement army. John assured the others that things inside were uncomfortable, but still safe, and Lacey remembered her conversation with Kevin, about John being one of the Three Nephites. Couldn't one of *them* simply "see" into the church, right through bricks? It made sense, in a crazy sort of way. Then again, wasn't everything pretty crazy now?

Lacey stood, leaning into Kevin, his arms around her, trying to keep her warm. Howks shivered underneath his waterproof coat, obviously miserable. The coat had been donated by one of the thugs John and Howks had overpowered earlier, and the four terrorists were now bound, gagged, and locked up in the church equipment shed near the back parking lot. Lacey thought the men must have awakened, because now and then thumping came from the shed, like feet kicking against the walls.

John wore only a denim jacket and jeans, his sandal-covered feet squishing in the wet grass whenever he moved. If the cold rain bothered him, he gave no sign, though he was the wettest of the three.

Howks was shivering so badly his teeth chattered. John reached over and touched Howks' shoulder through his coat, and immediately Howks felt warmer.

"It's good of you to attend church with us, Mr. Howks," Kevin joked, trying to lighten the tension.

Howks tried to smile back. "If you would have warned me in advance, I could have dressed for the occasion."

A popping noise overhead interrupted the conversation. "Trouble has arrived," said John, "Things are going to be very tricky. We'll need all the faith and courage we can muster."

The front door of the church opened slightly. "Tell your boss out there," a voice yelled to Penzatta's group, "to call 477-9090."

Ray punched up the number. "This is Agent Penzatta. Who is this?"

Vincent analyzed Penzatta's voice a moment, seeking a sign of weakness before responding, "Doesn't matter. Tell your goons to hold their fire. We're coming out."

"Are you surrendering?"

Vincent laughed. "Man, are you a dreamer. We're coming out, but not by ourselves. All these nice church people in here have 'volunteered' to be our shields. You start throwing bullets our way, and you'll hit them. Now how would that look in the papers? 'Trigger-happy police kill innocent hostages.'"

"Don't think we're going to let you just walk out of here," Ray warned him.

"Don't be stupid, man. We aren't walking. We're going to fly out of here, and you better not do anything crazy or the hostages will die. If we go down, so do they." The line went dead.

"Everyone, hold your fire," Ray called out. "No matter what." Then he asked one of his aides to get him the bottle of antacids from the first aid kit. His gut was killing him.

* * *

"Please, mister, just take me. Leave my wife here. She has a bad heart," pleaded a white-haired older man. But there was no response from the stone-faced terrorist who chained them both together in a line with the other twenty hostages.

"You can't do this. It's wrong, and you know it," Martin protested, placing the chains around his waist as everyone had been directed.

"Spare me your sermon," Vincent said as he carefully supervised the chaining. "If everyone is smart, we'll be gone soon, and all this will be just a bad memory. If you want to blame anyone, put it on the Gestapo troops outside. The American government is no longer of the people, but of the rich."

The crying and pleading of the innocent tore at Martin Davis' heart. He could only pray, and hope some miracle would stop a tragedy from happening. He wondered what had become of Kevin and Lacey. Were they dead?

* * *

10:39 P.M. As the hostage-shielded terrorists came out of the church, the four people in the bushes watched intently, their eyes now adjusted to see in the darkness. Sheets of rain continued to pour over everything.

The terrorists moved slowly toward the hill behind the church, the hostage-chained line forming a half circle around them. Attempting to shoot any of the terrorists without hitting a hostage would have been near impossible in the darkness, even with night scopes. Moving through the trees and bushes that landscaped the church grounds and then up the hill, shadows of law enforcement followed, waiting for Vincent's group to make a mistake.

John let the hostage group go past, then led his own small company on a parallel course, seemingly unaware of the heavily armed law enforcement army that was all about them. Howks kept looking around, wondering when someone would shoot at them, but as yet, no one seemed to have noticed the odd little group.

At the crest of the hill, the terrorists stopped the hostages. Vincent pulled out his phone to order the chopper down when suddenly headlights were trained on them. The terrorists lifted their guns reflexively, and the Burns' Point officers, exhausted from responding to emergencies far beyond their training and angry with being humiliated in their own jail, responded with immediate gunfire. The terrorists in turn began to fire back.

"Hold your fire, hold your fire!" Penzatta screamed, but his voice was drowned out in the gunfire.

Hyrum wheeled his wheelchair away from the van as fast as he could, while a storm of bullets struck his van, putting out both the headlights. Darkness covered the hill again, but the battle continued.

The white-haired man who had worried about his wife's heart caught a bullet in his left side and fell heavily to the ground, pulling his wife and the man behind him down with him in the chained line.

Terrorist return-fire caught Penzatta's leg just above the knee, and he cursed as he fell back against a fellow agent. A Burns' Point officer was shot and killed immediately.

"Now, Lord," John whispered, and immediately a powerful earth tremor shook the hill, knocking everyone off their feet.

Several seconds later, after the shaking stopped, Penzatta hobbled over into the midst of the Burns' Point police group.

Grabbing one of them by the collar, he shoved a pistol into the man's ribs, and yelled, "Tell them to stop, or I'll shoot you myself!"

The earthquake had interrupted the battle long enough that both sides had regrouped and were waiting to see what the other would do. As the silence held for several minutes, the chopper appeared and began descending on the hill. Penzatta stayed with the police officers, determined to shoot the first one who started something.

Kevin groaned. "They aren't going to let everyone go when the helicopter comes."

"No, they aren't," answered John, sounding preoccupied.

The chopper settled lower and lower toward the ground, until it was only eighty feet up. Vincent had begun to believe they were going to make it after all, when thick fog began surging through the trees behind them, completely blocking visibility and making it impossible for the chopper to land.

"Come down!" he yelled over his cell phone. "What are you waiting for?"

Without any way to check her position in the thick fog, Jenny drifted toward some trees and came close to wrapping a propeller blade around a tree trunk. "No way!" she shouted back at Vincent. "I'll come down when this clears."

"Listen, you little—" Vincent began, but Jenny snapped off the radio, missing Vincent's curse. Savagely she yanked the chopper's controls around, angry with Vincent and the police, and worried she might lose her chance to steal some of the ransom money. Immediately the aircraft veered off down the hill toward the chapel. As the helicopter began to plummet out of control, Jenny fought to regain control, fear rising up in her throat so fast she could hardly breathe. It was no use. With a concussive boom, the helicopter slammed into the LDS chapel, instantly demolishing the chopper and half the chapel.

Vincent slowly stood, his mind on fire, battling rage. He fought to clear his head enough to decide the next step. Obviously, no one was going to fly out that night.

"That's it," Frank said to Vincent. "We're dead."

"Then if we die, so do these people," snarled Jordan, grabbing a young woman by the neck and shoving his semiautomatic rifle barrel into her back.

Vincent shrugged. He wasn't ordering his men to kill the innocent, but he also wouldn't try and stop it. He expected to die that night, so what did it matter?

"Let's go," John said urgently, pushing Howks out ahead of him and helping Lacey move forward.

The thick fog that had come up over the top of the hill now descended as the rain abruptly stopped. A thick, white blanket of mist—damply cold to the terrorists, and strangely warm and comforting to the hostages—covered the crest of the hill. When touched by the fog, each of the terrorist's thoughts became jumbled and confused, until they had no idea who they even were.

John found keys for the hostage chain in Jordan's pocket and opened a lock on the hostage chain. As he passed the keys among the hostages, several wept and hugged him as he moved about healing with a touch those who had been hurt in the gunfire.

Howks, Kevin, and Lacey slowly followed John, helping people where they could, careful about the stupefied terrorists, but curious beyond caution at what John was doing. A peaceful, awed feeling filled their hearts, similar to what the Taylors had often experienced in the temple, but completely new to Howks. Moving past the gunmen suddenly seemed the most reasonable thing in the world to do.

Vincent grasped John's arm. "Who are you?"

John shook his head, as he released Martin, the last to be unchained, before answering. "It's time to give yourselves up and let these people go," he said kindly. "It's over."

Turning to Martin, he said, "Take these people down the hill."

Most of the terrorists had dropped their weapons on the ground and were sitting with dazed expressions on the ground. Vincent ground his teeth, furious but unable to reason out why.

Favoring his injured leg, which had been hastily bandaged by now, Ray stood and surveyed the scene at the top of the hill with a night scope. "I don't believe it," he muttered.

"What is going on up there?" the agent next to him said, looking through his own night scope.

Ray shook his head. "I don't know but we're going to take advantage of it. Pass the word for the net to tighten, when the hostages pass the tree by the clearing." Ray motioned toward the Burns' Point officers. "Keep an eye on them." However, in the sudden change of circumstance, five of the Burns' Point police officers had already managed to slip off through the brush up the hill.

As Martin gave the care of the freed hostages into the hands of others and hurried back up the hill, drawn by the hand of God, Hyrum Patches moved slowly through the damp woods. He was sweating heavily as he worked to propel his wheelchair, struggling to reach the small clearing where John and the terrorists were. Hyrum didn't know what he would do when he got there, but going he was. No one could have kept him away.

The Burns' Point officers came up the east side of the hill as Martin moved up the southwest. Hyrum arrived at the edge of the clearing on the north side as Ray and his men came up on the south. Between the police and the terrorist group stood John, with Kevin, Lacey, and Howks some distance away.

As if a plug had been pulled, the storm ended, the clouds drawing back to reveal a full moon above. Bright light washed over everything, illuminating the entire area almost as if it were day. Down the hill, the chapel burned furiously, with no way to put out the blaze.

The mysterious fog was beginning to dissipate, although it was still thick enough to make things unclear on the hill. One of Vincent's men tossed an ammo belt away and one of the police officers down the hill mistook it for a hostile act. He pulled a trigger and the terrorist fell to the ground clutching his shoulder.

"No!" John yelled. Hurrying to the stricken man, John pressed his fingers against the deep wound and helped the man to stand. Immediately the bleeding stopped.

Lacey stepped between the terrorists and the police, her hands raised high, her heart pounding with fear, not needing her eyes to feel the hatred on one side and the sickness on the other.

"Stop! Stop it right now!" she said loudly. She couldn't believe she was doing this, but knew she must, the Spirit touching her, strengthening her, pulling her to stand there, a shield to both sides against any further violence.

"No, Lacey!" Kevin cried out, running out into the clearing to bring her back out of the line of fire. When he reached her, he felt it, too—an overwhelming feeling of absolute power—as if the Savior Himself were standing beside them, putting his hand in theirs, forming a wall to block Satan from doing any more evil. All of Kevin's fears for Lacey, himself, or anyone else in front of the guns that night evaporated in a timeless moment.

Martin jogged into the clearing, panting heavily. He looked at the terrorists, who except for Vincent, had all dropped their guns, then over at the Burns' Point police officers whose guns were aimed and ready. Slowly Martin joined the Taylors to stand with them.

Hyrum finally managed to get his wheelchair to the edge of the clearing, but it would go no further. Seeing the police officers shoot first a moment ago, he recognized the act for the revenge it was.

"Get out of the way," the police called to the three in the clearing. "This is none of your business."

"Whatever happens here," Lacey said in a clear, strong voice, "is everyone's business. What these men did was wrong, and they will pay for it. But what you want to do doesn't make it better. Look at yourselves! Are you any better right now than they are? What gives any of us the right to play God?"

"Agent Penzatta?" John called.

"I'm here," Penzatta answered. He stepped into the clearing on John's right.

"You are an honest man," said John. "If you give your word, I know you'll vouch for the safety of these men behind me. They have caused a great deal of misery, and it is justice they need, not revenge."

"That's easy to promise," Penzatta said. He motioned for his men to circle around to join the Burns' Point officers, who, still angry and resentful, nevertheless lowered their weapons.

While John and Penzatta were talking, Vincent stood off to one side by himself. Still confused by the strange fog, Vincent fingered a grenade on his belt. He felt tremulous, unsure of exactly who or what he was, but the grenade gave him a feeling of power.

Hyrum was close enough to see Vincent, but he knew that calling out for someone to stop him would only make things worse. It had to be Hyrum who did something. He was the only one close enough.

Straining, sweat beading up on his forehead from the effort, exerting every bit of belief he had in miracles and faith, Hyrum slowly rose from his wheelchair. *God, please, help me now,* Hyrum prayed silently. *If ever I could walk, please make it now.*

Rising to his feet, Hyrum took one small step. Then another. With steps small enough to be a child's, Hyrum slowly made his way to Vincent's side and said softly, "Don't do it."

Vincent looked up, confused and angry. "Why not? Who are you?" he snarled, unleashing a lifetime of hatred on Hyrum.

"Give me the grenade," Hyrum insisted quietly.

John turned to look at Hyrum and Vincent. The look on John's face settled it for Vincent. Pushing his finger through the pull pin, Vincent yanked it out, releasing the firing mechanism.

Despite his age and still unsteady legs, Hyrum lunged at the grenade in Vincent's hand and wrestled the younger man to the ground. They rolled over twice, before Hyrum jerked the grenade away and rolled away from Vincent into the leaves beneath the trees.

With a blinding flash, the grenade exploded. Hearing the explosion so near, Lacey screamed in fear, unaware of what had happened. Turning away from the sight of Hyrum's maimed body, Kevin tenderly cradled Lacey in his arms. "It's all right," he said softly, as he told her what Hyrum had done.

"*Stupid* old man," Vincent grumbled, as Howks restrained him. "He was *crazy*. Why else would anyone do that?"

As John knelt beside Hyrum, he tenderly touched the dead man's face. "'Greater love hath no man than this, that a man lay down his life for his friends.' You were a better man than you knew, Hyrum, my friend."

"Why did he do that?" Vincent yelled again as federal agents handcuffed him and started to lead him away.

John rose from beside Hyrum's body. "Because only God should take a life, because only He can give it. Hyrum died for you, and all of us, because he finally remembered who he was. Perhaps, someday, so will you."

# CHAPTER THIRTY

Tuesday morning came bright and sunny, full of hope and promise, although repairing the damage to property and lives on the island would take many years.

Vincent's terrorist group was safely behind bars and would be prosecuted through the federal court system, but that wouldn't help replace the refinery that had employed so many people. A major source of income was gone in one day. And while most people were grateful there had not been more environmental damage to the bay, they wondered what would replace the lost jobs, homes, property, and health?

John and Martin surveyed the island from on top of the hill behind the church, which just last night had been a battlefield. Relief supplies were being airlifted and ferried in now, and the Army Corps of Engineers was already putting together a temporary bridge to the mainland.

"I wonder if this place will ever be the same again?" Martin said.

"There won't be another refinery here, that's for sure," John said. "Not with the island gone. Randolph Howks told me that's it for his company here. The refinery was one of the oldest in the system and not very efficient. He came here mostly to ease into retirement."

Martin sighed. He had been amazed and gratified at the cooperation demonstrated by the people of the island. The past dividing lines of race, income, or religious groupings no longer seemed to have any meaning as people helped each other sort out whatever belongings could be salvaged from the damaged homes. "I wish this unity could last," he said.

"It can, if everybody wants it to," John said.

"Do you think God was angry with the people here? Is that why He destroyed so much of the island?" Martin asked.

John suddenly felt tired. "God loves His children. He grieves even for those who have sinned the most against Him. The people needed a wake-up call. And not just the people here. What happened here can come to anyone who doesn't listen to the Spirit of God. The time for gentle reminders—of what is real—is fast drawing to a close."

Martin nodded in understanding. He picked a stick up and broke it. "I keep thinking about Hyrum Patches . . . giving up his life . . . actually saving the life of the man who took his."

"I'd say Hyrum died like he wanted to," John said. He started down the hill, and Martin followed. "He always wanted to look after others. That was why he became a police officer. To help. He died still doing it. Whether they deserved it or not wasn't something he wanted to consider."

An emergency pre-fab shed, hastily built by the National Guard, had been erected beside the blackened ruins of the church. The temporary structure served as a central supply distribution center for that part of the island. As John and Martin walked up, Bill Gibson, who owned the hardware store in town, was unloading sorely needed water purifiers.

"You sure got here fast with those," Martin called to him. "With the city water system off-line, things are getting pretty dry around here."

"People need water," Bill replied. "What we got coming out of the pipes around here isn't something I'd drink. But I hear your church members have water stored. Funny, when you think about it, since this is an island."

"Not when we remember that it's salt water," Martin answered. "Our church encourages food storage, and water is part of it. I wish more people thought that way."

"I've heard a lot about your church," Bill said as he unloaded the last purifier. "Maybe when things settle down, you could stop by and tell me more. I've been impressed with the kindness of your people. If that's what you teach, then I'm interested."

"I'm sure Bishop Davis would be delighted to teach you more about what Jesus Christ taught," John said, noticing Kevin and Lacey looking at the church ruins not far off. "Excuse me, there's someone I need to speak to."

"Hello, John." Lacey spoke with her back to him, before he was twenty feet away.

Kevin's eyes narrowed in surprise, then realization.

"So what tipped you off?" John asked as he came up beside her.

"Your walk," she answered, turning toward him, "and mostly your spirit. I won't ever forget what you feel like, John. You aren't like other people."

"Oh, I don't know. I'm pretty average."

"Among what crowd?" Kevin asked. "Average compared to the . . . Three Nephites perhaps? Or maybe even Moses, Abraham, Noah, Joseph of Egypt . . ."

". . . the twelve Apostles," Lacey added.

"See? Maybe a little less than average," John chuckled.

"*Are* you one of the Three Nephites?" Kevin asked.

John took a long, deep breath. "No," he said finally.

They waited for something else to follow, but he didn't say anything else.

"That's it?" Kevin complained.

Lacey reached out and touched John's arm. "What of the apostle, John, called beloved? You could be him."

John said nothing.

"Apostles don't lie, do they?" she asked.

"I'm sure they don't," he answered, a slow smile growing on his face.

"You aren't going to answer the question, are you?" Lacey said.

John embraced them both. "How about we let the Spirit answer that one. And I'll just say goodbye."

"Goodbye?" Kevin and Lacey said in unison. "Why are you leaving?"

"I've done what I was called here to do. Now it's time to move on."

Lacey kissed him on the cheek. "We'll miss you."

Shaking John's hand, Kevin asked, "Will you ever come back here?"

"I hope so. This is one of my favorite places in the whole world. So, if things go that way, I'll jump at the opportunity."

With a nod and a wink, John ambled down the road and took a right turn. Kevin watched until John was out of sight. Holding Lacey tightly in his arms, he said, "He *was* John, wasn't he?"

"I think so," she replied, snuggling back against his chest. "But I guess it doesn't matter much. He was here when we all needed him."

\* \* \*

John left the forest at a place where he could see where the Deception Pass bridge had been. Far below, still half in and half out of the water, was the bus Mary and he had fallen in. Thoughts about the resurrection and eternity floated through him.

"Lord, all things are in Thy hands. I accept better now that truth. It seemed my trust in Thee was complete before, but it is deeper now. As Thou hast always taught me, there are infinite levels of perfection.

"The one time, at the last Passover we all shared together, I remember Thy words, 'Don't get too used to seeing by the light, because the night will come.' I didn't know what that meant then, and Thou said I would, in time.

"I can see now, that the darkness is when we have to walk forward, not absolutely sure what Thou would have us do, so we can fully live the gospel. There has to come a moment, or even many of them, when we do what we feel is right, without direct, ironclad assurances that it is right. It is our own sense of eternal truth we have to draw on then, isn't it?

"Anyway, once again I thank Thee, Lord, for all that Thou hast done for me and for all here. I pray they will stay close to Thee, because there is much work to do now."

A dove flew over head, circling just a few feet out from the cliff, soaring on the updrafts from the ocean below. A quiet strength filled John's heart along with an impression of the rainforest in Brazil. There was a place there, among the native Indians, where they needed his help. Picking up a pebble, he tossed it into the water far below, watching it fall, until it landed with a tiny splash.

As he walked along the path back into the forest, John plucked a leaf off a Madrona tree. After a bit he tucked the leaf into his jacket pocket. The dove followed him, flying above the tree tops, catching sight of him now and then through the breaks in the forest canopy. As John walked, he whistled a thoughtful tune.

# CHAPTER THIRTY-ONE

Six months later, Lacey called from the car, "Kevin Taylor, church starts in two minutes, let's go." Even as she scolded her husband, Lacey rubbed her swollen belly, grateful to the Lord for sending them another child. Kevin paused on the front steps of what would become their new house. Every day he came by, inspecting what the contractors had finished. Smiling, Lacey called again, "Honey, I'm speaking in church, remember? This is my first time reading my new Braille scriptures."

"I'm coming," Kevin finally replied, reluctantly turning away from the nearly finished house. He had wanted to find another lot on the island, but Lacey insisted they get the old place cleared away and the hole filled in. Now that the new place was about done, Kevin had to admit she was right. No other place would have been as right for them.

As Kevin slid into their new station wagon—paid for by the insurance after their old one fell into the sink hole—he automatically reached for his planner. It should have been on the seat next to him, where he always put it when he traveled. "Where's my planner?"

"I don't know, sweetheart," Lacey answered.

Had he left it at the motel where they had been living for now on the insurance money? he wondered. Then he smacked his forehead. "Oh, shoot! I left it at the office yesterday. I'll drop you off and swing around to get it. There's a new home teaching roster in it I need for the personal priesthood interviews we're going to sneak in during priesthood."

"Daddy," asked his youngest daughter in the backseat, "when can I come be secretary at your new office?" Kevin had let his older daughter help him organize things at the new office Randolph Howks had arranged for, and he had promised to let his younger daughter come some Saturday. "Uh, how about next Saturday, honey? By then, maybe I'll be able to find some things."

After dropping his family off, Kevin pulled away from the Baptist church, quickly accelerating to avoid a truck in his lane that he hadn't noticed before. The Baptist congregation had graciously allowed LDS services in their building until the new LDS chapel was finished.

As Kevin drove off, Randolph Howks pulled up into the parking lot in his Cadillac.

"Good morning, Lacey," he called to Lacey and the children as he got out of his car.

Lacy stopped to wait for him. "Mr. Howks, I'm so glad you came again. Are you getting attached to our church services?"

If Lacey could have seen, she would have noticed the mixed feelings showing on Howks' face. As it was, she learned enough from the pause before he spoke and the tone of his voice when he did.

"I have to admit, I feel right at home. Maybe someday, I'll become a real member."

"How is your wife feeling?"

As Howks walked along the sidewalk to the front door of the Baptist church, he answered with a smile, "Better. The doctor says her heart is getting better all the time. She said she might like to try coming to church here with me next time." After they had gone up the stairs and he was holding the door for everyone, Howks added, "I still feel bad about her heart attack. If she hadn't been worrying about me through all that mess at the refinery, it never would have happened."

Lacey patted his arm reassuringly. "It's all right now," she said. "She's getting better. God is watching over the two of you. You don't know how often I have felt that in my prayers at night for the two of you."

Howks' eyes were moist as he followed everyone inside.

Howks nodded at Bill Gibson, and his wife, Janet, as he followed Lacey and her children. Mrs. Gibson leaned forward and spoke to Lacey, reaching out to catch her hand as she passed. "Today is the three-month anniversary of our baptism. Bill and I would like your family to come over this afternoon, about two-ish, for some dessert."

Lacey gave Janet's hand a squeeze. "We'd love to. What can I bring?"

"Just yourselves, dear."

Martin rose from a seat behind the lectern at the front of the Baptist church assembly room. Checking his notes for the sacrament meeting, he briefly looked down at his wife, Jan, and beside her, their two grandchildren. Martin's daughter, Julie, would be coming in from her job at the Burns' Point Hospital in a few moments. Julie and her two children now lived with Martin, and Julie was an aide in the pediatric ward, working with Janet Gibson. Things were still hard, but at least hope was growing.

"Brothers and sisters, welcome to the Burns' Point Ward sacrament meeting this fine Sunday morning," Martin began. "As always, we in the bishopric express our gratitude to our Baptist brothers and sisters for allowing us to use their building, until ours is finished. I'm sure we'll all be grateful when we can move back home."

As the opening hymn was finished, and the prayer given, Kevin walked in. He shook Howks' hand, then stepped past Randolph as Lacey and their three children scooted over in the pew for him. Lacey squeezed his hand. "Here I go," she whispered.

Martin had finished giving the ward announcements and introducing the passing of the sacrament as Lacey stood. Her Braille Book of Mormon in hand, she edged out into the aisle, using her white cane with the blue tip to make her way up to the front of the room. Carefully making her way up the steps, she sat in an empty chair next to Martin. He squeezed her hand.

Alone, Gary Stillman edged in the door at the back of the assembly hall, finding a place to sit by himself, alone in the far corner. His clothes were expensive but his face was sallow and tired looking. His physical therapy practice was on its way to failing, mostly because he drank too much. Gary couldn't find the same interest in his practice or money that he'd had before the earthquake that leveled his house and killed his wife. He and his boys lived in an apartment now.

Martin wished he could reach Gary and had tried several times, but for now, only Kevin was having any impact. Kevin saw Gary every day, one way or the other, and was determined to help him. The fact that Gary was here at all was something.

After the sacrament was passed, Martin stood again. "Today we have a special treat," he said. "Sister Lacey Taylor will speak to us. After she is finished, we will have a special musical number by the choir. Sister Taylor."

Lacey moved toward the lectern and opened her Book of Mormon up to Ether 12:27. "And if men come unto me I will show unto them their weakness. I give unto men weakness that they may be humble; and my grace is sufficient for all men that humble themselves before me; for if they humble themselves before me, and have faith in me, then will I make weak things become strong unto them."

She looked up toward the congregation, feeling their spirits. "The Lord invites all of us to come unto Him, so that He can heal us and help us become strong. Why then are we so proud, so slow to accept his invitation?

"When my blindness started, I made the decision that no matter what, I could get by without having to depend on other people. How prideful and yes, even foolish I was. None of us can get by without help, especially the Lord's help.

"For the past six months now, this whole island has been working together and helping each other to put back together our lives. I've thought about it many times, how it took us losing almost everything but each other, before we could see the truth. I hope we have finally awakened from the spiritual sleep we were in before, so we can keep our eyes on the Lord now. I know that is what has made me strong and happy now."

In a jail miles away Vincent thought about his trial, which would begin the next day. The federal anti-terrorist charges against him, including his connection to several deaths, would ensure his conviction and put him away for the rest of his life. Now and then, as he thought about the odd events that had prevented him from carrying out his violent plans, he shook his head, wondering.

Deep in the Brazilian rainforest, John looked up from the house he was helping an Indian man make for his family. A gentle breeze touched John's face and he thought again of Hyrum and of Mary. In his heart he could hear Lacey saying, "Wherever you are, John, thank you. We'll never be able to repay you for all you did for us." He smiled, warmed by the memory of the love he had felt there.

Lacey paused in her talk, catching a whiff of something exotic, like a breeze from a faraway rainforest. A picture of John, smiling at her, flashed in her mind for a moment. She smiled back.

"I guess," she continued, "when we come to see who we really are, and why we are here, every day is a miracle. So is everyone around us. Maybe when we realize that, a true awakening goes on inside each of us. Maybe then, we are really alive, in Christ."

## ABOUT THE AUTHOR

Thomas D. Eno has been a practicing counselor for over twelve years. He has served as Mental Health Director for different counties in three states. His diverse and varied experience has enabled him to understand, help, and relate to people of differing backgrounds and needs.

Thomas enjoys music, history, martial arts, nature, as well as telling puns, laughing, and spending time with his family. He is the author of the best-selling novel, *My Name Is John.*